More praise for Kathryn H...

'Never a dull moment . . . A...

'A highwire act of fiction, ba...
multicultural microcosm of ...
female bushranging, migratio......, the pain of losing
children, and the way a spark of inspiration passes from one
generation to the next. Sound ambitious? It is, but in *Captain Starlight's
Apprentice*, Kathryn Heyman pulls it off, playing ringmaster to this
crowded bill of ideas and weaving them into a kind of magic' Judith
White, *Bulletin*

'A serious and beautiful meditation on exile: emotional, physical and
psychological' Rebecca Abrams, *Bookmark*, World Radio Geneva

'Powerful and accomplished . . . Heyman reveals her pedigree as a
playwright and poet in stunning language and original imagery . . .
profoundly moving' *Scotsman*

'A pleasure . . . this is a novel which never betrays its promise. The
rawness of the emotion and the beauty of its conveyance into words is
a potent combination which will not easily be forgotten' *Australian
Book Review*

'Heyman has produced a riveting blend of wit and poignancy,
harmonic in structure, that triumphantly confirms her reputation as a
great literary entertainer' *Scotland on Sunday*

'This is a remarkable novel, funny and heartbreaking at the same time'
Glasgow Herald

'I loved it. I was swept along by its exuberance – and like all true
comedies, sensed the underlying sadness, so subtly touched upon . . .
very deft, never lost momentum at all' Margaret Forster

'A superb mix of lyricism and economy' *Sunday Herald*

Kathryn Heyman's previous novels are *The Breaking*, *Keep Your Hands on the Wheel* and *The Accomplice*. Her work has been longlisted for the Orange Prize, shortlisted for the West Australian Premier's Prize and the Scottish Writer of the Year Award and won an Arts Council of England Writers' Award. Both *Keep Your Hands on the Wheel* and *Captain Starlight's Apprentice* were adapted for BBC Radio.

CAPTAIN STARLIGHT'S APPRENTICE

Kathryn Heyman

headline
review

Copyright © 2006 Kathryn Heyman

The right of Kathryn Heyman to be identified as the Author of
the Work has been asserted by her in accordance with the
Copyright, Designs and Patents Act 1988.

First published in 2006 by HEADLINE REVIEW
An imprint of HEADLINE PUBLISHING GROUP

First published in paperback in 2007 by HEADLINE REVIEW
An imprint of HEADLINE BOOK PUBLISHING

1

Apart from any use permitted under UK copyright law, this publication
may only be reproduced, stored, or transmitted, in any form, or by any means,
with prior permission in writing of the publishers or, in the case of
reprographic production, in accordance with the terms of licences
issued by the Copyright Licensing Agency.

All characters in this publication are fictitious and any resemblance
to real persons, living or dead, is purely coincidental.

Cataloguing in Publication Data is available from the British Library

ISBN 978 0 7553 0218 5

Typeset in Perpetua by Avon DataSet Ltd,
Bidford-on-Avon, Warwickshire

Printed and bound in Great Britain by
Clays Ltd, St Ives plc

Headline's policy is to use papers that are natural, renewable and recyclable
products and made from wood grown in sustainable forests. The logging
and manufacturing processes are expected to conform to the environmental
regulations of the country of origin.

HEADLINE PUBLISHING GROUP
A division of Hachette Livre UK Ltd
338 Euston Road
London NW1 3BH

www.reviewbooks.co.uk
www.hodderheadline.com

For my mother, who made it home.

And, as always, for Richard.

If we could embrace, even in the house of the dead, we might gladden each other in our icy grief.

Homer, *The Odyssey*

The lights begin to twinkle from the rocks:
The long day wanes: the slow moon climbs: the deep
Moans round with many voices. Come, my friends,
'Tis not too late to seek a newer world.

Alfred Tennyson, *Ulysses*

Rose, 1956

The deep shine on the floor of St John of the Cross Rest Home for Women was not the result of the bee-sweet wax poured on each Friday and licked into the surface with a white electric polisher, but of tears. Each woman housed by these cool walls was crippled by her own unhappiness, and there were usually tears. Once or twice there had been blood, but these were accidents and only to be expected in the course of discovery. Not ideal, but hardly the rule, either; though detractors would suggest that blood ran endlessly in here, trickling across the floors, running down through the corridors and out on to the city streets. To hear them speak, you would think that everyone in there, in that building, in the whole city, was coated with blood, which rose from the room in a great tidal wave of distress. Which wasn't the case at all. Healing: that's what this place was about. Being made right.

Like all the others, she said, 'It's a mistake. Please. I shouldn't be here, I'm just—'

They all said that, or versions of it: *Why am I here? You'll regret this; it's him who should be here, not me*. Protestations were parcelled up and sent flying, like yellow kites, to the high ceiling of the grey-green room. You could see, if you looked hard enough, the scuffmarks along the paintwork, the places those cries had hit the walls and bounced back, fruitless, to the crier. Rose had not struggled, not once since she arrived, which was a blessing.

'Lay her down,' said a tall, snake-mouthed nurse. She looked down at Rose and said, 'I'm Nurse Sich.'

'Sick?' Rose was croak-voiced, weak as a bird.

The nurse's lips folded down, touching her chin. 'Nurse Sich. My father was Mr Sich and my mother Mrs Sich. Next year I will marry Dr Kingley and I will be Mrs Kingley. I will escape, you see. Like you.'

'Oh,' Rose lifted her head, opened her eyes. 'Have I escaped?'

The smaller nurse, pink on her cheeks, looked at Nurse Sich, looked only at her chin, not at her whole face. 'Perhaps we should be silent?'

'It does no harm to talk.' Nurse Sich pushed Rose back, pulled her jaw down towards her breasts. 'Here. This will help. Take it now.'

Liquid slid in, sleepily, shimmied down through Rose's veins and she slipped back, watching, watching everything.

And then she remembered. Her tongue was a thick eel in her throat, swimming for her gullet. She pulled at it with her hands, pulled it out, slapped at it, trying to give it shape, substance.

'Sammy,' she called. 'Sammy.'

It came out as this: Shmmme. Shmmme.

The small pink nurse leant close and whispered, 'Your baby is fine. You just worry about getting well. Your husband——' A pink flush appeared on the nurse's neck. 'Everything is under control.'

Sammy. Her mouth was closed, but the word was there, darting about inside her head, looking for a way out.

Sand was in her blood, her eel-tongue flailing in her mouth.

Dr Kingley prodded at her belly. 'All right, are we? All right?' He leant close to her ear and called, 'All right in there?'

'Shmme,' she whispered. 'Shmme.'

'Yes,' he said. 'Everything's all right, isn't it?' He nodded at Nurse Sich.

'Yes, we'll be working with her. Later. Do we have straps?'

She nodded, lips folded neatly.

'Here we go, then.' He tapped Rose's arm, pulled a grey strap tight around it and stabbed with a white needle. 'This will help you; help you forget all that trouble.'

But she would not forget; not for a day, not for a moment.

The strap across her ankles cut into her, though she noticed the thickness of the leather, the coolness of it. There was nothing more to say, so she didn't speak. Metal, heavy as teeth, bit into her wrists, one, two, buckle-my-shoe. Another buckle on ankles, waist, chest; like being tied to a tree, or to a mast. She thought of the story, taught in school, of Odysseus, roped to the mast to stop him leaping into the depths of the sea, called by the singing of – what were they? Mermaids?

Pressed back with the weight of those woodthick straps, she became as weightless as water. She dissolved into it: she thought of her darling Vincent's powders, collapsing into glasses of water. Back then, when she bothered mixing them with water. God knows, when you're downing eighteen powders a day, you don't notice the slight grain in the throat, the tightening of the tongue: there was only the relief from the pounding head, a moment of silence while each granule tickled its way down, down. Nurse Sich's hands were wet with heat, slipping against the skin on Rose's forehead. It was not unpleasant: the being strapped, the hands on the forehead. She had only to give herself over, Vincent's powder to water, to dissolve away, and she would be free. That was what they told her: she had only to let this happen and the unhappiness would stop.

Glass-cold metal discs pressed against Rose's forehead – one at either side. Dr Kingley nodded at the smaller nurse, who stepped back nervously. Dr Kingley was a curved frown, grumping over the bed, tugging at the straps round Rose's wrists, slipping the metal discs closer to her eyes. He stood, raised one arm and nodded at Nurse Sich. Her hand was on a red lever, attached to a black panel. Batonless, Dr Kingley conducted Nurse Sich. She pulled the lever down as though bowing a cello: one fluid stroke. The sound was a harsh note, a catapult of a noise, as low as a cat's underbelly, as strong as a siren.

Restrained by the straps, Rose's body pressed skywards, seeking flight, seeking a catapult of its own. Dr Kingley was always amazed by this, how the body longed to soar, as though called by some far, wonderful music. Nurse Sich looked at her hands, at the narrow lines flecking her nails, at anything but the arching body in the bed. It wasn't the body that bothered her, but the way the face pulled back into itself, so that you could see the skull beneath the skin, so that you could feel the raw terror lurking in your own flesh. Dr Kingley watched, observed the arcing upwards and saw the shadow of a tall birch tree, held briefly in a wild kiss of lightning. There was one once, he recalled it, on the lawn of Trinity College. He had spent the whole night sitting alone, watching the storm rage across

Cambridge, and had found himself weeping when the yellow crease spliced the sky and left the birch bent over, halved. He welcomed Australia with its lack of birches, welcomed the grey stubble that passed for countryside, welcomed, too, his own lack of tears. The woman – Rose, he knew her name, it was simply easier not to notice certain details – the woman was shivering, which was unusual. He stepped over to the board, lowered the lever himself, and watched the woman on the bed rise again, several inches off the white sheets. Watched her hit the surface of the bed with the sound of a house falling. He checked his watch, made a note: 11.05 a.m.

She could feel the volts pass through her. Each cell in her body readied itself, became taut with waiting. Her bones pushed back, melted, collapsed into themselves: as her body lifted she saw a light, then a ridge. Rocks. Red sky. A woman on horseback leaping across a rocky ravine. Words on a poster: *half girl, half horse!* A whitegum, twisting out of black earth. Lightning striking: it spliced her again; her eyes drifted back, back in her head; voices were whispering; singing; calling her name.

~

Jess, 1914

You want to watch me leap, watch me fly, watch my body blending with the lightning and with the horse, but you only want the pretty pictures. I am not a diversion. That is not what I am here for, and I am calling you, asking you to stay; I will show you what is possible and I will help make you whole.

Look at this, my tumbled body: ha! How strong I've been, and as fast as lightning, it's true. That eagle, circling, watching, casting its shadow larger than the trees. Wirripag, he's called by Billy's mob. Oh, and I've been as fast as you, Wirripag, as high. Hard to see now which is blood, which is dirt, which is bone. Perhaps, in the end, they're all part of each other.

When I was a child, I longed for adventure. Lying awake on the small metal bar bed, listening to my parents' voices murmuring through from the room next door – sometimes louder than a murmur, sometimes sharper than a voice; a thump, say, or a slap, these things have a different sound. I would lie there, pressing my hands into the bones of my hips, even then – and, Lord, I can't have been more than eight – even then, I would look straight into the dark and say, 'I am not afraid of you.' They were the words, anyways. Words aren't always same thing as feeling; but they've got a big, sharp, overfull way of making one like the other. Would seem that way, anyhow, if you wanted to spend some time looking at this chickadee's life. Cripeys, when wasn't I frightened? But so what? Fear is just fear – can't eat you, can't buck you off it, can't even punch you in the face. No – fear is not the thing that causes pain or danger. So this is my rule: know what does cause pain and danger. Know it, and then run at it with your head down, before it even sees you coming.

Here I am, just twelve, even barely that. There were four of us in the house, if you want to know, and I suppose you do or else why would you have gathered me up, called out to me like this? So, then, if I was going to be truthful with you, really straight-up, I'd tell you that it wasn't even a proper house. Half a house more like. One room for sleeping, one for eating and farting in. Sorry. Too long on the trot, me, too long in my own company and too long before that in the company of men. For her, that woman (my mother, technically, but I'd hesitate to say it out loud in case it burnt my lips down to my arse), he was a come-down, a let-off, a never-was. As for straight answers about why she walked herself down the aisle with him then – because, Lord knows, no one was asking her to, I could bet you that much – well, nothing came out of her mouth but regret. And regret doesn't give you answers, doesn't give you truth. Doesn't give you anything except a belly-ache and lips wrinkled like a sultana's bottom. Apologies for the 'arse' earlier. I know how to say bottom, behind, posterior, as well as the next person; know how to say *derrière* better than most. Four of us, and him with his glorious plans all the time, his schemes, his useless, brilliant hopefulness. It was the hopefulness that did us in the end, if I got the story right. What to do but farm us out: Mikey to the priests, and me to the circus. Thinking on it now, I could bet my *derrière* that I got the better deal out of it, got the better life. Yes, I would, even now, with everything I'm going to show you, I'd still say that.

Look: me and my daddy. You can feel the heat coming off him, feel the need pouring out of his skin along with his damned gin-soaked sweat. My hair in two tight braids: they pulled at my skin, stretched me so tightly that I would burst if you came near me with a needle. My mother did the braids, the blue hairbrush pulling roughly through my hair, that woman's sniffles of tears plopping into my frizz. I knew where I was to go or, at least; what the Plan was. My mother held me tight, whispered into the braids: 'Know that I love you.'

And there I am, tugging at my temples, smiling in that same tight way at this man, Mr Ariel, of Ariel's Great Circus Show. Behind him a green tent, round and pale like spit, fluttered weakly. The Big Top! The centre-stage! With each shred of breeze I could see the threads of canvas, spooling out like fine green worms. Two wooden caravans, white paint flaking off, leant alongside the tent. Untied swag tents were spattered about the brown-green grass; plopped down like cow dung, you might say, if you weren't a lady. On the other side of the field, a lady in pink bloomers and a red dressing-robe was poking a billy on a fire. Nearby, a woman on a bicycle rode – standing up! – until a man as tall as a small sulky shouted at her to piss off and she toppled almost into the billy fire. It was like

9

a laundry, that humphing field – the steam of activity puffing up in delicious bursts. The man who had shouted at the bicycle lady played a tiny ukulele and the plonking notes caught in my fingers, my hair, pulled at me everywhere.

My daddy said: 'She can ride like a demon or like a feather sent down from Paradise, Mr Ariel – whichever one you want, she can do it. Do it, Elizabeth.' I lowered my head, bent my neck, yes, a dragonfly wing softing in the wind. The smell of need on the man. I cannot even imagine that he is my father.

'Elizabeth.' Mr Ariel, his face a yellow pat of butter melting on the bread of his neck, bobbed down to me. 'Elizabeth? Would you like to have a ride on Prince Vic?'

I kept my tongue firm, tucked behind my teeth, kept my words from tumbling out in a shock of loud, just nodded. Once, twice. A smooth-faced, liquorice brown man was currying a palomino. Eighteen hands, I reckoned. Plaited tail and mane; too ruddy fancy for a gelding. Mr Ariel called to the bushfire-skinned man, 'Billy, the girl's going to have a ride. Good, you think?'

A pearl-coloured wedge pushed into Billy's face, a slice of smile puffing him out. 'Good luck, hey, if you can manage him. He's *yirrakato*, this one, hey? Bloody wicked fellow, him. No good for pulling them wagons, no good for nothing but looking. Try him, but.' He squeezed on the barrel of the horse and pulled the stirrups up.

I always knew how to blend into the breath of the horse, how to make myself liquid on the horse's back, how to be upright and firm, yet loose as air all at the same time. I don't know where it came from. Neither of them had it, that mother or that father. My father, if you could be bothered calling him that, he was loose as wheat on a horse's back: he flopped around like an old hat on a fat man in the rain. Soggy and not much use. Any horse could feel it, of course. And that mother! She was worse, if such a thing were possible. Nervous as a sparrow in a flock of cockatoos. Fluttering and waltzing around, never sure which side to be on, how close to stand, whether the horse would just rear up and snap her in two with its huge yellow teeth. But me, now, I was another thing entirely, always, from the beginning. My daddy put me on a horse – for a joke, I think, though no one ever said as much – he put me on a horse when I was three, my black hair still curled round my dumpling soft face, if what they say is true. I can almost remember it, though I'm never sure whether it's a true memory, or the memory of something that has been told so often that I believe my body recalls it. Both of them watching me, laughing, clapping; my mother calling, 'Oh, clever darling, brave girl,' until the rattle of a wagon somehow started the young mare, quite as if she was a locomotive engine, and off she trotted across the little paddock, with me on her back, the tiny child who seems like another person, holding on tight, sitting upright, rising and falling in time, bless me!

That woman who was my mother always wiped her eyes, said, 'We'd never have believed it possible, but that child, well, she comes from somewhere else.' You could tell she believed it, too. Believed somehow that the scramble-faced girl that I turned into had come to her, ready formed, from some far continent and she, the mother, had no say in any of my strange skills, or in my whip-sharp unhappiness.

*

11

Look: Prince Vic arching his goldy neck, staring down at me, snorting. I leant in close, palms out, body soft, and snorted softly back. Stepping around, careful as a colt, I pushed one foot into the Great Ariel's cupped hands. I kicked him away as my leg scissored over the saddle, foot sliding neatly into the other stirrup. Knees squeezing, I tugged on the reins and gave a poke with my heels. I didn't need to kick; Prince Vic had my scent and knew what he was dealing with. Just a walk at first, my hands loose, back stiff. My daddy called out, 'Give him a kick, girl, do a gallop, do some of your jumps.'

Listen to him buzzing on to the Great Ariel: I could hear him just before I dug my heels in, flicked the reins, and leant in close to the neck of Prince Vic.

'Go, boy,' I whispered, so soft that it was just thought, passing straight between me and the palomino. 'Just go and I will come with you.' And the horse knew I meant it, knew I planned on staying put. The heels slivered down, balleting on the grass. The paddock was a long thin one, barely big enough to pasture a horse this size. Smack in the middle was a three-bar jump, nowhere near as high as the fences I could leap even without a flaming horse. Prince Vic's back was rippling with pleasure; I could feel the length of him as I leant down, flying with him over the jump. Ariel was applauding, and I kept the horse going, galloping on. I was laughing in his ear, and there wasn't a moment of hesitation between us, not even when the Great Ariel called out behind us Stop, no, Stop; the fence was nothing like a proper bush jump, and we took it easily, and I couldn't help the neighing laugh that bucked its way out of me. I reined him in, stroked his neck, cantered back round to the paddock entrance. Ariel was there on his own, teeth the colour of clotted cream spooned on to his face.

'Yes,' he said, 'yes, indeedy You will be our girl rider. A horse rider. Yes, that will do fine.'

It was then that I noticed the empty space beside the Great Ariel. Beside Ariel, where my daddy should have been, was my red-stringed hat-box, its round lid dinted.

Ariel held up the box, said, 'Your things are in here. Your daddy said to wish you well. He's –' His face melted into pity, clotted-cream teeth curdling. 'He said he'd take your first month's wages. But you mustn't worry, not a bit. We'll take care of you here, we'll always do that.'

And that was that, really. Scheming bastard sold me for the price of his debts and one month's rent.

That first night, I sat up on the high row of ladies' seats and looked down at the men standing and swaying near the front, but I didn't see the sandy hair of my daddy. Ariel stuck me up there, watching and waiting and watching and waiting. Night after night. An apprenticeship, of sorts. That was what he called it. There were four rows of wooden seats, banged together by Ariel and the ukulele man, just for the ladies. Never even half full. Standing to the side of the seats, the clumps of men swayed like grass, in time to the snake girl's dance. Her name – the snake girl – was Gladys. After my daddy swam away, to whatever ruddy sewer he'd come from, Ariel took my hand and said, 'Come and meet your new family.' Family, ha! Circus people always like to say that, family. But, good Lord, it's only folk who haven't known it who would think of 'family' as a word of praise. There was a scrap of stained canvas dangling over a rope – one end wrapped round a fat gum and the other hooked on to the paint-peeling caravan – looking about as clean and pretty as the back end of a sheep in summer. Sticking her head out of the tent, Gladys looked as stained and rumpled as someone's knickers, too. Nose too long for her face, the point of it trying to stretch for the crooked line of her upper lip. On her shoulder, the diamond point of a brown snake. Both of them – Gladys and the snake – squinted their eyes up at me and I could practically see Gladys's sharp little tongue whip-flicking around. That brown diamond on her shoulder, though, glinted and looked as cool as a bag of nails; I held my hand out flat and rested it on the dry skin. That was when Gladys smiled, her nose moving upward, and a laugh rumbled through Ariel.

At night during the shows, the men standing at the front smelt of the sticky-sweet hair cream and they pulsed together like a breath when Gladys peeked her way into the circle. The horse-tall ukulele man, Heap, with his moon-bright bald head, picked out delicate notes while Gladys stood, swelling, with two pythons licking their way round her almost-bare belly. I was the half-shadow at the back of the ladies' seats, barely flickering. The snake girl was the peak of interest, all that breath being held while they eyed that bare belly. After that, it was all shuffling and pulling out of pocket watches. Heap lifted Tilly, the bicycle girl, still on her bicycle, high above his head, while the wheels spun, and I was the only one who clapped. Two wooden flats, painted with stars, covered the tent flap, but even so you could see the hefty ruddy gape when Heap pulled it open. Ariel squeezed in, huffing past Heap, wearing a red cape. Even to me – and I was, let me tell you, more than a little unsophisticated then, in spite of being able to leap on a horse's back and make a stockwhip cry out louder than three galahs – the cape looked like a curtain, yanked down from a drawing-room window in a mad hurry. Ariel stood straight, his palms pointing to the stars, I held my breath. He took his time, letting them take him in, his bare palms. Standing there, as still as darkness, the man was the centre of the world, was the one shining star in a cloud-darkened sky. He was someone else, there in the tent: not the head-bobbing man of the paddock, no. Someone like a parade leader, or a general, or a king. He rumbled a word – I couldn't tell what it was, it sounded like thunder – and his hands blinked shut. When they opened again, he held three silver rings in each. I clapped and stamped and shouted until my eyes stung. Every night, for eight nights, I sat on the harsh wooden bench, watching the ladies clapping politely and the gentlemen swaying along with Gladys; I watched Ariel turn into a king, and I stamped my feet and shouted More. And every night for eight nights I looked for my daddy, and then I knew he was never coming back.

We packed up on the ninth day. Billy, who broke the brumbies, showed me how to hitch the horses – three Clydesdales, a chestnut mare, Prince Vic and a newly broken brumby – to the caravans and to the loaded-up wagon. For three months, in twelve towns, I watched the show from the wooden seat, fourth row. Daytimes, Billy started teaching me smart tricks with the whip, and with the brumbies. Flicking a whip round his ankles, then up to his waist; he could do it back to me so that the whip landed as soft as butter round the curve of my belly. By the time we got to Gundagai, I could leap from the back of Prince Vic and land one-footed on the stubborn ruddy back of the piebald Clydesdale. When we got to the South Australian border, I taught myself how to flip into a handstand on Prince's back: still I sat in seat four each ruddy day and each ruddy night, while Ariel counted out the flaming ticket stubs, sighing so that he rattled like a flame-torn paperbark tree. I stood beside him, tugging on his shirt, asking, When, when?

In Tabulum, two crumpled-looking men sauntered past me and Ariel after a matinée and the traces of their words flew back at us: 'The snake girl was all right, but, Jeez, the rest of it wasn't much, hey, and a bloody chinky ringmaster, jeez.' Beside me Ariel stood still, his long face sucking in on itself.

Out the back of Tabulum we were camped in a wide, flat crater: a dry lake, curved into the shape of a keyhole. We could hear the packs of brumbies – those mad, wild horses – thundering above us on the ridge top, leaping over logs so that, from the lakebed, you'd swear they had wings. By the fourth day, there was no one in the audience. Not one person. A girl called Maggie had insisted on joining us in Gundagai. Mad about bicycles, and men. That one, that show, was supposed to be her great flaming début. So she lurked at the backflap, hopeful as a red-eyed coot, until Ariel called out that no one would be going on – no one at all – and he had a bloody headache like the billy-oh, and that we should all rest up, then get ready to pack up and move on to Somewherebloodyelse. Right next to Cape of Lost Hope, if his face was anything to go by. Up on the ridge, a herd of brumbies thundered past. Billy called out, 'I'm gunna go up and catch some, boss. Good for workhorses, or for this one, this *wungunbai*: she a good jumper, hey?'

I watched Ariel stalk off to the other side of the lakebed, his back a dry stick. Look at me: my braids have gone and I'm all frizz and freckle and already hard-skinned. Ariel, he's another thing entirely. Hard-skinned, yes, but burnt orange, and his tilted eyes with a way of holding the sun, shining it back out at you. I can trace my hands across his shoulders: in my imagination, I do.

Stretching one handspan after another across his back, that's what I imagine; counting out twelve spans as I push my palms across the thin bones, the brown shoulders. Once, in Nambucca, he said his shoulders weren't big enough, that he couldn't carry us all, though he wanted to, wanted to find a way. There had been some blokes outside the big tent, calling out something about *Chinks, Chinks,* and one had spat at Gladys, too, called her Lady Slut. Ariel stood in front of her, his big chest bellowing in and out, a firebolt coming from him. Maybe they saw the hulking great shadow of Heap creaking around, or maybe they could see that firebolt – but they muttered *sorry* and scampered like a pack of half-shot ruddy wallabies.

On the other side of the lake, he was creaking, stretching up and down, his hands pressed against his head. He looked up at me, watching him like I always was. He didn't turn his back on me, so I counted myself invited, and ran to him. Could barely speak when I huffed to him there on the other side of the lake.

'I'm thinking, Elizabeth, thinking.'

As if he needed to explain the act of thinking to me, as if I didn't understand the great pressing weight of thoughts that jumbled out of your head, trying to push out and be born.

Then he burst open, like a cloud, his face splitting with a smile. 'Yes – I have it, I do.'

And he lifted his bony knees, took my hand, and swung me round, laughing so hard that I laughed too, though I had no idea what the ruddy joke was, or if there was one.

'Here it is.' He stepped, all magical flourish, to the side, and waved his hand, as though demonstrating a theatre curtain. 'The whole show needs to change, to become new. Something new. And

17

you,' his hand flicked towards me, an extra flourish, 'are the key, Elizabeth. Oh, indeed.'

I stopped nodding, sat up and took some ruddy notice then, I can tell you. 'The leaping on those brumbies of Billy's. And cracking whips and – we'll be the World's Greatest Buckjumping Show. Forget the regular circus. Rough riding, that's the thing. With a story. Yes! A girl, taken from her farm – no – wait.' He pressed his hands to his head again. 'My head is aching with it. Oh, the billy-oh. We'll still have the cycling, and Heap, but – I've got it – it's an outlaw story. We'll have the story of Captain Thunderbolt himself, we'll act it all out, with horses, and cycles, and sharp-shooting and whips: him emerging from a poor family. Oppressed—'

'How will we show that by rough-riding and circus tricks?'

'Yes. So perhaps only the cattle duffing, bailing up the police. Him becoming a hero of the people—'

'The traps themselves wouldn't like that, us showing them being bailed up. Wouldn't they?'

'No. No – not that. You will be disguised as a boy – a wild boy – perhaps a young wanderer, lost, aimless – no work, no hope – you'll wear a goatskin, then you'll come on as a man – riding in different styles – yes—' He was shouting then, 'You'll be the damsel in distress, and the mentor of the boy, and the wild boy, and perhaps even one of the traps – a mistress of disguises, queen of horseback. You will be – I've got it – *Athene of the Antipodes*.'

'Athene?' I didn't like fancy names. Still don't. Flower names are fine, but not these fussy, dancy fancy names like Zirinthia, Vanessa, Clementia. 'I don't even like Elizabeth. It's too—'

'Fussy.'

'Yes.'

He grinned. 'You need a name that is strong and brave, beautiful, but plain and – Jess.'

I loved it. I wanted to be Jess.

'Rhymes with yes,' I said, and he lifted me and swung me round, a planet orbiting the sun.

Ah, I tell you, it was all so long ago that it seems only like a sigh, seems to be right here with me now. And this is where it brings me to, though, this love of him, this clumsiness of me. Here, with this crooked body, the grey and yellow stone around me; the earth beneath my skin.

Rocks below me, sky above.

War is beginning on a faraway rock of land, that's what they said; but I am here, knowing the battles have ended, gloriously ended. I feel that I've been swallowed up, that I am shouting from across a ravine. I am caught, twirling, in a swirl of smoke, and no one hears me across the crackle of the fire and the singing of the earth. Except you. Finally you are listening.

~

St John of the Cross Rest Home for Women was a progressive institution. Experimental, attempting to cure rather than to hide. Rose could see all this, she was no fool, and understood that the machine, the straps, were meant only for her good, meant to save her from herself.

Rose's breasts were milky round, the day Joe brought her in. After the kicking and shouting, she stood staring away from him, letting the weight of her hands pull her arms straight down so that you'd think she had rocks in her fists, or gold. Even when Joe left, without a kiss on the cheek, without a by-your-leave, she kept her arms, legs and face as calm as bark. Only when the echo of his footsteps began to gentle away, only then a sound, a sigh, a whoosh: the sound of a tap being turned on. Damp began to spread on her new regulation green tunic, began to spread first across her chest and then to spurt, so that pale milk dripped down her front, drenching her to the waist. The days merged with the nights. Several times Rose woke and rolled over to see shadows of her wardmates moving as though flying, flitting like moths.

On Tuesdays — the nurse said it was Tuesday, as though it mattered — a doctor would appear at her bedside, a white badge on his lapel: *Dr V. Dwyer*. She thought he was Japanese, perhaps. Oriental-looking, anyhow. Each Tuesday, when Dr V. Dwyer arrived, he held his dusk-coloured hand out to her, as though she were a friend, not a woman losing everything. He walked with her to a cream room with a print of sunflowers on one wall, two framed diplomas on the other. Two chairs, that was all; no desk. He sat on one of the chairs, and she sat on the other, staring at the diplomas.

Each Tuesday he said, 'What shall we talk about today, Rose?'

And each Tuesday she shook her head, unable to find words. Sometimes, he sat in silence, while she wept. Once, he said, 'It is not good, to separate a woman from her child. But,' he stretched his hand out towards her, smiling, 'you will become well, that is the thing. You can survive all manner of things, Rose.'

'I've always been happy, before. I didn't plan – I don't know how I got here.'

On the other days Dr Kingley came to collect her. He held his arms out to her, and though there was no corsage offered, she had the feeling that he would like to waltz with her, that he was planning dance steps in his head, even as he placed one foot neatly in front of the other in a plain straight line. Together, they swayed down the corridor to the blood-swelling room, where Rose obediently stepped behind the white screen. Slipping into an open-backed gown, Rose tilted her chin and straightened her back. She could try, at least, to be brave. *Like Athene of the Antipodes*, she thought. Then: *Now where did that come from?*

She stepped out from behind the screen, head lowered so that you would think she was a new bride showing off her trousseau. Almost did a twirl, though she stopped herself in time. The long bed was covered in crisp sheets, as though it were for sleeping, or resting, reading. Without the panel on the wall alongside it, without the wires dangling on to the edge of those inviting sheets, it would seem a place for quiet slumber, for peaceful nocturnal activities. Dr Kingley smiled thinly at Rose, waved his hand in the direction of the bed. When she hesitated, he said, 'Come now, you know this is for your own good. We are here to take away all that terrible weeping.'

Rose knew it was true. Indeed, she had no desire to give in to the weeping, she did not call it on herself. She drew a picture in her head: of Joe, of Sammy especially, but not just of them. Of herself. The way she could look, could be. When she was dreamed out. She thought of it like this, being dreamed out, cleaned out, and the shocks were not unwelcome. She did feel – how to put it? – clearer. Less silted by muddy thoughts, by the effort of pushing every thought through sand. She had a picture of herself, not entirely plucked from the photographic pictures of the *Women's Weekly* but owing something to them. She was mildly, healthily, distracted in the picture. Wearing a pink dirndl – no, she tried again, strained for something flatter, sensible. Cotton pants, with a grey striped pinafore knotted over the top. There. One hand was on Sammy's head, the other was engaged in something motherly, competent. Perhaps cracking an egg? Rose strove again, here, to create the perfect picture, wanting to be concerned with the whipping of the egg and timing of the vinegar, concerned with effortless mayonnaise creation, with the pleasure of it. She could remember the pleasure she had in such moments. Careful, too, with where she placed Sammy in the picture. Too close and her stomach knotted, her cheek burnt where she imagined him placing his hand, reaching up to touch her. She could see him, could see that his face was button-sweet, and was able to notice the pleasing fatness of his ankles, the way his toes kicked up when he was tired. Yet all his softness was not enough to pull her back, to stop the dull dread that had struck up inside her chest every morning since her long-awaited boy had pushed out of her with the pummelling of a violent storm.

*

All that hope on the ship, rocking across two oceans. Joe with his teacher's certificate folded like a kiss in his black leatherette case.

There he was, Joe. Yellow dusk shifting round him, the Isis slugging past. Icicles gathered on the outer edge of the window; inside, steam sucked across the panes. He spread the two-page advertisement across the new red laminex table and looked at Rose, just looked.

Finally: 'There now. What do you think?'

Rose sat opposite him, her bare hands linked in her white-skirted lap.

The wireless was on in the sitting room, Doris Day calling out 'Secret Love'. 'They need teachers. British workers of all sorts. Think of it, Rose.' He reached his hand up, left it hovering, waiting, then lowered it again. 'A beginning, an adventure.'

'How many beginnings can we have?'

'Rose.'

Oh, when he put that ripple in his voice, she turned to silk, rippling herself. He's thirty-five, she thought. Too old to have waited so long for a child: a first, second, third. Where were they, those small ghost children who had never arrived? All those seeds that passed unnoticed until neither of them could bear it. Sleeping alongside each other nestled back by back; this was no hardship. Desire had long ago settled beneath a lap blanket, rarely purring. Joe's belly rounded over his belt, his face was beginning to fall down around itself, and he rarely touched her any more. Rose, barely thirty, still held herself neatly in, had a daily walk and made sure Ada gave her a manicure each Wednesday. She did book-keeping once a week for the Hinksey doctor, and bought new fashions and lipsticks with the earnings. There was no need to let yourself go.

In winter, they had found a block of shining smooth ice, neatly kissing the edges of the tin bath, left outside since the summer. Rose slipped off her shoes and skated on the tiny pond in white woollen socks, arms waving as she tottered, laughing like Doris Day. After, steaming wet and red-cheeked, they'd all sat at the wood-stove drinking hot cocoa. Rose's mum, Ilsa, and Joe. All of them shaking off the winter, while Joe pulled out the map and pointed to Australia, to adventure.

Sunday. It was a Sunday. The sermon was from the Book of Ruth: *Where you go, I will go; your God will be my God*. After church, Joe was warm with her, his hand nestling on her back. 'I feel led,' he said. 'Really, Rose. That the Lord is telling me.' The air sparkled, and Rose felt suddenly fresh, felt twenty-five; believed that they could start again, on new soil. That a new land would even take Joe's memories, return him to himself, and to her. And Joe was full of light, full of the old rollicking way, before disappointment took him: the mouth curving on one end, the deepdark eyes, which had caught her in the first place. She remembered, that night, all the pleasures of desire. His hand pushing against the dimple on her back; the rough skin on his cheek pulling against her own cheek; the shocking fit of them, like keys, or cogs.

Here she is now, trying to have this sudden, unexpected misery zapped out of her, vamoosed away. For Rose, flicking a switch to have light was still miraculous, but here, the thought that it could cure her, make her well: the idea was like angel dust. She had seen women leaving, too, with their trouble packed up in their old kit-bags, or so it seemed. One woman who scratched at herself and then lay bleeding on the ground: the treatments had made her almost well, she said it herself. Rose, though, did not feel the swords of electricity hewing into her unhappiness: she felt only bruised by the invasion. After each session her skin was raw and she trembled for several hours, a violent shiver as if she had been pulled from an icy lake, the cold waters of her mother's memories. *I have swum the waters of a loch*, she thought. *Loch Lomond, Loch Katrine, Loch Ness*. Each time a different body of water. Each time, the same uncontrollable icy tremor.

She was still obedient; she was not so far disappeared into herself to have forgotten her training in obedience, though Joe would dispute that fact. When Dr Kingley pointed silently at the table-like bed, she leant against it, let her legs swing from the ground and tipped herself back in a smooth movement. Scissors, that was what it made her think of somehow: a pair of scissors, kicking back and down. Smooth, sharp ones, not the blunt kind that always snagged at the fabric. Face pointing to heaven, or to where she imagined heaven to be, Rose breathed in as tightly as she could. It was a different nurse this time, a tall girl with a dark fringe hanging limply round her eyes, which Rose longed to snip at. It was so often silent in this room, at least before the treatment began. There was the fierce concentration marking the face of Dr Kingley, and the anxious breathing coming from the table. Rose steadied herself, lay back and thought of England; truly, thought of England, her England, not the dark grey one of the Thames bleak and thick, but the England with long white days endlessly stretching into slow nights, England with the glitter of summer afternoons sprinkling on to her shoulders. She longed for it, longed for the pallid light—

The limp-haired nurse stretched the straps across Rose's waist, chest, ankles, wrists. She looked down and smiled; it was so unexpected that Rose called out, a sharp 'oh'.

Dr Kingley looked over at the nurse. 'Problem?'

'No.' The nurse barely glimmered. 'I can't see anything—'

'We'll move on, then, shall we?' A razor poked through his voice: warning, warning. Rose was silent; it always came to this, to this silence. She could feel a tear riding down her nose, could feel it trickling towards her mouth, was suddenly hot with fear, irrational, hysterical. She knew it to be so, but could only think of this: water and electricity, water and electricity. All the warnings she'd seen on the magazines: *Ladies, no wet hands with electric lights*. 'Please, please stop.'

Dr Kingley paused, looked right at her, as if she was there. 'Problem?' His voice did not have the razor in it, this time, only honey and music and warm eiderdowns.

'Please. Wipe my tears away first.'

The young nurse hurried over, but Kingley raised his hand in a blunt stop sign. He took a checked handkerchief from his pocket, dabbed at Rose's cheek, and then her nose.

No tears, no water. And then the tears came again, a flood of them, breaking through, pushing the logs aside. She could see herself toppled, kneed sideways by the force of the water, her branches split, the whole of her tumbling down. *Loch Tay, Loch Linnhe, Loch Earn*.

'I will drown, don't let me drown.'

'No.' The young nurse stroked Rose's forehead. 'Let it go now.'

'I want to remember.'

'It's better to be clean. To begin again.' For Dr Kingley, there was something of Jesus in this. The doctor stretched tall and, experimentally, swept his hands in an act of benediction: *Go forth and be well*.

Rose tried to push breath further than her throat, tried to push her thoughts elsewhere, to remember anything, anything at all.

Joe coming from his Men's Breakfast, buoyed up by the Word, calling her to the kitchen and flicking through the fine pages of his English Revised Edition: here, here, there, all the commands, the instructions. The sweet comfort of rules. They were both to obey, there was no question of that. Only that Joe seemed to hear the instructions more clearly. Yet she had been full of God, herself, full of the Word; everything certain.

She concentrated, tried to see, to remember. The sparkle of the ring, when he'd opened the maroon box, standing underneath the Osney bridge. 'Will you, Rose?' Such unexpected shyness in his voice. Later, watching him shake her father's hand, saying, 'I'll take care of your daughter, sir,' and 'I'll hold to the promises of the Word, to be yoked with her, to care for her.'

Frank, her father, nodded and Ada left the room, giggling into her hand.

It was the one glimmer of light in the darkness of the war, that was what Joe said, finding the Lord, or being found by Him. Some nights, she'd roll over in the darkness and find him at the little table in their cold room, crouched like a hunter as he turned the pages, making sure the promises were there, trying to hold tight against a storm that Rose couldn't see.

*

She was eighteen. They thought the war would end that year, and Frank let her go – just for six months, mind – to make blankets and bandages at a little factory in Rhyl. Three girls roomed together, bickering over the pennies for the gas meter. Mair, one of them was called, and the other – an Edinburgh girl, wasn't she? – her name was gone. Not her face, though: she was a pink-faced girl, with flat cheeks. Laughing, all the time, with her broad mouth. They all laughed, the three of them. Everything was hilarious. Even folding the bandages into neat packages didn't stop them, and Rose was the worst, telling jokes about bottoms and wind, as though she were a child, or a man. The glory of work, of being useful, twirled all of them like leaves in a storm, and made them giddy.

The Rhyl Methodist Guild had a picnic, a day out for the soldiers in Rhyl on R&R. Rose wore trousers – wide-legged, narrow-hipped – and a Betty Grable swimsuit tucked underneath. She couldn't wait to show it off. And there he was: Joe. The way he was then – nothing would sluice that memory from her. She was a tiny bird next to him: his wide chest, that long straight back, hips like a girl's, eyes as brown as mud. The beach was scattered with metal tank traps, their pyramid tips glinting benignly in the sun. Like giant's toys, Rose thought, though she knew they weren't playthings, or a laughing matter.

The church group had spread blankets, were gathering for a round of songs, but he stood with his hands dangling, his eyes scanning the beach. She reached right up to him, bold as brass, stood in front of him with her hair untucking from its pins. 'What are you waiting for? Which do you want to do – sing with me, or swim? You have to do one or the other.'

'Aren't there landmines?' His voice was as deep as peaty soil.

She shrugged. 'What's your name, before we swim together?'

He smiled down at her then, the eyes looking down from the sun, squinting right at her, and she was suddenly as light as the sand. His hand shielded his face. 'Give me yours, first.'

She picked up a blown branch from the sand. Between the tank traps, stepping through their painted shadow, she etched lines into the sand, arcing her arms high and deep, carving furrows as long as her body.

On the first furrow, he called out, 'Don't – you don't know – if there's anything there—'

She kept drawing, laughing over at him, making the furrows longer, curving them round until her name was spread across the sand. The shadow of a tank trap formed a thick exclamation point. Rose!

He wanted to kiss her when she put both her feet neatly in front of his, her chin pointing up, she could see that he wanted to, and she slipped her hand into his, her liquid to his air.

At the end of the day, his commanding officer – Mair's lipstick smeared across his cheek – said they had to go back, the next day, that the war was still on after all. Joe touched his finger to the end of Rose's nose, and she knew then that she would be at war too, until he came back safe.

Once, she had been a girl with a Betty Grable swimsuit, and no fear, and an exclamation point at the end of her name.

What else? She tried to recall the scent of blackberries, tried to remember the twelve times table and how to spell Mississippi backwards. Not the ship. Better to leave that, to stay with forgetting.

*

Heat fused against her; her lips widened. A tremor pulsed on her arm: a sudden emptiness, a sieving of memory. One hundred and forty-four volts of electricity passed along the metal cable to her skin, and from there, spiralled, spun, to her nerve-endings. Everything jolted, jumped. Water ran. A girl leapt. Surging through her, a swirl of pictures, as if in death: she and Ada, red-cheeked children, playing by the river in Hinksey, mud caking red wellingtons; Joe kissing her nose, along the Willow Walk; a sudden gush of blood, clotted and hard; Joe's back, straight and cool, as he walked across the pale green fields; words on a poster — *You'll Find it In Australia!*; rows of curved metal army huts, the migrant hostel. And others too, bearing no relation, mixed in with equal parts. Rose's mouth hung open as another one hundred and forty-four volts shrieked across her skin and the shots of memory fluttered through her like a tattered flag. Another poster, *The Great Ariel*; dry hands, snipping at long hair. Someone — perhaps it was her? — sobbing, or singing. She had forgotten this, the voices; the beautiful, beautiful voices.

~

You're not the first one to be in pain, oh, no.

Heap and Billy rode ahead of us at each town, spreading posters on town hall noticeboards, handing out cards to gentlemen of the press. All legs I was, and half horse, or so they used to say. Even the painted posters, dotted about the towns we passed through, proclaimed: *Half Girl, Half Horse! Athene of the Antipodes! She never falls!* And I didn't. None of them could throw me, and that was a record even Billy couldn't claim. He'd been thrown by twelve brumbies, he said, though you never saw a bruise on him.

Me and Billy started the show by pretending to be sharp-shooting each other, leaping back and forth; then I got the hang of proper rough-riding, won the ruddy medal against half the men not just of New South Wales but the whole new ruddy nation. Hold the barrel of the horse with your legs and let your back be a wave of water, that's all, that's the trick. Strong legs, soft back, simple as that. And let me tell you this, too, in case you ever need to know: when you've outlasted a brumby, trying to buck you off, you'll have a pet sweeter than life.

One time we rode into Ballarat and they saw me and Billy up front with our whips, and a lady in the main street – all hatted up and dainty – started screaming. Thought we were some new breed of ruddy bushrangers, outlaws copying the dead old Kelly gang. Ariel, flicking the reins on the caravan, called out to me, 'Might be more money in bushrangering,' and I laughed for a second. Then I stopped laughing and said I wasn't doing anything for money, only for love, looking right at him. Ariel stopped flicking the reins and looked back at me, long and quiet.

*

It was Ariel and Billy between them thought of really making it an outlaw show: *Captain Thunder and His Fiendish Friends*. Me and Billy cracking our whips, holding Tilly and Gladys hostage while Heap tried to rescue them. Ariel said he would be the honest Chinese storekeeper, getting robbed by the bushrangers, and when I said, no, why shouldn't he be the copper fighting the good fight, he put his hand on my arm and said, 'I don't think you see how I am seen, dear one.'

One night I lined up four ladies from the audience all in a row and cracked my whip so that their bonnets came flying off and after that we had to turn people away, we had such crowds.

We were in Quirindi, the first time Ariel came to me. Storms had ripped through New South Wales, leaving farms with their insides torn out. The first night, the show tent was full of people desperate to be entertained, to be frightened out of their misery by enactments of modern bushrangers, wooed by cycling girls and snake dancers. But the storms didn't stop, and each night the tin box rattled less. On the third night, Ariel had called everyone in to his caravan, said: 'We'll pack up tomorrow and move on. Head back to Maitland. Night.' Billy and the others left in silence, but when I stood up to go, Ariel said, 'Don't. Please, Jess. Please stay. I need——' And I'd stayed, what else was she to do? His body was long and bony, and he'd wept when he pushed himself inside me, wept when I cried in pain and kept weeping after he'd rolled off me, his hair drenched with sweat. The man was a great ocean of wetness; I could barely breathe for all the water of him.

On my seventeenth birthday, in Wodonga, he had Heap and Tilly play 'Lady Greensleeves' while he somersaulted down on to one knee, magic rings still in his hand, and said, 'Jess, will you be my wife?' And I said yes, because who would say no with an audience of six hundred and thirty-one people watching? I felt like he'd taken his ruddy time about it, that's what. Everyone wore white for the wedding, except me and Ariel, both of us in jodhpurs and boots. My hair was tucked under one of Ariel's caps; I wanted to look like a boy. Ariel said he couldn't wait to tear that brown jacket from my shoulders. After that first night, when Ariel pushed inside me and then lay weeping, our activities became more advanced, more – how to say it? Can I be frank with you? – more acrobatic. He loved me to wear the cap, my hair tucked under it until I flipped myself on to him; he would pull it from my head then, bury his face in my hair, and wrap himself in it as though it were a blanket.

After Wondonga, there was Ballarat, then in and up, as far as the Queensland border. We traced the state of New South Wales up and over, in and around, like fine needlepoint. In Cessnock, Ariel rode out with Billy to catch some brumbies to use in the show, rode out as far as Nullo Mountain. Leapt across the ravine. He wasn't the world's greatest horseman; no one could say that. God, he knew how to run a circus, though, how to pull a show together: his patter; the girls on the trick-cycles. No one had done that before, can you believe it? He was the first – Tilly and Gladys, dressed in sheer knickerbockers, talk about saucy. Almost gave an old man a heart-attack one night back in Gundagai, when Tilly swept round the ring, tilted at the front of the cycle. You could see right down her blouse. Deliberate, of course. Kept them coming back, shouting for more. In its day, our Buckjumping Show was the greatest in New South Wales. After Ariel – well – everything changes sooner or later, doesn't it?

*

That ravine, one of a hundred up there in Nullo Mountain, is an open mouth, grey teeth, green fringe. Ariel could jump, though, when he needed to. Almost as fire-free as me, when he was on the fly. Poor old Billy couldn't even catch him, couldn't trail him. All the things I'd taught him, flowing with the horse, all came to him. Flying, Billy said, like a cloud. Ha. Who'd have guessed?

It must have been, oh, just before the Wodonga show that the white-haired man came creeping round. I hadn't had my crick-kneed proposal from Ariel, though I had been proposed to by eleven men, if you included the two drunks who shouted out at me when we rode through Albury. None had taken my fancy enough to lure me away from Ariel and the darling grey stallion, Lordship, that Billy and I had broken. Every so often, Ariel would take me aside and ask if I felt worried, frightened, by all these men and I'd slap at him. How could they frighten me? I'd been a grown-up since I was twelve, tougher than most of the drovers who hiked their way through New South Wales.

It was always Ariel who checked the tent before a show, counted out the audience, kept the hawkers out of the way. Ludicrous prices, they'd ask, for tiny slips of silk – and right before a show. I never cared for silk, anyway, unless it was slipped under a saddle. Most shows, especially near the cities, they were there, snooping around, trying to trip us up, trying to make Ariel fail. It's the truth: there were more than a few making noises about who had the right to take money from good pure Australians. Not that I'd agree so much with the 'good', not for some of them – burning sticks poked under our tent; crushed glass in an envelope addressed to *Chinky Ariel, Poste Restante*. Oh, I know I sound like a madwoman here – no offence intended – but it's true. *Yarakai*, Billy called them, staring them right down, Lordy, that man was afraid of no one. *Yarakai*, hissing like snow; you wouldn't mess with him and you didn't need to ask what it meant.

One night we were in one of those ruddy over-rich towns, Bowral, perhaps, or Mount Wilson. Feathered hats everywhere, bobbing about like birds in the audience. Tweet ruddy tweet. Me and Billy were doing our trade-off, the getting up, hands out, the watching each other as slow and careful as velvet; and these three blokes in the audience stood up and started stamping, cheering. One of them blew a whistle. Spread out round the tent they were, one in each bank. Prince Vic pigrooted; I had no grip, how could I? Hit the ground with one hell of a bang, and Prince's hoofs would have belted down on me, too, if it weren't for Billy leaping off Galah and rolling me away as if I was a fat rug. Bloody Billy. I was always worried he was going to break his neck.

Don't know if it was the same blokes who poisoned Lady and Prem, but someone did that, too, and it cost us the takings from four shows to get new show-horses and even begin training them up. Usually, they kept aim at Ariel, but we all copped a bit – Billy, for being a black, me for marrying a Chinaman who was busy taking all the work from good honest whites. Not that I saw any of them shifting off their arses and dragging their way round the country, training up girls and lads, callusing their hands from tugging at ropes and folding heavy canvas, sweeping up shit and hay and staying up nights to care for sick horses.

There was a sign up, once, in Windsor: *Go Home Chinky*. It wasn't the only one, though. Alongside it, there was another one, just for me: *Women Should Be Women. No Unnaturals in Our Town*. I was touched, I really was. If Ariel had to take the dictation test – in case you're asking – there'd have been no problem, unless they gave it to him in Indian, which I wouldn't have put past them. He was born in Ballarat just after his mama found a half-ounce gold nugget, plonked right in the middle of her pannikin. Ariel always said she was in the middle of the creek, her bloomers up round her elbows, when she felt the first tug in her belly. Ariel and gold, discovered together, that's the way he told it. Born in the middle of the goldfield, he was, with only his mama for company. His papa was scalped that same day, left to bleed to death on the side of the find. Once, Ariel danced through a field of wildflowers in Ballarat, right there near the same fields where his daddy was killed; he danced like a dry river, bending and rasping, as awkward and as joyous as a yellow-crested cockatoo. Revenge, he called it.

In that town, as always, we'd pitched the sleeping tents in a half-circle, with our newly painted wooden caravan in the middle, a glorious red beacon. Drongo, the bay Clydesdale who pulled sluggishly at the caravan, was head-down beside me, chomping at rough-stemmed dandelions. There were two other Clydesdales who pulled the wagons, dragging the canvases and hoops and banked seating and lamps about as willingly as we set them up. We formed a minute village on the edge of the show tent, making a courtyard of stubby grass for the Clydesdales to chew on. The show-horses sniffed at the grass as though it were filth – spoilt ruddy things they were, used to oats and hay and sweet chaff. So, there was Ariel, doubled over, counting out the pink ticket stubs, while I curried Lordship.

The blond man lifted his hat to me, then tapped Ariel on the spine. Leant down to ask, 'Mr Ariel?'

Ariel stood up then, scrumping the stubs in his fist. 'There's no free tickets, not for press or government. All government tickets are gone.'

'Just wanted to give you this, is all. If any of your men are interested, I'd be happy to discuss payment.' He uncreased a poster: *From Dampier's Stage Company comes a new Story of the Wild Bushranger for Cinema! Danger and Adventure in* Captain Starlight!

Ariel read the poster, then handed it to me. 'Cinema?'

'I've all the fittings and kitty from Dampier's. They got out of it well. Sorry. Forgetting myself. Alfred Dibbs. If you have any men—'

Ariel nodded at me. 'This one's my best.'

Mr Alfred Dibbs raised his eyebrows. 'It's a woman.'

Ariel handed him a ticket. 'Go in. See for yourself. But you won't be able to afford us.'

It. Inbloodydeed.

Inside the tent, I could see the blond moustache glinting in the front row, could see the sweat on his lip when he leant forward, watching me. There were always some men who came to see – I think you'll understand me here – more than the tricks. They came with the wrong sort of hopes. This one, though, it wasn't that sort of look. Still, that stare cut across the ring, I tell you. With him there, even flipping upright on to Lordship – which really was a simple handstand, legs flicking neatly into the air – made me feel giddy. After Tilly and Maggie did handstands on the penny-farthing, me and Billy rode in, all upright and dressage, for the trade-off. Waved to each other, waved to the crowd – which in this case amounted to seventy-two paying adults, including Blond Moustache. So we criss-crossed, and we waved neatly; and who could tell what they were more amazed by? Me, a woman, or Billy, an Abo? This was Parramatta: we weren't counting on much in the way of brains. Lord knows, I should have an opinion about it – my daddy came from there, and he was as brainless as he was gutless.

Billy rippled like water; he shimmied up, a smooth flip on to Prince Vic's back. Wild applause. They barely noticed me haul myself up on to Lordship's rump. Once I was up – the trick is to push back against the knees, that gets rid of the tremble – Billy and I eyeballed each other, Billy's dark eyes making me as still as red rock. He was like a snake, sometimes, Billy, with his deep eyes and the way he breathed down at me, making me calm. Our hands came up, one, two. Everything is in the hands, in keeping them slow and steady, so that was what you noticed, what you thought about, while the back of the horse rippled and pounded and your toes curved round to meet the spine of the horse's back. Hands, arms up, watch, eyes, breathe. Legs soft, feet hard. Lordship and Prince Vic pounded in a circle – don't let anyone ever tell you that horses aren't smart, that they don't know where their food is coming from – the sparkle on my jodhpurs glinting like diamond. Not that I ever saw real diamond up close: even my wedding ring was made from copper.

We waited for the rhythm to pound into the audience, waited until it was a drumbeat that dulled them to a trance, then Billy stepped on to Lordship's back, as neat as if he was stepping on to a stretch of cloth. Lordship jolted, unable to hold the weight of us both, and I breathed in, pushed against my bare toes and leapt across, one foot, then two, catching on Prince Vic's rump. He stumbled when my foot tipped his spine, double-stepped, and I felt my feet flick. Landed with my face in his neck, arse-up. I wasn't going to let Mr Cinema have that as the last sight of me — my legs dangling like a sheep's dag — so I flipped myself round, arms out, face to the sky, and lifted my legs in the air. Scissored them up and down until I could hear the thump of seventy-two pairs of boots, stamping for more, then slid myself down, along Prince's Vic's whiskery tail. Believe me, even if I was wearing a skirt I would have done it. Better have it straight now, once and for all; I stopped talking, thinking, behaving like a lady way back when I believed it mattered. Contrary to opinion, to legend, whatever you want to name it, contrary to all that — no, it wasn't the cave did it, wasn't the cattle duffing. God, no, by the time you could properly call me an outlaw ladylike language had long since stopped passing my lips.

I knew I'd won him; I could see the gold in his teeth, glinting as he leant forward. Even the spot of spit on his lip: the lights caught it, and I saw it all. Afterwards he draped an arm over Ariel's shoulder and called him Mate. I could see Ariel softening like lard while I cleared the ring, paid the boys, got the sawdust out of Lordship's hoofs and boiled a billy on the fire outside Billy's tent. He waited by the main tent, glimmering as brightly as cash, while I sifted black leaves into my blue Ricketts teapot because, unlike Ariel, I had nothing to prove, and I wasn't going to be drinking tea from a billy, not for any man. Nor any woman, for that matter. Once I'd let the tea draw darkly, and scraped off four chips of sugar, I sat myself down on a bag of chaff.

'Jess.' Ariel was fluttery, nervous as a feather. 'Mr Dibbs here—'

'Alfie. Please.'

'Yes. Alfie.'

'Pleased to meet you, Jess. Quite a performance.'

I looked right at him and didn't say a word.

He kept babbling, though, making less sense than a creek drying up. 'Yes, just – that bushranger show, very, erm, lifelike. Scared the ladies, didn't it? A lot like our moving-picture show. All about Captain Starlight, gentleman bushranger.'

I kept silent, watching.

Ariel sucked in all the air around him, so that his cheeks went hollow. 'Jess. It's cinema and—'

'Thought we despised cinema, thought it was the enemy of honest touring troupers?' Somehow, I wanted to poke at them, both of them, sitting on the only two wooden chairs and rubbing their hands as if a deal had been done. There was sweat on Ariel's cheeks. 'Our name will be at the end. Big letters. Hundreds—'

'Thousands.'

'As Mr – Alfie – says, thousands of people. All seeing the name: Ariel's Buckjumping Show. You'll be the star.' Ariel rubbed his hands against his blue chaps. 'Jess. You know it will make the difference for us. For all of us.' And so I nodded, and held out my hand for him to shake and tried not to notice the scent of need that wafted off Ariel and reminded me, suddenly, so much of my daddy.

~

Dr Dwyer folded one hand over the other. A thin gold band twisted round his ring finger. 'Hard, to leave home. To find home again.' His black eyes creased at the corners.

Rose looked at his hands, at the worn band, then at the flecks of grey at his temples. 'There's nothing here' she said. 'Nothing.'

Dr Dwyer whispered back, as though she had a right to quiet, as though it were not strange or wrong to want it. 'It just takes a little while to see it.' He smiled again. 'Victory, Rose: sometimes I think that victory, for what it's worth, is in finding home where you are. Dr Kingley's treatment,' he clicked his tongue behind his teeth, as though spitting out poison, 'it is one way. One approach. Not mine. It's difficult – believe me when I say that I know this – it can be terribly difficult, to discover yourself without a past. But it is possible. I believe that it is.'

She had heard them – Dr Dwyer and Dr Kingley – arguing outside the wardroom. Dr Dwyer, calm and steel-edged, saying, 'You can't believe the shocks work for everyone; you're blinded by your enthusiasm.'

Dr Kingley, snapping back, 'It works, that's the thing. *Doctor*. As for being blinded, at least we're humble enough to call it a treatment. Talking cure, indeed. Talking cures nothing.'

'That's not what I see. I remain unconvinced by your enthusiasm for your machine.'

'Why bring your talking treatment here, then? Why not take it elsewhere?'

The pause was so long Rose thought that he'd left, gliding quietly away on the polished floors. He hadn't, though. He spoke again: 'I believe I can help, here. To provide some hope, some other way forward.'

*

'Rose?' Dr Dwyer tapped his hands together, took a Biro from his pocket. 'Is Dr Kingley's treatment – by which I mean – how is your memory?'

Rose rubbed at her forehead, tried to recall the name of the nurse, or to remember what was on yesterday's lunch tray. She knew it would happen, they had told her, warned her. Holes, small ones, would appear in her rememberings: they would not be significant. What she had for breakfast. What happened last week. The name of the thing she slept in. Odd words. Not this, though: her sister's face. There was a name – Ada – but a blank oval where mouth, lips, eyes should be. And today, or yesterday, Joe came, saying Sorry. Sorry: again and again. She counted four, five times, each time wondering what it was, the terrible thing, which made his eyes go wet and made him so terribly sorry.

She remembered coming in from the rain, shaking it off like a coat, shaking it off with their laughter. Both of them, she and Joe, pulsing through the door, rolling with laughter, while Ilsa and Frank tut-tutted around them.

When did this cloud come? This wading through treacle to reach any thought, to see even a speck of her far-off self, or the baby. She tried to see him, longed to, but everything pressed against her. As for the place, this country he'd brought her to: she looked around her, she did; looked out at the tall white gums ghosting across the window, smooth pale bark stretching up, grey leaves pointing earthward. The very grey of it suffocated her; she could not understand how Joe could see beauty in it. She tried to see the loveliness he spoke of –

though she saw only the absence of her past, or of a present she could understand.

His hands were warm. She remembered that, loved to remember it. Back from the war: he asked her to walk across Port Meadow and they kept walking, all day, with Joe stopping to tie his laces, or hold a round stone in his hand. They doubled back on themselves, Joe getting more and more anxious. It was along the Willow Walk, the slippery path linking North Hinksey with Oxford town, that he finally stopped and turned her to face him. 'Be my wife,' he said. It didn't seem to be a question. She nodded, of course – what else was there to do? – and he shook her hand, as though she were his father. Cool and compressed, his lips nailed her cheek. The green wash of the willows tinted his eyes, tinted her own hands, with a pale green glow. She had seen men grab their fiancées – wives, too – in sudden, fierce embraces. Joe simply rubbed his hands together and said, 'Good, then. Good.' Then, remembering: 'We should pray. Give thanks.' So they sat on a damp log, with the sodden field behind them, and rattling bicycles clunking past, and gave thanks for their good fortune.

Rose rested her hand in his wondrous palm and her whole body gave thanks. In the middle of the prayer, she pressed her face to his, hands on his cheeks, and he stopped. Pulled back for a moment to look at her, then squeezed her to him, so close that she lost her breath, and his was fast, caught in his throat. Their backs pressed into the curve of a willow, and rain dropped from each leaf, scattering like music.

They left everything except what they could take in three cases.

Ada squeezed their settee against their front-room wall, just in case. Everything else was sold off for five pounds and two shillings. Rose had two long dresses, both crusted with diamanté. One had a long chiffon sash, floating down to the ground. The other, marquisette round the collar. Shoes to match. There was a photo somewhere, the two of them: she was thin – you could see her bones – and her hair was smoothed into a curled bob, a dark Grace Kelly. Lips curved under her nose, you could see that she was trying to hold them together, to look mysterious, resisting the desire to burst into a white-toothed grin.

She left the dresses with her mother, mothballs tucked into the creases.

Before they travelled into London, to Australia House, she had pulled at his arm, tugging like a child, and said, 'Joe. Please listen.' She showed him the doctor's scrawl on a yellow sheet, the lists of things she should eat and the things she shouldn't do.

'I'll be needing my mum. And Ada. Wanting them, you know. Wanting to be here, with them.'

'Trust me,' he said.

And so she did.

There was a brochure on the low brown table in the front office: *Australia! A British Home from Home*.

The thin man behind the desk had brown spots on his cheeks; asked Joe, and only Joe, about his family. Two brothers, both killed in the war, what was the point of staying put?

And the man nodded, adding, 'Bloody war.'

Joe was silent, staring down at his brown shoes.

'No children?' The man lifted his head, and looked Rose over.

She opened her mouth, ready to speak, to be heard.

Joe pushed his knuckle against her lap. 'No. Perhaps in Australia. I've heard the sun does wonders.'

Both of them — Joe and the brown-spotted man — laughed together, and Rose laughed too, at the thought of the sun unfurling them like flags, and of her child being born beneath its brightness.

As she grew, ripened, Ada tutted around her, folding baby clothes into the black case. Rose's mother knitted four bonnets, drooped as she handed them over. 'I'll no see him, my own wee grandchild.'

Rose imagined the child, saw herself wrapping him in small versions of man clothes: brown corduroy trousers, flat at the front, the cosy warmth of them filling her with longing; collared shirts, the lapels flattened out like Joe's; laced-up shoes with heavy black soles. He was a child, never a baby, in these imaginings, and always surrounded by birches, elms, bluebells. Moss, not sand.

When they left, Southampton docks were a surge of colour and Ada was the brightest, weeping in her bobby socks and red dirndl.

'Red!' Rose poked at her sister, tutted over the way the colour washed her skin out, and at Ada's bare hands, creasing in the sharp wind. 'You'll freeze, too, without gloves. What were you thinking?'

That was when Ada let the weeping come: 'I wanted to wear black, funeral black, but I will not. I am not dressing for a funeral.' A pearl button caught at her wrist-watch, and she tugged at it, impatient as a fly. 'I can't bear to lose you, Rose, and I feel terrible, hateful things for him, taking you away to that forsaken land. I've heard that there is no water, and natives running with——' She stopped then and her thin, gloveless hand whispered about her mouth. 'Come back to me,' she said.

Rose looked away, up to the great blue ship, waiting for her.

Ada gave her a knitted stole, deep green, the green of hawthorn leaves in summer. Rose held it over her shoulders, nuzzling into it, even when they passed the equator and sweat began to weep at her earlobes, heat prickling beneath her fingernails. She spoke only to the shawl, whispering into its glossy green wool.

On the ship, the whole journey, all they'd talked about was the sun. Sunshine. Glorious golden sun. And oranges. There would be oranges everywhere, in Australia; the smell of them would infuse the air. Doreen and Arnold from Kent, emigrating for Doreen's health, said that the sun in Australia was warmer than the South of France in August. Doreen hadn't been to France, hadn't left Kent before now, though they had almost travelled to Spain on their honeymoon, could you believe it?, at the end of the war. Doreen insisted that the sun in Australia was worth a thousand Spanish summers, she swore it, would swear it on her mother's life – Arnold interrupting here to point out that her mother was already long dead, but still – the sun, the sun. They'd eyed Rose warily, as if she might pounce. Lord knows, she felt like a cat that whole journey, cooped in a cabin with June from Ely and her baby boy, who howled the whole time like a flaming air-raid siren. And the sickness! Joe felt nothing, stomach like iron, barely even flinched when he slid past the vomit outside the lavatories, the putrid marks of those who didn't get there in time. Buoyed up as he was with the excitement, anyway, nothing could touch him. Rose, though, queased and quailed the whole way through the Suez, growing as round as the oranges she was assured would be endlessly available in Australia. She imagined golden sands, she and Joe in brightly coloured swimsuits, wandering along the beach.

Joe lined up, waiting his turn on the deckchairs, smiling at the boys from the darts room, and sat himself down. Besotted, he absorbed it all: the oceans, the constellations, the changing light and the changing time, while Rose doubled over, weeping and vomiting by turns. Games nights in steerage were full of shrieking, hopeful couples. All the singles were on deck, canoodling or looking for canoodles, anyway. Hokey-cokey. Ten green bottles. Loverly bunch of coconuts. Rose and Joe joined in with them in the record club, trying to swing to that Fats Domino, the songs and clownish actions merging into one. Waving hello to their new land, most of them, and not looking back, not looking back at all. Rose felt glued on, her smile pasted, and her head tilting the wrong way, back towards England. The Kent couple, Doreen and Arnold, tried to take Rose in, to protect her. Rose thought only of the low, wooded hills behind Hinksey, the yellowish light at dusk, of the cold May-morning walk into Oxford, even the grey-green silt of the Thames dribbling past.

And endlessly, with the rocking of the ship, the prodding of the questions. *Where are you settling? Who are you leaving?* There was an understanding among them all, not to be challenged, that they were braver than the ones who stayed behind. Rose didn't dare to speak out what she believed, that staying was its own act of courage. Leaving everything, beginning again, as if the act of new land could wipe everything clean — was it courage in the end, or vandalism?

As they drew closer to the equator, welts began to appear on Rose's body. Great strips glowing red down her stomach, grown as swollen as a beehive. The sun burnt above her, so she sought out dark, cool corners. Twice a day, a purser darkened the games room and pulled out a film reel, to be shown in two halves. *Summertime*. *Marty*. *Sabrina*. Even *The Seven Year Itch*. Sometimes, reels showing bright Britons leaping in the Australian surf, showing how they'd never go back, never have it any other way. Often, a grainy silent film.

Rose let the shadows fall across her: the silent ones were her favourites. Australian films about outlaws, horses, wild doings. It wasn't the story — she barely read the words on the bottom of the screen — but the comfort of the black and white and grey; the cool flickering shadows. In one, there was a woman on the screen, throwing herself on to a white horse. Dark, bee-stung lips, a cap pulled down over her eyes, so that she looked like a pretty boy. Rose let the awkward piano music clunk over her, washing past with the grey cinematic shadows. In one scene, the girl — or perhaps it really was a boy? — rode closer and closer to the camera, until Rose could see the horse's hoofs, and the girl's head thrown back, laughing. In another, she waved a pistol and rode off, leaving a young policeman bleeding grey blood on to the dark grey grass of a wide paddock. Rose flexed her fingers, imagining pulling a trigger, the cold hard metal of a gun. She lifted the trigger fingers, fired, then quickly folded her hands back in her lap. Smoothed the lemon cotton of her skirt, checked that she was alone.

*

The night they arrived they rattled up to Westbridge Migrant Hostel with four other migrants, huddled against the window of the hostel bus. Wire, a remnant from the hostel beginnings as an army camp, stretched the perimeter. In the half-light of the moon, it looked murderous, scissor-sharp. They shuffled behind the other couples, Rose clutching the terrifying smallness of the baby, trying not to breathe too deeply in case everything inside her fell to the ground. It wasn't supposed to be this way: she should still have been swollen, the baby ready to arrive in Broken Hill, where Joe would take up his teacher's post. There was no whistle blowing now, no hope of it either: the doctor had made it clear – she wasn't to squeeze on to a train for eleven hours with a too-soon, too-thin baby. There was nothing for it: she would need to be near doctors. Surely they would have doctors, here, among the dust and the wire.

Counting off the rows and rows of narrow tin Nissen huts, curved like slugs, Joe muttered something about army camps, and the man leading them down the path said, 'Don't know why youse lot bother if all you're gunna do is complain,' so they were silent, except for the violin-scraping, the keening of the baby. When they finally flicked the light on in their one room, Rose lay on the grey settee with the baby on her stomach, and shook all night.

In the morning, she stood at the door and watched the hordes of bright-eyed ten-pounders stepping into the burning heat. Squeezed onto this patch of brutal army land, they looked around them as if it was not the most disappointing patch of nothing anyone could hope to see. The paths between the rows of metal huts – each one divided into four dark box rooms, one per family – were covered with blue gravel. A monstrous grey gum was the only tree, looming at the wire fence near their squat hut. Rose stared at it, imagining a silver birch in its place, or perhaps an elder, and was startled to find her collar soaked not just with the wet of her tears but with mucus as well. Joe curved over himself beside her: what was he to do? He wouldn't get another teaching post, not now, having turned his back on Broken Hill. Factory work would have to do, like the lines of migrants before him, climbing over the barbed-wire fence before the gates were opened at dawn to travel into the city and queue for work.

In the unaccustomed heat, Rose sweated so badly that lines of water dripped down her throat and on to the baby. She couldn't eat, feeling the weight of all that hot air bricking down on her, on the food. There was a dry ripple floating above everything, a haze that swam on the surface of everything she looked at: the linoleum floors; the narrow laminate table; the three cups lined up on the wooden bench. Everything was made double itself by its ghost floating above it. Rose wondered if she had this haze about her, this reflection sitting on her own lap, staring down at the mottled newness of the baby.

She wrote to Ada: *It's warm all the time. The flowers grow so quickly, so does the baby.* She wrote: *I wonder whether the birth would have been better at home, with you and Mum. I didn't expect so much bleeding, didn't expect it to be that way, like a battle. It's fine, of course, we're all fine—* Then she stopped, crossed it out. Tears started to fall on to the bond paper, making the ink run. That was the first time, the first time they came and wouldn't stop, not even when the baby woke from his nap and cawed out for her. She lifted him all right, but it was through a wave of tears. His toes were curved, and touching them, she almost felt the rush of tenderness a woman is supposed to feel for her baby. His sharp face was tilted up at her, a yellow bead of wax shining on one pink ear. The tender rush slipped away, as quickly as it had come, leaving only bewilderment and stabbing absence.

Other women could do this, she knew that. The heat made everything – the air, her blood, her temper – bubble. Sammy's face was red, his skin slippery. Nothing would settle him, though she patted his back and tried to latch him on to her nipple, cracked with his desperate gnawing. Four of his nappies, thick towelling, were dangling like puppets on the rope strung across their half of the hut. Rose drenched them in cool water, then laid two on the concrete floor. He stopped whimpering when his skin touched the wet towelling, and he gurgled, back in his throat, when she laid the two other cloths across his sweating skin. Her head was pounding, throbbing.

On the ship after Sammy had made his early, shocking entrance, the younger doctor – freckled skin, fine reddish hair – gave her the powders. Vincent's, Bex: fine grains in delicate, rustling paper. She tipped them onto her tongue, gagging at the thick glug of graininess filling her mouth. The young doctor handed her a red Bakelite cup, a moonlike sheen on the surface. Washing the powders down with one swallow, she felt the sudden ease, the loosening around her temples, her chest. He patted her hand and said, 'You should take a couple of these a day, just until the worst is over.' The worst. How would she know when it was over?

There were no powders left in the box beneath the sink, and no pink pills, and Sammy was beginning to whimper again. Cold water trickled on to her skirt as she splashed his face. Then she hurried down the dirt path between the huts until she got to the tin shed that served as the migrant kiosk. She bought two boxes and swallowed three powders, right there, in front of the woman glaring at her behind the kiosk counter. Granules stuck to her tongue and to her cheeks, until the sallow kiosk woman relented and handed her a dirty Vegemite glass, with a gulp of water in the bottom.

Later, she wrote: *The migrant hostel has flowers everywhere. It's just a stepping-stone, anyway, until the Department lets Joe have a teaching job. Everything's fine.* She stared at the letter, then screwed it into a ball. On a new sheet, pressing carefully, she began again. *Dear Sirs.* She closed her eyes as she sealed the letter into its pale envelope, and tucked it into her underwear box. Each morning for five days, she took it out, ran her fingers across the writing: *Department of Education.* On the sixth day, with the heat booming down, she tucked Sammy into the oversized pram, and wheeled him to the hostel shop. The sallow, tooth-sucking woman was there, making notes in the margins of a paperback book. Rose stood, waiting, hands resting on the bar of the pram. Finally: 'Stamp, please.' Her voice had become watery, barely audible.

The woman glanced at her, keeping her pen on the paperback, she grunted out, 'In a sec,' then underlined another word. Rose could see the edge of the book's cover: *How She Loved Him*. A glimpse of blonde hair.

Rose tried for a louder voice: 'Stamp. Please.'

The woman flicked at the page, said, 'In a minute. Love.' The word – love – came out sounding scratched, and hard as thorns.

A burst of her own self – the way she was before this sodden treacle-walking, this half-light self – flashed through; a peek of hard-edged anger, something with substance. Rose leant across the low counter and snatched the pen from the woman's hand. 'My name is Rose.' And she wrote it down, in the margins of the woman's book. Rose! The exclamation mark scratched hard into the rough paper. She could hear the woman calling after her as she left, something about bloody rudeness and whingeing Poms, but she kept walking, holding on to this moment of vigour that might return her to herself. Her feet crunched on the pale gravel, then glued themselves to the sun-softened Tarmac, and the pram wheels squeaked in the sun. Sammy's hands were above his head, as though in surprise, his eyes squeezed tightly shut. She pulled the shade of the pram down, tucked his muslin cloth around him. Her hands rested on his soft chest, feeling the rattle of his heart. *Precious boy*. She tried to send the words to him, to pulse them through her hand. If she could harness some of that – the vim she used to have—

It was possible. Perhaps it was possible. To find home, here, in this place of heat.

She walked back to the hut, straight-backed and rigid with fury. Left the pram outside while she pushed into the darkness of their one room. Gathered a bottle for Sammy, her wrist-watch, then pushed out, past the hostel wire glowering down at her. She walked, and kept walking. Letting the pram lead her, she walked, and kept walking. She still felt sliced up, her body still creaking. The letter was face-up on Sammy's muslin wrap, the address inked in black; and then she knew where she was going, where her feet were leading. Mouth dry and sweat-baked, hands slipping against the metal of the pram handles. Outside the hostel walls, the black bitumen stretching ahead. As she pushed further along the road – stopping every now and then to swallow, to create a sense of moisture in her mouth – the trees got thicker.

The sun was baking her by the time she reached the station, and Sammy had woken, had started his regular howling. She rocked as she pushed, walking curved over, as she called in to him: 'Sssh, ssssh, we'll get you there, we can do it, I can do it. I'm trying, sssssh.' There was a low, white, hand-painted sign: Station. A road turned off the Tarmac one, and she followed it, still curved over the pram: ssssssh, sssssh. Near the station, ahead of her – like a mirage – she could see a spread-armed tree, with deep green leaves; green as deep as hawthorn. Its shadow stretched across the road. As she came closer, she could see clusters of pink and white, scattered across the green. Petals, pink and white, feathered and full, covered the branches. Closer, with Sammy's howling sliding into a steady whimper, Rose tilted her face towards the petals, feathered so perfectly. She eked into the shadow of the tree, and leant in to lift the baby out, trying to hold the bottle to his mouth. Several of the flowers squawked, and some flew away. Birds. Pink and white birds, as gentle-coloured as magnolia petals lifted into the air. In a second, the tree was empty, and the sky above it was a collage of pink and white, and Rose – sitting beneath the tree, with Sammy, amazingly, guzzling from the bottle – felt something like a laugh cricking against her teeth.

There was no one at the railway station, so she waited. A drinking fountain shone in the sun, and Rose gulped a trickle of warm water from it, even splashed a little on her temples, careful not to wet her hair. Sammy's eyes had closed again, and she waited in the afternoon silence; her vigour edging away with each long minute.

It took three hours: the waiting; the tugging the oversized pram on to the train carriage, standing, rocking with it all the way into Sydney. Yellow-grey arches heaved above her at the city terminus and she followed the stream of people out into the tiled concourse, swarmed with them. Rustling through her, the thought that if she could change one thing, just this one thing, perhaps she could be changed. It – she – could be the way she had imagined: glowing, attentive, happy.

She took two wrong entrances before she found the plaque: *New South Wales Education Department.* A carving of round grapes, or pebbles, surrounded the lintel. She wheeled the pram against the wall and lifted Sammy out, and the letter. Sammy stopped crying, a startled pause. She was unsure, suddenly, why she was here, what right she had. She kept moving for fear of what might become of her if she didn't; for fear of the shadowy fog of exhaustion waiting to engulf her. Holding the baby against her, she pushed against the door with her back; she imagined the carved grapes as rocks, ready to be rained down on her, and she ducked her head. Behind the door, a narrow band of steps glowered, covered in a rock-brown carpet, Climbing the stairs took all her breath; she gagged through the smell of sour hops, or yeast, infusing the air. The room at the top of the stairs was dark, too dark for a room so high. Blue walls were interrupted by narrow, long windows looking across to a grey building. One desk was flanked by brown chairs, and behind it huddled two doors. Doors lined the other wall as well; it seemed to be a room of doors, a dizzying number. Rose tried to imagine pushing on each door – six or seven, there must have been – until she found the right person. She tapped on the nearest, then banged harder.

'Yes?' A man with eyebrows thick as clouds looming over his eyes swung the door open. 'Are you lost?'

She rocked back and forth, desperately trying to keep Sammy from squalling again. 'No. No, I'm not. I'm here about my husband. Mr Joseph Dobell.'

'We don't—'

Rose swayed faster, talked faster, anything to keep moving, to keep trying, to keep the fog away. 'My husband – he's – we've come on the assisted passage. There was a job – promised – Broken Hill. But then this one came, you see, so we couldn't – that is, the doctor ordered – I was – it wasn't an easy birth – bleeding, you see and—'

The man's hand twitched on the doorhandle.

'I'm sorry – I'm a little flustered. The point was, is – he couldn't take it, not his fault. And – we can't afford rent, anything, not with factory work, and – leaving at dawn, home late at night. The baby—'

'Yes. I see. The normal channel for enquiry is via letter initially and then—'

'No. No. My husband is—' She stopped, tried to get calm into her voice. Calm expectation. 'My husband came to this country on the promise of a teaching post. My baby was born – prematurely – on the ship. Do you see?'

The man began to back into the room, closing the door. 'I'm afraid you'll have to put your concerns in writing.'

Her foot was in the door before he'd finished speaking. 'We could not go to Broken Hill; I – we were in a medical crisis. He did put his concerns in writing. And now I am expressing them in person. My husband is hammering wooden pegs in a machine three hours from the migrant hostel, where I am attempting – *attempting* – to recover. Australian children need – so we were led to believe – skilled teachers. My husband is a skilled teacher. You need to give him a posting.' She pushed the letter into his hands. 'Here are my concerns. In writing.'

The eyebrows clouded further down, drawn into a cavelike squint. 'When a contract has been turned down, there is no substitute offer. There is a careful protocol in place, madam. Which has, I'm sure, been followed in your husband's case. Please close the door at the bottom as you leave.'

Rose could feel the tears coming before she started speaking. 'You can't – please – we've come all this way – and it wasn't his fault – we have no one here, no one—'

'Thank you for your visit. I really don't see how you can help your husband by—'

'His name is Joseph Dobell.'

'As I said, I really don't see—'

'Then you're blind. You're a one-eyed fool.'

'The porter will see you out, Mrs Dobell.'

She stood for an hour on the blistering footpath, staring at the brass plaque on the brick wall, rocking the pram with one hand, barely hearing the crying coming from it. When she finally turned to trudge back to the station, Sammy's sobs had subsided to intermittent whimpers.

*

Joe pulled her to him when she finally came into the dank hut-room. Outside, the night was thick and cool. 'I thought you'd – I was worried sick, Rose. I thought you'd done something stupid. Something – I didn't know what you'd done. Where were you?'

Nowhere, she said, just bloody nowhere.

With her back to him that night, she asked, 'What did you mean, something stupid?' and his silence bounced back at her while the small, sweet burst of vigour seeped away, like mud.

She waited, just in case, for a letter. For days, she kicked at the grey dust outside the door, tried to talk to the baby and waited for something to happen, for her new life to begin.

Here it is, her new life, right here: leaving the calm cream room, with the sunflowers and the framed diplomas, following Nurse Sich down the corridor to the grey room, stepping back on to the bed, hands flat.

Pushing her nails into the nurse's wrists, as the discs pressed against her temples, she was swallowed by the thought: *What will happen? What will become of him?* Catlike, she clawed at the nurse: 'My baby – he's in the hall.' She stopped. 'Not the hall. He's – there isn't anyone looking after him, feeding him. He's only a baby.'

'You – I mean, he—' The nurse stopped, looked over at the doctor.

Dr Kingley took one, two steps. He rested his hand on Rose's temple. 'Everything's fine. You concentrate on getting well, that's all.'

He kept repeating the words, softly, like a song: everything's fine, everything's fi-iiine while he stretched out his hand to push at the metal column. He took his hand from Rose's head as he pulled the column down, but he kept smiling, soothing, kept the song going: Everything's fine, everything's fine.

~

Dibbsey was at the wedding. Which is only strange if you think about it. Mud was all over the ground, splattering up over my legs, even on to my face, and we laughed like drunkards, all day. Three weeks later, we parked ourselves in the same field as our circus tent had just blown down from. One Mr Alfred Dibbs – Dibbsey, he insisted – had a tin megaphone in his hand, which he used for nothing more than swatting at flies. Not once did he raise it to his mouth. He was there, all right, and I suppose you could say he'd never led us astray, never told anything but the truth. Still, fact is, me and Ariel, both – and Billy, too, who had more brains than the whole of Parramatta put together – well, each of us had somehow got the impression that Dibbsey was the ringmaster. *Mistakenly* got that impression, Dibbsey pointed out: he'd never said any such thing, never led us to believe anything other than the truth. He was third in command to Mr Rolfe and was scouting out riders for him, when did he say any different? He was, in fact, a little runaround, a hand-holder, an apprentice. Not that we minded one way or the other. Mr Rolfe, who had the money, and the moving cameras, and the wheeled wagons to put them on – and, as it turned out, the handsome face of the leading man – was happy to stump up cash for me and Billy to add what he called 'real muck' to the moving picture. Ha. Real muck, my lady's arse. Dear old Ariel was sweating like a sunburnt emu over Lottie Lyell, who appeared to be the star of the show. Not, as was promised, me: Athene of the ruddy Antipodes.

Oh, this Dibbsey had plans, though, he promised he did: a vision, a picture in mind. He was on his way, Mr Rolfe was going to help him, and I would be perfect. All I had to do was wait.

I'd somehow got it in my head that a film stage would be like a circus tent, all darkened and private. Hadn't counted on the shovelling, humphing hordes of people. Everyruddywhere, like ants. A man to hold each camera. A boy to wheel the trolley along for the camera to sit on, a girl whose job seemed to be wiping dust off things – faces, cameras – and a dozen bit-part players. Gladys, Tilly, Heap and Billy got to play at being townspeople held up by the bushrangers. Tilly particularly enjoyed throwing her hands up, making her eyes round with terror, but I felt like I was being drowned in a swell of people. Ariel, though – even without the promise of a starring role for Ariel's Buckjumping Show – thought he was home, he really did. Dibbsey had plonked him in a slatted chair, and Ariel was propped up with one of Mr Dunkerly's new Akubra hats perched on his head, a wad of tobacco beside him. And me, a one-woman movable trick, covered with mud and water and slime. Not that it hurt me at all: I got to leap on and off Lordship, spitting the dirt up as we galloped across the stage.

Mr Alfred Rolfe told me I had an exciting future ahead of me if I wanted it, and his eyes were definitely below my neckline, and I told him I already had an exciting future, not to mention a spectacular present, thanks very much, *not* to mention the expectation of a paid-up promise with Mr Dibbs over there. Ariel was the one who wanted it, after all; me, as long as I got to throw myself on the back of a horse, as long as I could lean down into a whiskery back and feel that I could keep going, just keep going for ever, well, that was me, happy and plain. Wanting to keep moving, that was the thing, never wanting to stop. There's nothing like movement to keep you satisfied or, at least, to stop you noticing that you're unsatisfied.

I tell you, though, the talk of the money! My goodness, the

paddock, the stage, was rife with it. One Mr Charles Cozens Spencer planned on opening a Lyceum Theatre just to show the film he was making, right then, that very day, very moment. Ten thousand pounds! God's truth, that's how much it cost. You can imagine, I turned my nose and sniffed around all disinterested, but my God, my ears were pricking pretty sharp. Nellie Stewart was going to be paid seven thousand pounds for appearing in Mr Spencer's film. Saliva was trickling round my mouth as if someone had run a slice of lemon across my tongue. It was a story, was all; but stories can make you hungry and cold, can't they?

Miss Lyell told me she was making a new film, straight after this one, so she said, starring in, even adding some words, perhaps some directing. *Australia Calls*, it would be named. All about the 'yellow peril' — and her eyelids stretched right up when she said that, just as though she was a little *ingénue*, being married off to the Head Villain.

'Aren't you worried?' she said, all breathless, managing not to notice Ariel sitting there with the shadow of the Akubra casting over his face, and his stupid great grin and his battered boots shucked up on a wooden box in front of him. Damned fool, couldn't see a tornado coming if it blew in his face.

I looked at Ariel, real slow, then walked over to him, pulled his Akubra off his stupid ruddy head, bent down and gave him a long, slow kiss. 'No, ma'am, Miss Lyell, I don't think I've got any need to worry on that account.'

On the second day, Mr Rolfe gathered a circle around him: Lottie Lyell; me; the camera boys; the limp man with an overloud voice playing one of the outlaws; Maggie, Tilly, Heap and Billy; a red-headed boy who giggled like a cockatoo; three of the roundish looking men who were playing bit parts. 'Right.' Rolfe was a boomer, voice like a freight train. 'Here's the story – much as you need, that is. Rich bloke, falls on hard times. Girl loves him. He loves girl. Bloke goes to find better times, can't find them, holds up homestead, girl still loves rogue. Shoot-out at homestead, local copper shot by Starlight, et cetera, et cetera. The end. Okelly-dokelly?' It was clear he was about as interested in the finer points of the story as he was in the finer points of serge bloomers. He clapped his hands, said, 'Now go,' and we stayed sitting, none of us knowing what to do next, until he hauled me and Miss Lyell out. Told me to ride alongside Miss Lyell, dressed, mind you, in ridiculous lace skirts; I was to be her sister, weeping as she rode off to her Captain Starlight, Gentleman Outlaw.

'Alfie, dear man. Don't you think she – I mean, she rides well, doesn't she, but like a man, do you see?' She was as upright as a post, that Miss Lyell, propped up on her handsome chestnut gelding.

Mr Rolfe, if I remember right, had his head turned somewhere else – looking at a line of painted flats spread out on the paddock edge. Or, possibly, shouting at the poor young red-haired boy whose job seemed to be to stand alongside Mr Rolfe and receive thwacks on the back of the head or the leg. Anyway, in this case, he looked up and muttered something like 'No, no, I don't see. She rides well, she looks like a girl, your sister. What am I missing?'

Miss Lyell smiled at me, lips closed. 'Sometimes, I think I'm the director.' She rubbed her horse's ears. 'Think I should be, anyway. Ruddy well could be.' She called out to Mr Rolfe, then: 'Put the girl in some men's breeches. Let her ride like a man.'

'But your sister—'

'There's no sister in the book.'

The book! It wasn't just me and her, on a horse, in a paddock, and Mr Rolfe being Captain Starlight, waving his pistol and seeing off the troopers. Someone had put it all down, all the words, and now they were ours. My head swam with it, the way it swims with this, too: that it isn't just me, here, now. That I was joined in with his story, Mr Rolfe's, the way that you're joining in mine. You are, you'll see. I have a plan.

And so I squeezed myself again into my jodhpurs, and tucked my hair under Ariel's cap and felt all the happier for it. Mr Rolfe called, 'Marks, set,' which was the signal for us to gallop, all across the muddy, stubbly field. Up front of us was a stretched paperbark, its thready bark peeling like eyelashes down to the earth. Even in the mud, even in the spit of winter, this bleak stubby paddock – well, if you'd not had the cameras there, you'd have seen what I could see, the stretch of the gum, the aching arch of the streaked sun. The whole of this horizon, the bush, and all that surrounds it – it's like a stallion, it's so hazardous and dangerous and – you can't take yourself away from it, once you've loved it.

Mr Rolfe stayed at the paperbark end, his camera rolling, his hand waving like a bee above the mounted camera. 'Keep coming,' he called, 'don't stop, come right up, right up close,' and he was getting as excited as a whole ruddy bunch of galahs on a fruit tree in summer. I leant myself down into Lordship, thinking like a man, facing like a man, and made myself air. We were right there, alongside each other, beautifully one. You could have sworn we were shadows of each other and she looked at me and grinned, this time not with her lips closed. Mr Rolfe was leaning back, his head scraping against the paperbark, the camera pointing up; he wanted close, didn't he? So I pushed my heels into Lordship's side, and twitched at the reins. As we galloped towards the tree, I tugged again, and Lordship swerved, his face nearing Mr Rolfe, nearing the camera. We side-cantered at the last minute, and it was all I could do to stop myself leaping on to Lordship's back, performing a little dance. Paperbark strands dangled from my cap, that's how close I brushed. We soared past Mr Rolfe and I heard him shout as if he'd just been born, and I was laughing as if I was the sun and the wind, both.

Ha! Applause rattled from the other side of the paddock – though it was thinner than I might reasonably have expected. Just Ariel, in fact. Standing on top of the rickety slatted chair, his Akubra thrown into the dust, and his dry hands thundering applause.

'Get her off, get her out of here.' Mr Rolfe was a shaking, shouting banshee, his reedy voice sending Ariel's applause scuttling.

'I never met a woman who rode better than me.' Lottie Lyell was still on her horse, had to lean down to offer her hand to me.

I took it, and shook it as though we were generals. 'I never met a man who rode better than me. Still haven't, in fact.'

The red-headed boy who followed Mr Rolfe around holding his notes, his baton and his whisky, ran to me, hands out as if I was an escaped elephant. The crooked-faced cameraman ran with him, other side, footballish.

'Just take her. She's a bloody danger. Almost killed me. Almost destroyed the camera. Circus clowns. They're not theatre people,

Dibbs, no bloody idea. Get them both off. Her and the — him.' Mr Rolfe's hand pointed over at Ariel. Two pairs of hands yanked at me, one in either direction, or so it felt.

'What's the problem, Alfie? You got the shot, didn't you?' Lottie Lyell slid from the horse, her crop tucked into her belt.

'Use your eyes, Lottie — look at the camera, look at the mess.'

'Do we take her, Mr Rolfe?' The red-haired boy had dropped his hands. Stood waiting.

'I said escort her off the stage. And him, too.'

I shunked off their hands. 'I'm going. Hell-in-stirrups, you never been around a horse before?'

Billy was hunched over his tin tucker-box, as miserable as you could hope.

'Go on, get,' a thin-necked assistant shouted at us, as though we were ruddy hawkers.

Ariel turned back, and stood burning in front of him. 'You have just witnessed the finest horsewoman you will ever see — with all respect to Miss Lyell — and you are incapable of rising to meet her. You are — you are — not worthy, and your cowardice will destroy you. You want to be great? Be brave. But you—' Ariel lifted his hand, swung it round so that it took them all in, and I had not seen him blaze so brilliantly since he swayed and danced in the wildflowers. 'You are all cowards.'

Dear, darling Billy stood up, applauding, and walked over to join us.

'You stay, Billy.' Mr Rolfe boomed, but his voice was hesitant.

'You lot about as smart as that *niriti*, hey.' And Billy spat a load of his words out at them, fast and proud. Odd words I heard: *niriti*, *kumbal*, *kumburikan*, *untelliko*. That one I knew — dance. Billy whistled for Prince Vic to follow him, offered his hand to Mr Rolfe, about as polite as the captain of a ship might be, then reached out for us and we danced away, to the tune of Ariel's rasping laugh and Billy's clicking tongue. We kept our heads up, and Lordship and Prince Vic trotted beside us, joining in the foolish dancing. Just before we got to the paddock fence, Lottie pounded behind us, put her hand on my shoulder and turned me to face her. Kissed me straight and cool on the lips. Her mouth was soft, as damp as moss.

We'd pitched a camp on the edge of the town; Tilly sat at my feet and rubbed them with camphor and lavender. That night, me and Ariel wrapped ourselves round each other while the wind whipped the caravan so hard it sounded like a dingo being squeezed through a metal wringer.

Sun burnt into the open doors of the caravan in the morning, and not a peepo from any rain. There was a great hump of a shadow, though, sticking his face through the gap in the wall, all cheery as if he was our best friend in the world: Mr Alfred Dibbs. 'Mr Rolfe wants to see you immediately. He's very excited.'

'Bugger off. He was very excited yesterday. Bloody over-excited.' I shuffled back down into my swag, stuck my face back under the grey blanket.

'I think you should come.'

Ariel lay like a dead snake, his skin empty, shed of everything but breath.

'Ariel is sleeping. Go away.' This from inside my swag, swallowing stale air.

'He's changed his mind. You need to see why.'

Bloody mind indeed. 'Changed his mind because he was flaming well wrong in the first place.'

'Just come.'

Magpies were quieter than the gathering of galahs down at the film stage, I can tell you that. Cackling, backslapping, oh, you wouldn't know the half of it. Mr Rolfe lifted his arms when he saw me, shouted, 'Here she is, horse-riding star, Jess A.' Didn't hold out his hand for Ariel, though, I noticed, nor for Billy. 'It's brilliant, what you've done. My God, you've – and to think I nearly missed it. Come. See.'

We straggled up – the cluster of two-legged galahs and me – to the tin shanty on the edge of the paddock. At the door to the projector shack, Mr Rolfe turned and called to the crowd of cameramen, runners and bit-part actors, 'You lot, carry on. Go on, get back to what you're doing.'

There was a group murmur, a discontented chorus as they stepped back. Magnetism, that's what Alfred Rolfe had: force of repulsion as strong as the force of attraction.

Inside the shack, it was as dark as an eye. There was just me and him and Dibbsey and Ariel, and the sound of the honking, squawking gathering outside. Dibbsey fiddled with a clinking piece of metal, lighting match after match. Three times he burnt his finger, swore, then burnt it again. Then: 'It's ready, Mr Rolfe.'

On the sheet spread on the wall in front of us, there was suddenly light. More than light: shadow, movement, a flickering that was alive as water. Something shadowy, grainy, covering the sheet; I had to peer into the darkness to make any sense. Beside me, Ariel drew his breath in, sharp as a kingfisher's beak, and then I could see: in the distance, two figures, two horses. Me and Lottie. Coming closer, closer. I held my breath, too: the boy on the pale horse was flying, trembling along, right towards me in that tin shed, I could see the horses coming closer, could see the neck of the horse. Closer still, each shadow on the neck of the horse, the boy riding small and thin, looking down, a wild face, then the hoofs: my hands were over my head, waiting to be pounded. Then a splattering of sound, a clicking, and Mr Rolfe's voice: 'Quite something after all, eh? Magic of film. God, I love it. You never know, you just can never quite tell.'

Dibbsey leant on the door of the shanty, to make it swing open, and Ariel squeezed my hand so tight I thought he'd poured himself into me. Me! That was me, that boy with the wild face. Me, there, racing towards me in the shed, both at once, here and now, just the way I'm there, now, in the film, and in the paddock and even back in my daddy's house, and all the time, just as much, here – right here – with you.

~

Rose dressed carefully, as though for a date, one of the early ones, back at the end of the war when Joe was shy-tongued and hopeful, after a year of letters and longing. There was herself, someone in the mirror, that was her, surely? One eye smaller than the other, which she could fix, almost, with makeup and the trick of rolling her hair. It dated her, she knew that, knew that it wasn't in keeping with the new modern time, but she liked it, clung to it. Hair curled up from her temples, and under at the nape of her neck; it reminded her of being happy, that hairstyle. Red lips, blotted three times – which reminded her: Joe's lips were cold, on that first walk after he'd come back, with three medals and a deep line across his forehead. Would you call it a date? A walk along the towpath, her hand tucked into his pocket, they'd walked right along the Hinksey Channel before they drew breath. He did first; stopped talking, touched her lips, said, Rose, Rose. She could see him, for a moment, Joe, and then he fluttered like cloud and was gone. She opened her mouth to speak, there by the Thames, and there was nothing, only silence, the echo of footsteps shuffling past outside, in the corridor of the ward.

Hand shaking, just keeping still enough to get the Rich Red sheen on to her lips, Rose was startled by a sudden, shimmering thought: *I am there, now, and all the time, just as much, here, right here, with you*. She tilted back, looked over her shoulder: *Here, with who?*

There were no mirrors on the ward, not on the walls, for fear that women like Rose would see ghosts, shadows, portals behind their own faces. Nurse Sich, though, offered Rose a small compact. Blue, with bevelled edges, and a mother-of-pearl square in the front, it was a rare mark of favour. Rose pressed her nose to the powder, breathed the soft pink hush of it.

She scratched at a smear of lipstick on a tooth then rubbed it away with the corner of her sheet. You couldn't say that she didn't try – no one could say that. That she hadn't worked on it, tried to do it well. Wifeliness, motherliness: all that was expected. Feeding, ironing; not just the sheets, but the underwear too. She'd stayed up until midnight once, ironing Joe's underpants, pressing the heavy iron against the wood-burner in her mother's house. Mad, he'd called her. But in a soft way, his hand resting on a collarbone, his thumb stroking her neck. Lipstick too, and eyeshadow. Everything. But it couldn't stop her falling, slipping into the gap between people, between thought and breath.

The red was too harsh on her lips; she could see that, in the daylight traipsing through the windows. It washed out her skin, made it flap on the side of her face, like gills. She looked like a bag of leaves.

There was the Christmas Day, the first Christmas in this new country, first Christmas with her new, early baby. Rain steamed down on to the flat pink face of the hostel shacks, pouring in through the half-hammered-in sheets, whipping the sidings apart from each other. Rain hammered into the crowded tin roofs and shook the sharp wire fences. All day Rose sat next to Sammy, trying to smile, parting her lips, clapping her hands, failing. She hadn't expected the rain. It wasn't in the advertisements.

Outside, she knew how it would be. Him not meaning to be late, but he would be, it was to be expected. He would roll the cuffs of his sleeves back, oh, he would have an opinion, all right, about why he was late, and why she was in the thin, quiet ward. Endless words of sorry, he'd have as well. Sorry, he said, sorry. Tears sometimes, too, though Rose would not have imagined him a man given to tears. She couldn't remember him visiting her before in the ward: what would he have said? Sorry, with no explanation of what or why. Rose held out her hand in front and counted the freckles on the back of her wrist. Three.

Sammy would be—

She stopped, confused by her own thoughts, her own stumbling. Sammy. Her baby, she knew that, but something was missing: his face? The smell of him?

Blood. That was the smell she thought of when she tried to get a scent of him, her baby; when she tried to call him to her. The thick ripe smell of blood.

On the *New Australia*, they'd grown restless and loud as they sliced through the ocean, closer and closer to the equator. Rose could feel her back creaking with every move. At night, rigid on her side in the cabin, she tried to catch her breath. Joe, on the men's deck, could at least sleep through the snoring. On the women's deck, though, the squalling of babies shrilled through most cabins, and Rose was so swollen with the baby that half of her body hung over the edge of the bunk. Absorbed in the life of the ship, Joe was his own captain. He'd taken over as a volunteer teacher in the ship's school, and spent his mornings setting minor arithmetic problems for a cluster of ten year olds. At the dinner buffets, he found her, stood beside her, sometimes wrapped his gruff fingers round hers. Daytimes, though, Joe swanned round the decks, joined the Record Club, the Departing Migrants (South-west) Club, the Men's Bible Group, the Morning Watch. Rose wiped her face, and her enlarging welts, with cool towels. There was an announcement on the ship's Tannoy, while Rose lay, queasing, in the darkness of the cabin one afternoon. She heard the mumbled sounds of the voice, but not the words. Short, sharp pains were creasing across her back and stomach, each one forcing her to stop breathing until it passed.

In the queue for dinner, Joe crept behind her, slipped his hands over her eyes and whispered, 'Guess who?'

She rested her hands on his, trying to ignore the pains.

He stepped in front of her, bobbing down and trying his rascal's grin. 'Crossing the line tomorrow. Nearly there. More than half way, love. More than half-way there, if you look at it north to south.'

Another pain accordioned across her back; she held her hand out to Joe. 'I'm getting all sorts of pains, Joe.'

'See the ship's doctor, perhaps? Baby's due in two months, and you'll need to be well when we arrive. It'll be quite a journey, so Doreen was saying, up to Broken Hill. Imagine, Rose, our own house, a car, a room for the baby. Room to breathe.'

'I could breathe at Mum's. I know it was—'

'It was, Rose. It was impossible. For me, it was impossible. I couldn't stay.' He looked over her shoulder, at the horizon. 'Maybe she'll come out. Maybe Ada will too. Look at this lot. Everyone's coming.' He laughed. 'There'll be no one left.'

Behind them, there was the round slap of a hand on a bottom, a shriek of a laugh. They were all at it: married men, singles. Unleashed from the land, not yet grounded again, they were unloosed, as wild as children. Rose had heard groanings and gigglings coming from closets and lifeboats and the echoing metal stairwells.

Was it the next day? It must have been, surely, that the great foghorn sounded through the ship. She was resting in the cabin, gathering strength for the dinner noise, the rush of bodies and voices. June from Ely, sharing the dingy cabin with Rose, was nursing her baby; the piping sound of absorbed, greedy gulps had been the only noise before the siren honked into the cabin. June grabbed at the baby. Someone rapped on the door of the cabin: when Rose swung it open, no one was there. She scuttered in the cabin and felt the beating, the sudden ache across her back. Again, a rap at the door: three taps. She pulled the door back, ready to shout, be all kinds of rude. The young steward from Coventry was in front of her, face painted black with some kind of tar, his eyes looking oddly moonlike in among the clown-black.

A flash of white teeth: 'Down you come, now, all ladies as well as men. It's the Crossing of the Line!'

Behind him, a swarm of women and men too, even on the ladies' deck, buzzed towards the lower recreation area: Rose couldn't tell if they were laughing or shrieking, what the noise was. The steward grabbed her hand, pulled her from the cabin and into the river of people – passengers, mainly, but there were stewards too, and children. Joe was nowhere; she let herself be pushed, pulled along. In front of her, two men with broad backs stopped every few steps, letting out a shout, 'Half way there, half way gone.' Each stop they made jolted into the tight drum of Rose's belly, the neat cocoon that she carried now in front of her. Someone slipped on the stairs, and someone else – a child, perhaps – started screaming, though it merged with the laughter, and it was hard to tell where one sound began and the other stopped.

On the pool deck, stewards were painting the faces of the passengers, caking them from tubs of black polish, and everyone but Rose, it seemed, was as full of the late-day sun as a field of corn. One of the stewards called her, pointing to the tub of paint. Rose shook her head, backed away so that she was pressed against a wall. She wanted to call out, shout, for Joe, wanted to flare out her panic, loudly, but she didn't dare. Two men, blacked up and with yellow scarves on their heads, grabbed a woman in front of Rose and, with a single swing, hurled her into the pool. Rose pressed against the wall, a silent patch in the shouting crowd. Around her, they danced and swelled; Rose felt herself caught in a wave, tumbled about, breathless. Four men were stripping off, at the end of the pool, right down to their underwear, and one was trying to squeeze into a ladies' dress. Someone – it was Joe! – stood behind them, miming a hula dance. He had a bottle in one hand, and what looked like a sceptre in the other. A crown tilted over his head and, even from that distance, Rose could see the flush on him. He was busily bobbing the sceptre on people's heads, before the purser pushed them into the pool. She lifted her hand and tried to wave, and as she did, something in her blood, or in her bones, undid itself. She could feel a sudden surge of liquid between her legs, a knifing across her chest, and her belly. Everything swam. She called, or tried to, to Joe. He looked up, waved, kept dancing. A narrow-hipped, black-haired woman stood in front of him, swinging her hips in time with his. Liquid was seeping out of Rose, now, and breath was being punched out, one, two, three. Before she fell forward, she whispered to the woman beside her, 'Please help. I need a doctor. Get my husband – there – King Neptune.'

*

Rose opened the pearl grey vanity case, looked again, tried again. Soft peach was a better colour; less hard on her thin lips. Polished and double-buffed, her nails gleamed. Rose smoothed her hands across the cream dirndl skirt. She listened to the passing of the footsteps in the ward, to the soft murmurings of Nurse Sich and Dr Kingley. She smoothed the skirt again, and waited.

~

I'm not going anywhere, if you're wondering. Seeing it through with you, because we're caught up together now, whether you like it or not. Who knows if you have invented me, imagined me, or not?

We were in Eden when Dibbsey turned up again, barely a month since he'd waved us off from the scrubby paddock on the edge of Parramatta. Underneath his arm, he had three bottles of cherry beer, and on his face, a self-satisfied spread of smirk. His yellow moustache was quivering with it all, how clever he was to have found us. He'd scouted all round New South Wales, so he said, trying to hunt us down – as if we were snakes, or wolves. 'Well,' I said, 'all you have to do is read the *Bulletin*, we always have a picture advertisement in there and, Lord knows, we haven't got so broke that we can't afford a fly-bill.' I shook his hand, as though we'd just met, as though I couldn't tell he was shaking with some excitement or other.

He came to the night show, let himself be called out of the audience by Heap the Strongman, and lifted up in the air, laughing the whole while. It was a decent crowd, that one; no town hall in Eden, no room for picture-houses, so we'd nothing to compete with. When the show finished and the cold dark had hit the air with a whistle, Ariel lit a fire at the back of the camp and we plonked ourselves down on logs around it. It was as cosy as a house. Heap the Strongman brought out his tiny ukulele and we all sang along to 'The Old Mill', 'Alexander's Ragtime Band', and some old ones as well: 'Down By The Riverside', 'Give My Regards To Broadway'. Dibbsey started up with 'Mary's A Grand Old Name', but he changed the words to 'Jess is A Grand Old Dame' and we all shrieked and caterwauled so much you'd have thought we were on fire.

After the singing, Dibbsey sidled up, squeezed himself between me and Ariel and told us his plan, as pleased with himself as a dingo on the kill. It was all of us he wanted: me, Billy, Ariel. Another film, but this one, he swore, with him at the helm, and me as the star. *Mary the Outlaw*. I've said it before, and I meant it, I couldn't really give the parson's nose for being the star, but I could see that each show we did we were losing numbers. In Burke and Temora, both, there'd been no room for our posters, only for film displays, advertising pictures shown in the town hall. Tilly and Gladys and Heap the Strongman stood on the corners, shouting, calling people in, but even so we only managed to fill two rows. And, I confess this too, there was some sort of magic in it, seeing yourself reflected back, bigger than you were. My name wouldn't even be on *Captain Starlight* in the end, I could bet my mother's plaits on it. Even so, there was something about it all that made me breathe better. So I listened, is what I did. And, later, I signed my name on a piece of paper, and Ariel signed his and we'd had so much beer by then that all we knew about that paper was that we'd agreed to something about the property owned by Ariel's Buckjumping Show, and something about me, and then we fell about laughing.

That night, Ariel pulled me to him, the way he hadn't for months, not since we'd been away from the show, and he let his whiskers tickle me all over until I was sizzling like fat and I thought his face was going to split in two, the way he cried out.

In the morning there was a good deal of creaking and cricking; I could barely walk down the caravan step for the wobbling in my brain. Tilly and Heap were lying right by the charred circle of fire, and Dibbsey stumbled out of Gladys's tent with his hand over his head. It was Sunday, church day, ha! The closest we'd get to that little rickety ritual was gathering to clear the bottles and sweep the tent. Still, for the horses it was a day of rest at least. Not for Ariel, though, no day could hold rest for him. That man was an ocean of movement. Even when he was lying beside me, on the swag, he'd twitch and slap at the air. In sleep, too: rolling to each side, kicking his legs out. Nothing could contain him. I surely couldn't.

So Ariel woke up that Sunday, head like a hyena, and called for Billy, and shaved his face over the brown enamel bowl balanced on the ledge of the wooden caravan. I lay on the swag, watching him through half-dozy eyes. He nicked himself with the stupid ruddy cutlass he used to slice at his whiskers – he was rough with them, with his own face, hacking at it like grass. He watched the blood lick into the bowl and pressed his fingers into the cuts. Shook out his chaps, used my hoof-pick to clean under his nails, then rode off up to Nullo Mountain to catch some brumbies to use for the show. Planned to be gone up to three days.

He never came home to me.

You knew that, of course; saw it coming.

Damned fool, trying to jump a ravine that size. Ariel was like a sick cockatoo on the back of a horse, if you want the truth. What even possessed a man like that to tour a horseback circus? Well, Ariel was more mystery to me than God, I can tell you that for nothing. Billy rode back on Prince Vic, with Galah trailing along like a dried leaf. Not a mark on Galah, though Billy had a few scratches slashed up and down his arms. Face too, some still inking blood. *Yarrakai*, Billy said.

We closed the show down. Put out a call in Rylestone, and handed all the tickets back. Strands of hair scattered across my tent sheet, across my knees: I snipped it all; would have wrapped my own neck in it if I could. Burnt my dresses too, wore only jodhpurs, men's shirts, the brown jacket, the checked cap. Blood had marked the enamel bowl from Ariel's last shave, and I kept it by me when I slept and when I woke, touching my finger to the rough edge of dried blood, but carefully, so that I wouldn't rub it away. It was all I had of him.

Two days after Billy rode back alone, they were there again, the stampeding men with their spittle and their painted sheets. This one was spread across the front of the camp, left lying there like a bit of old washing. Spread out neatly, though, with the painted words face up. *No More Yellow Peril*. Stupid as a pod of blind possums, the lot of them, couldn't even figure a way to hang it from a tree, to make a statement as big and as bold as their ruddy stupidity. Oh, yes, I know where it's all led, don't get me started. You'd be surprised what we see, what we keep track of. Anyway, when Billy saw the sheet lying there, he did the only decent thing, which was to pull his daks down and piss all over the painted words.

I waited for him. Waited for him to rouse himself from wherever he'd disappeared to, and to ride down the track with a meek, broken mare behind him. For a hundred, a thousand minutes I thought Ariel had moved into my body, his salty darkness sifting into me like flour, fine flour. Grief wrenched at my body, changed it. My nipples grew darker than Ariel's eyes. Funny thing: when

Dibbsey came the first time, maybe even the second, he wouldn't believe that I could ride like a man, though he saw what I could do on Lordship, and I'd shown him the plaque. *Australian Rough-riding Champion 1908*. Mother-of-pearl, it was, and still glowing then, even then. After Ariel disappeared into that bastard ravine, Dibbsey lurked around, waiting, waiting. By the time he came back, waving the piece of paper we'd signed, he knew what he was dealing with. Or at least, more to the point, he thought he did.

He said: 'He would want you to keep going, to get up and ride.'

He said: 'He was old enough to be your father.'

And: 'You can't carry on like this for ever. You're the woman who can outride any man – anyway, we start filming tomorrow week.'

He showed me the paper with all of our drunken, scribbled signatures on it. Each of the horses, all of the circus stock, everything owned by Ariel's Buckjumping Show was to be used in the filming of *Mary the Outlaw*. The show would close down until the film was made.

'What about the girls? And Heap?'

'We'll find them something to do. Your name will be everywhere, you'll be bigger than Lottie Lyell. Bigger than the Vitagraph girl.'

'I'm not ready, Dibbs.'

He waved the paper under my nose again, ran his stubby finger under a line of narrow print. 'It's all agreed, doll. You've put the circus up as collateral.'

I felt swollen, heavy-tongued. Around me, all that we owned, all the makings of our little show, were packed and folded, stored on top of each other. The show tent, folded and packed under heavy canvas; three caravans; two bicycles; seven saddles; the trapeze that

Tilly jumped from, landing one-footed on the bars of Gladys's moving cycle. One snake cage for Gladys's snake dance, and a collection of stockwhips. It wasn't much. Heap owned his ukulele, Tilly owned her flute. It was the horses that were the real worth, each of them trained and fed and sleeked up. And me, to tell the truth. I was worth a ruddy fortune. Ha. You couldn't buy what I could do. All of that, though, all the flimsy gatherings of Ariel's efforts. Twenty years' driving ahead in the leaky sulky, posting up notices, writing to the press: it was all there was of him. That and the bloodstained enamel bowl.

So I said yes to Dibbsey, as if I really had any choice in the matter. I cooked up a stew from a roo that Billy had shot, and Billy baked a damper and me and Gladys and Billy and Tilly and Heap sat on the ground, with the fire scorching our fingers, and I said, 'This is what we're going to do.'

The sickness started just then, as I dabbed a hot chunk of damper into the brown liquid of the kangaroo stew, watching the fat from the tail begin to congeal. I guessed that it was Ariel, settling in, letting me know he was there. It was my guess, too, from the queasy way my stomach flipped itself around, that he wasn't altogether happy about the state of affairs, the black and dribbly signatures on the end of that buff paper.

Well, what I had to say to him in that regard was this: why the hell did he sign it? Instead of lurking around, trying to sneak back into my body, why didn't he just show up and answer me this: why the hell did he insist on guzzling so much beer that his head couldn't have been screwed on straight? And while I was at it, what did he think he was playing at, anyway, taking a twelve-year-old girl off, and letting her daddy go away without calling him back and giving him a spank, or a kick up the arse? Which was what was needed in that particular situation. And also, while we were on the subject of getting complaints in, what the hell did he think he was at, calling me to his bed, when I had nothing to compare it to, nothing to know any better with? But mostly, and most hatefully, this: why the hell, why the bloody hell, had he ridden out to Nullo, to a back-end arse of a mountain, without me? Why had he let himself be chased, run down, into that ravine, and why would he never come home?

Anyway. Filming was pretty straight up, really, when it came to it, and a damned sight easier than pleasing a circus audience. There was Dibbsey with that ridiculous blue cap on – he said something about Mr Cozens Spencer wearing the same thing, which I didn't believe for a second; men can be such fools – and there was only one camera, though he did have a wagon for it, and a boy called Roy to wheel it around while another boy, who also seemed to be called Roy, stayed behind the camera. Those cameras were bigger than me. Not that I was ever anything other than tiny: Ariel could lift me on to his shoulders with one hand without even pausing for breath. Me, I was sick again, doubled over in the corner of the paddock, way out there in Parramatta. Straightening up every twenty minutes or so to jump on Lordship and gallop around behind the lad playing the Evil Villain. I had to be three different people, and in one scene, I was the villain's best mate. I had no idea where I was or what the story ruddy was and, to tell you the truth, I don't think Dibbs did either. Not then: he was stringing it together, whatever came to mind. Ride on a horse. That's it, leap off. Now, let me think – chase him with a gun. And me, switching from *ingénue* to landlord. When you're as flat-chested as me you'd be amazed at how little it takes to convince folk that you're a man. Someone did once ask if I was a powder-puff. Did I like men, he asked. What was I supposed to say? Which bit?

I was starving by eleven o'clock, and no one was mentioning food. Dibbsey got his black megaphone and shouted, 'Robbery scene, places.' No one was further than a couple of yards from him, we could hear him if he whispered, so why he had the megaphone was anybody's business. Worrying about my gut, and what was going to go in it, was all very well, but it meant that I missed the vital clue about what happened next. Billy leaped on to some white brumby he'd caught for Dibbs, and I was doubled over, wiping sick from the corners of my mouth. Dibbsey came over and said, 'This is where you have to be Mary again, leaping on to the villain's horse.'

He handed me a long petticoat and I slipped it on over my jodhpurs.

'No,' he said, 'bare legs.' He watched me all close while I slid the jodhpurs over my legs. I tried to slide them off in one fast go, but they were tight, and I had to wiggle, and every time I wiggled, Dibbsey drew a breath and, believe me, I knew what that meant. When a man draws breath like that, snapping like a branch breaking, you can bet your petticoat he's not thinking about his lungs or his heart.

Mind you, I have to say, for all the fuss, when it came to it, it was barely even a ride: anyone who could gallop a brumby could do it, but he loved that it was me, in a dress, with a flash of bare thigh, pushing the burly villain bloke (who I have to say was a powder-puff if ever I saw one) off his horse. Leaping without touching the stirrups – it's a cinchy trick, anyone could do it, but they loved it, he loved it, even though he said it would never happen, couldn't happen, that a woman could outride a man like that. Then he slapped his thigh and called out to the fat man to get the Constable's costumes and I stood there like a dumb duck, waiting for the next step, waiting to say, 'Well, it could happen, that a woman could outride a man.'

For instance, I wanted to say, for instance, I could outride any man here, or any man in almost any town in the whole of this new and over-bloody-confident country. Instead, I stood, quiet.

Until Dibbsey looked at me, surprised I was still there, and said: 'You're the woman I need to marry, Jess.'

Ha. Because I knew that I was still married, that Ariel hadn't gone anywhere. I knew, sure as love, that he was lurking around, watching and waiting, just in case I needed him. And I knew that I would always need him, that I would never stop. And I would have told Dibbsey so, too, without a flicker of worry, if it weren't for the sudden twist of sickness hurling its way round my gullet, like a ruddy shooting star.

~

'Rose?' Nurse Sich held out her hand out for Rose quite as if it were a dance, another one, perhaps a barn dance, and they were partners calling, taking to the floor.

Rose stepped, then stopped. What if the baby — what if Sammy didn't remember? What if he hid his face, she had heard of it, whispered among the women here, some who returned, aching worse than before, hiding from the machine?

Everything was beating, pulsing, louder in her; her eyes blinking more rapidly, an excess of saliva in her mouth. After waiting so long for the shivers of terror, she knew the signs. There was much she had sliced away from her memory, but she remembered this, the sensation of sudden imbalance. When she stepped out, into the cool grey corridor, she could see Joe, hunched over himself, the filling pulled out of him, and for a moment she thought it was a child, a thin boy, sitting there. Rose fluttered near him, a moth, unsure where her hand should go, unsure how to place it. Touching — for both of them, it had been a long, long wait between flesh and flesh.

Peach lipstick. That was another thing. And the sweet clean smell of their trembling, the night she finally agreed to this — an adventure, Australia. Travelling by train to Southampton, with Ada and her mother rocking opposite her. Her father's face, averted at Oxford station as the train pulled out. 'I can't go,' he'd said, 'I can't bring myself to watch you leave.' Ilsa, her mother, didn't speak, the whole journey, though Rose tried three times to make her. Smoothing her hands over the low oval of the baby, whispering, 'It will be fine.' Only Ada threw streamers up on to the ship, and Rose watched, as the *New Australia* horned its way out of the harbour, waiting for the last streamer to break. The last tie.

*

There was this, too, rising up, unbidden: she was a child. Thirteen, perhaps. The war had just begun. Ada, the younger sister, insisted that they run away, go into hiding. They took a parcel of jam sandwiches – pieces, Ilsa insisted on calling them – and walked up to Boar's Hill. Ada wanted to see the boars. Rose insisted that there were none, not here, not in England at all, but Ada was so sure, and so full of hope, that Rose was swayed. It was summer; the days unwound for ever, and the sharp scent of grass was in the air. When they finally found the woods, they'd eaten the jam pieces, and Ada was complaining of blistered heels and a bellyache. The woods swallowed them up, enclosed them in a sudden, splendid darkness and a loamy silence. Ada's hand gripped Rose's and she whispered, 'Where are the boars?' Rose was about to say, again, patiently, that there were none, when there was a stampeding, a scuffling. The harsh sound of heavy bodies pushing into the woods, the smell of sweat. Rose pulled Ada back, pressing against a pine tree, and Ada whispered, 'Is it them?'

The woods seemed to breathe open, to explode into noise: a group of soldiers pounded past. They ran in a clump, their breathing as loud as the fierce booting of the footsteps. Storming past, so close that the girls could smell them, the soldiers seemed like one being. They were a sudden, solid wall, and then the woods swallowed them again. The chestnut leaves beneath their feet folded into their silence as Rose and Ada trudged back down the hill. They rode back from Cumnor with the rag-and-bone man, counting out the bluebells.

They swam in the river, all of them, stripping down to their cotton underwear. Rose held her father's hand and listened to Ilsa calling to him, 'Hold her tight, Frank.' Every summer the same, Ada leapt in with her limbs flung wide. Even Ilsa waded in, her grey bloomers billowing out. It was a sign of summer, as reliable as the first daffodils in spring. The first cuckoo. Frank's hoot of a laugh: 'You'd never get water like this in Dunbarton, Ilsa. Freeze your bollocks off there.' And, always, Ilsa's sure, sharp slap on his wrist.

There was none of that, now, wouldn't be again. Those familiar signs, the markers of the seasons, of daily changes. It was an alien language, this new country, though the words were the same. There were no places that marked her memory; she had no childhood here, no trace of herself, no past. Her own child would be alien, his childhood an unfamiliar country.

A breath, a heartbeat, and there she was again: awake, lying on the ship-surgery bed with Sammy beside her. White film covered his body when he finally pushed out of her, in between the stirrups on the hard bed in the white ship-room. It was unexpected; none of it was expected. She had planned – they both had – another two months of her welting and swelling. They would arrive, rattle up to Broken Hill, set up house in the teacher's quarters, and then, when all was clean, Rose would have the baby. Instead: Rose, the red-headed nervous doctor and the fiercely capable nurse on the *New Australia* had held her down – so it felt – shouting to push or not push and no one, no one, had warned her to expect so much blood. For twelve days she lay in the ship's infirmary, her eyes barely flickering while the baby suckled desperately. The nurse had named him Sam, after Uncle Sam: a winner, she said. Expect great things. He pinked up after ten days, and she noticed his black lashes spidering across buttery cheeks. She lay awake, feeling the heat stampeding through the portholes, everything in the infirmary condensing. She traced her finger against the porthole and watched the baby's upper lip shift with each breath, the leaflike sheen on his skin. 'Where were you?' she asked Joe. 'Why didn't you come?'

The corridor at the end of the ward swam up again, appeared as though through mist. Rose let go of Nurse Sich and moved towards Joe. Tried to – wanted to – offer her cheek, without any tears but could only bob down, as though curtsying for the Queen.

'Rose.' Joe's hand was held out, calloused. Waiting for what? A handshake? It was that sort of gesture, formal, one she couldn't possibly offer. After bringing her to this place? Not just this building, with its whitewashed linoleum and its watergreen walls, but to this country full of strangers, and full of silence, too. Absence, that was what it held. The absence of her history: how could she survive, how could she be expected to, with no past?

Joe dropped his hand, lowered his head: 'The taxi's out front.' He paused, cleared his throat. 'Costing me the week's wages. Not much money in factory work. Well, you know that.'

She tried not to ask after Sammy, guessing that the drive was too long, that he was being dandled on the knee of one of the women in the hostel. The lady from Dunbarton, perhaps, with the three girls. Something – there was a gap, there, a hole where he should have been. She could wait. She knew she must behave well, behave properly. Must memorise the actions, the correct words. It would come to her, the words, the actions, perhaps even the deep pleasure in the scent of her child. Nurse Sich had said it would, and the other nurse, too, the limp-haired girl. Sometimes, it was true, since the treatment began, Rose could feel herself swimming back to land. Joe was so far away, though, an unbridgeable distance, and she remained bubbling away below the surface, just at the point where water meets air.

Nurse Sich nodded encouragingly at Rose. 'All right, Rose? Enjoy your weekend home. You've done so well. Back on Monday for your treatment. You'll be all rested, won't you?'

'It's not home. It's a migrant hostel. A line of tin army shacks, crowded on a patch of dirt. The kiosk worker has a gun under the counter. How could it be home?'

The nurse smiled nervously at Joe. 'Well. Home is where the heart is, isn't it?'

Which reminded Rose: 'Why didn't you bring him?'

'Bring?' Joe stood, waiting for a touch.

'Sammy. Sammy, of course. Where is he?'

Joe stepped back, as if she had kicked him. 'Rose – what—'

Nurse Sich bustled over. 'It's fine, Rose.' She turned her head to Joe. 'Go gently, that's all. We talked about this.'

Rose spoke carefully, like someone drunk, expelling each word out slowly, rounding it off neatly. 'Why did you leave him behind?' She breathed in and out like a factory machine, laboured, loud. Honestly, how hard a question was it, really? Joe seemed huge next to her, a swampish monster. He seemed, even now, so far away.

Joe glanced at Nurse Sich, then put his hand under Rose's arm. 'Rose, you remember this, you do. I couldn't do it on my own, couldn't—'

At last, Rose nodded. 'You're right. We agreed. I forgot. He would stay behind while you came in the taxi.' She grabbed suddenly at Joe's forearm. 'I do love him, Joe. I do. The smell of him. His eyelashes.' But she could remember nothing else of him, only his name.

The taxi – a brown and white Austin – was loud, reverberating with a mess of clangs and lumps and minor poundings, and it made talk blessedly impossible. Rose tried to be a beacon. Tried to pretend – to herself, to the driver – that they were an ordinary couple, an ordinary family, coming home from an outing. Going home to their baby, who was being cared for by a lovely neighbour.

When the taxi pulled up outside the hostel gates, they sat for a moment, while Joe scratched in his leatherette wallet. The taxi driver stared at the barbed wire, at the huts huddled together, at the scrape of dirt that passed for a garden. 'Gawd. Nice bloody weekend leave here. I reckon I'd rather stay where you were. At least there's trees there.'

Joe handed him three shillings.

'In fact,' the driver clinked the coins into a wooden box, sitting on the passenger seat, 'I don't reckon I'd have left old England for this. I mean, why?'

A trace of red silphed on to Joe's neck. 'It's temporary. Only until we get – until we find our feet.'

'Heard that one before. Heard about folks being stuck out here for two years, saving the money to go back.'

'I suppose, in our case, we felt, erm, we felt led, really. That the Lord was instructing us.' Joe's voice wavers, briefly.

'Yaaaaair.' The driver spread the word thin, like poor people's butter. The square face looked into the long rear mirror. 'Quite often hear voices, myself.'

Joe left a Bible tract on the back seat, just in case.

*

It seemed more alien than before. She recalled nothing of this: these scraped-out paths between the tin buildings; the brick laundry shed wheezing in the centre. Joe marched ahead of her, the stubble at the base of his neck slick with Brylcreem. Rose watched her feet on the path, marking the squares between the huddled shacks. Dirt fountained round her patent leather shoes, shining with the force of a twenty-minute polish. In the dust, she could see her footprints, the pointed toe, then a gap, and the prick of a stiletto mark. Two women in the laundry shed stopped talking, holding a yellow sheet between them, and watched her pass. Her handbag – patent leather, beige to match her shoes – made a reasonable shield, clutched against her chest. A snide of teenage girls hipflicked their way past her, staring, and she couldn't see Joe, not his back, not his face. The humped-together hostel buildings were faceless; she had no memory, none at all, of ever having walked here.

Sammy: she could remember his skin, pale with jaundice in those first days, while the ship's doctor tried to pump oxygen into him. And stepping off the boat with him cradled as carefully as a bag of hedgehogs. But, not this: being with him here, perhaps wandering on these hacked-out paths with him? She stopped her feet moving, stood still, between two rows of the Nissen huts. Heat swelled from the ground, and from the mustered migrants beginning to throng to the dining shed; she looked beside her, ahead of her, for Joe, the only familiar shape.

On the ship, she'd been carried by the two doctors. One called, across the blacked-up faces, the shrieking of women and men being hurled into the sharp surface of the pool: 'Get the woman's husband. Get him now.' And Doreen from Kent had been close by and nodded and ran towards Joe, his cardboard crown beginning to sag over his face.

Rose held her hand out for the tin edge of a hut. Tried to find some bearing: she remembered a tree. An oak? An elm? Everything was faceless; she could hear, for some reason, the sea in her ears. Screaming his name wouldn't do it, she was sure she'd done that on the ship, screamed and screamed for him and still he never came. She couldn't sit; not in the terrible dust. With people watching, too. Even crying, which was all she wanted to do, weep until she became a lake herself, even that couldn't work with such an audience. Sammy was barely a minute away, and she would wait until dark, or knock on each tin door demanding her baby. For once, she would be as hard as metal with Joe, would let him know what was what.

She stood, bewildered until she felt the weight of his hand on her shoulders, his face, close up, nose to nose. 'Rose? Come back, can't you? When will you come back?' And there was something wet on his face; but he couldn't come closer.

'You left me.'

'No—'

'You didn't come. I waited and you didn't come.'

'I went in – I thought you were following. Look – it's our hut. Right there, the same one, it hasn't moved.'

She looked at the rows of huts again, all full up with waiting, and wanting, and limbo; you could practically slip on the smashed-up hopes of all the migrants who got stuck there. She remembered that, knew that all right.

He stepped ahead of her, looked back, pointed to the narrow, dark doorway. 'Here, where it was before.'

Nothing. Her eyes on him, blank as he tugged her inside.

'Where we've been for eight months, Rose. Where Sammy—'

'Just give him to me.' Air suddenly hissed from her, she clawed up, ready to scratch, to fight.

He wasn't ready for it, for her, for the unexpectedness of all that she was determined to forget. 'Rose.'

She reached out, as if searching for a railing. 'Where is he?' She was a blind woman, leaning against the tin wall, peering at Joe, peering at her feet. His name, again, trying to tumble from her mouth, but nothing coming: *Shmee. Shmee.* A sheep, a ewe, bleating on about something or other; made mute, made animal, by the pungent smell of his absence.

Joe stood in front of her, his shadow stretching, rippling on the tin ledges of the hut wall. Arms folded, the way they often were.

'Where is he?'

'Rose.'

'Where?'

'Don't make me tell you this. You know this.'

'Where is he?' Mucus, tears, spit, they all leaked from her. She was a river; her words were watery, incoherent.

'Don't.'

There was no crib. No line-up of bottles. No white scrubbing brush. She pushed her hand to her mouth, bit on the heel of it until blood speckled the skin.

'Rose, please. It was – have you forgotten, or have you made yourself forget?'

Forgetting. Remembering. She was unsure which was which, and which memory was real. The woman on the horse? Was that real?

Or this: she was on the floor, in the one room of the hut, the linoleum burning into her knees. In front of her, the china teapot, shining with a pale blue, pale as water. She'd packed it into the case, shipped it out with them from home. Home. She still thought of it like that, like home. She knew it drove him mad.

She was on her knees and the baby was beside her, still yowling, when Joe pushed into the door. Rose stared into the space beside the baby, her mouth open, one tooth shining, the teapot in front of her. In her hand there was a cloth. Perhaps it was cotton. Perhaps – she could not remember now – perhaps she had been polishing the teapot, the beautiful blue teapot. The baby was howling, his mouth a pink pie, wet and uncooked. Yet, somehow, all that she heard was the deep wail of whatever noise was calling her into herself.

Joe stood in front of the baby, knowing he should pick the child up, rock him in his arms perhaps. He reached down – he got that far – but it felt awkward, didn't fit. Midway to the child, arms outstretched, and he turned instead to Rose, called into her face: 'Where are you, you stupid woman? Get yourself back here to your responsibilities.'

She had expected to be full of life. Even with wanting to stay, with feeling dragged away from her life, she'd still hoped for – bounce, that was it.

He'd endlessly said it: sorry, sorry. About the woman, the one night: a mistake, an ache. He should never have told her.

It wasn't that, Rose said, it wasn't simply that.

The baby was still shrieking, his face blotched red and white. Rose had not moved. Joe leant his face close to hers again and shouted, the way he never had: 'Get yourself back here, you get back here now.'

This was what he'd said, before, in Hinksey, when she said she didn't want to go, not to Australia, not to Canada. Not anywhere. Not even to the other side of Port Meadow, beyond the tame ponies and the wild geese. Home was there, Hinksey, with her mum, and her sister, and the familiar scent of rotting leaves in autumn and fresh buds in spring.

It was spring when Joe came home at dawn after that night. Some party, to wet the head of a baby: a wife of one of the teachers was at home with a fine-haired newborn girl, and six men were out drinking till dawn. Or not drinking, not entirely, not only. Not quite. He crept in the back door, sat beside her on the bed until she woke up. 'Don't tell me.' That was what she said, and she wished he hadn't, wished that he'd kept it quiet, just – people went on, didn't they? Keeping their mouths shut. The men's Bible study meetings started up after that; the Morning Watch – the dawn prayer meetings – the poring over the Word. The bright new soil of Australia was a gift, direct from the Lord, he knew it. A place to redeem himself, to prove himself worthy.

He was gentle with it, when he said it: 'Rose, love. This is a chance to begin again, to forget that mistake, that— It would never have happened, you know that, if we had been Man and Wife.'

'But, now, Joe – with a child. It will be a beginning anyway, won't it?'

He was firm then, as he had to be. 'You know this, that the man is the head of his wife, the way that Christ is the head of the Church. And I know, I do, Rose – I know that the Lord is asking us to go.'

This shouting, though, this putting his face close, red-eyed with frustration: when did Christ ever shout at His church? When was the Lord so busy drinking beer and doing the hula that he forgot about his church, left his church bleeding with strangers? When, indeed, had the Lord spent a night with another church, just, one mind, and then insisted on dragging His people away from home?

Oh, Israel. Yes. But you could hardly count that.

She wept without knowledge, noticed afterwards, and could not stop herself. Midway through the very beginning of a sentence or a word, Rose would touch her own cheek and feel that the tears had already begun, had been waiting, longing to slide down her face. There was one great comfort of disappearing into the great lake of tears: there were no thoughts that were unwelcome, that were not allowed. I will die, she thought, I will go down to the foul-smelling creekbed and lay myself in the water and simply disappear there.

Joe tried to make her see him, trying to call her back from that other England, which she was lost in. Really, he said, didn't she think he felt it too? Didn't she think he was sorry, hadn't he said so? But he had to obey, and the Lord had told him, he was sure of it, to follow the path to this new land. Like the Puritans, those Israelites of the New World. New land would heal them, him, would make a fresh start. It wasn't his fault – how was he to have seen? – the early labour, the impossibility of Broken Hill, the loss of a teaching contract. Not a chance, the department said, once you've turned down a posting. He was trying, Joe was, trying to make amends, to heal the damage he knew he'd done. The Lord well knew that he, Joe, had no desire to be putting small wooden blocks in a machine all day. And it would get better, he promised, she was just simply to trust him. Even the place, with all its strangeness, she would learn to love it.

She had trusted him. Before.

At least there was something to love in the desert. At least there was manna. And pillars of cloud to provide entertainment. But this place – she could see nothing, only trees that were alien, light that was too sharp. Some days, she could let her lashes dapple her view and imagine that the scrabble of rough grasses in front of her window was a low rise, the mound in Cumnor Wood. She could, if she concentrated hard enough, imagine the thick bracken, the layer of bluebells, the prickle of blackberries. She could breathe in deep, imagine the sharp whisper of the air, the lush scent of wild garlic.

It was not the absence of the baby that she wished for: she wanted to find him, to adore him, to feel his adoration in return. She knew that it was possible, that other women did, that other women fell so in love with their babies that they did not notice such trifling matters as shapes of trees, the wrong taste of the air.

She remembered this: days and days of weeping, of losing words, then clawing at her neck, trying to breathe, feeling hooked, caught, trying to tug at the metal hook that pulled at her lips, her skin.

The baby crying, still.

And then: hooked. Gone.

Nurse Sich, Dr Kingley. The coolness of the metal discs.

She swam back, surfaced. The tin room. The metal bed-settee. The narrow table, the two chairs. Behind the three walls, the sharp words of the other migrants: something about a factory, someone was saying; in another room, there was the blurred murmur of a song.

Sammy. Shmee.

She held out her hands: 'I want to hold him.'

'You're doing this deliberately. I'm trying to be patient. You're doing this to punish me, Rose, and it's not your job. I've already been punished, haven't I? Don't you think I'm punishing myself?' His hands fisted up, he seemed to swell, to redden. 'I can't – Rose, I'm trying to obey, all I've done is try, and, he, our baby, God— Gone, and all those bloody powders – and you wonder—' He pushed past her, toppled her as he swung out on to the dirt path of the migrant village. She could hear him, a kind of howl, as his feet pounded. Where had he been all those years? All that time, in Hinksey, and later, when she'd waited for him to cry out with love, or pain, or – anything. Waited for a sign of his blood, there was the truth of it, not of the Lord's. She didn't need to see the Lord's blood.

Blood.

Joe's howl, the echo of it, settled beside her, as dogs or wolves might. He was gone. The powders, he had said. Gone, he had said.

There was no moment, no memory of her child. She strained, tried to recall. It was clear that Joe believed she knew. Nothing came to her, no picture of Sammy, no smell. Only there, his absence. That he was disappeared, with the other odd patches of memory. Something about the powders. Something – only a thread of memory, knotted. Ice sliced at her, the creeping fear of discovering something more terrible than she could imagine.

She was gone, too, gone; there was nowhere to be, now, with this swallowing, this unmemory. Her body withering, not just with her undoing, but the shame of being unable, unwilling, to mother.

The box was still in the asbestos cupboard beneath the one sink in the room. Washing dishes, hands, faces, bodies, teeth; everything happened at that sink. And this, too, the mixing of the powders, the swallowing of the tablets.

It wasn't the first time she'd imagined this, thought it possible. All those days, keening, half down on the floor, her mouth hanging open, she had known that this was there waiting for her: the line of pills and powders, courtesy of the hostel doctor, and the weekly store. Bex. Vincent's. The small white pills with scrawled labels: '3 per day, after meals. Mrs Dobell – take daily'.

Sammy held her, here, in this milky world; and the hope – she could admit to it now – that they could, would, gather themselves, leave the squat red of the hostel. The hope that she'd find herself again, find strength, fight, that they'd abandon the notion of the quarter-acre, or of the farm, or the beach, that was going to change everything, open their lives, their worlds. Abandon Joe's talk of the Lord's Guiding Hand, abandon his determination to be right; his knowledge that he'd get another post after all, the past would be forgotten, Rose would move on, and they'd be home, they'd all be home.

But not for Sammy, who was gone. And who would, in any case – she was sure of it now – be better off without her.

Sammy. She could see him now, smell him. He was a tiny drip in a basket, his fist balling into his mouth, his eyes squinting shut. His skin smelt of oranges, the promised scent of Australia. Suddenly it was all there, awakened. And the way he might be, too, later. The way she might be, might have been, if she had been made well:

His hair is curled at the back. It's morning and he stands in the doorway, the light behind him. Hair sticks up on his head in grassy tufts, small birds of wishes hiding in nests. His pyjamas — flannelette, dotted with alphabet letters — crease round his ankles and dangle over his wrists. Light spears the morning around him, cutting away from the tumble of his hair, sharp as a lion's breath. For a moment, he is still, watching her. She can feel him, the hot ice of his gaze wakes her, and then he is a ball of tumble, a flame-footed runner. He is the weight of sixty men, jumping on her chest, her face, her shoulders. Beneath him, she can barely breathe. There is an abundance of laughter. Joe has no need to say, I'm sorry.

This moment never was, never had been, never would be, not with her gone, not with Sammy gone.

Rose leant her head on the edge of the toilet seat and watched tears pool on to her wrist. She was a drain, an absence, an invisibility. She didn't count the pills, or bother mixing the powders with water: she just lined them up and swallowed, one by one by one.

~

If it's rest you're after, don't come here: it isn't what you think, what you imagine. But remember this, that what you long for isn't necessarily what will satisfy you. Or maybe this is more the truth of it: that what you long for might wear a disguise, might require some — and I don't want to be rude here but, still, it needs to be said — some sticking power. Are you with me?

You'll think me a fool, it's true — but even when I was tender in the belly and hadn't bled for more than two months, I was slow to notice. I know. Thing is — with all my being on and off horses and often not eating much more than a slice of Madeira cake for tea, I never was too regular in that department. Chewing tobacco didn't help, I suppose — I did, I did chew it and, believe me, it's a fine habit, if you just keep it private. Why not? Can't go around putting everything in the closet, and from the time I married Ariel I'd caught more than my share of disapproval from the rest of the world, so I must say that particular feature of mankind and his wife doesn't concern me one little bit. Weeks after Ariel was gone, the sickness still wasn't going anywhere. I thought it was him really settling in, letting me know he was there, inhabiting me, and, well, I was half mad with the loss of him and — anyway. Enough of that, because it's as clear as gin, isn't it, where I'm going? It seems ridiculous, a woman of my temperament, being so ill informed — but there you have it, how it was.

Ariel's Buckjumping Show had nothing left in the coffers. I thought I knew all of Ariel's troubles, I thought he halved them with me, but when it came to me trying to sort out what we had and what we didn't — well, there was more of what we didn't have than what we did. So having my own little seat, with my own little name, in a real-life moving picture, meant something more than seeing my face, all made up and pretty. It meant being able to pay the girls, and Heap, and Billy. Bloody Billy hadn't let me give him proper wages since Ariel took his stupid running leap – since he did whatever the stupid old bastard did out there, on Nullo. Well, *Mary the Outlaw* was filling up the little pot in the red caravan, nice and steady. Dibbsey kept his mouth shut about where the cash might be coming from, and he kept his eyes on me, the way he had that first day in the show tent. Gleaming.

But here, look – it's the third day of filming. I was tender as a turd, if you'll pardon the rudeness, but that's how it was: I was soft and achy and waiting to be tripped on. We were making the moving picture, if you'll believe it, in Rushcutter's Bay. It's true: twenty miles from the bush and nothing but water in our view, flat and blue. Somehow, Dibbsey had called in a favour from Lottie Lyell, who – it turns out – was pretty fine friends with Mr Raymond Longford, who knew Mr Dampier himself and there we were, in Mr Dampier's studio, with the roof lifted right up to let the sun in. Didn't take a genius – or me – to make it clear that a better way of getting the sunlight is to be flaming well outside. Well, mind you, there were three different cameras, each with one of the Roys behind it. Tilly and Gladys were allowed to be girls from the bush, and Heap had the job of holding any equipment Dibbsey had on hand. Five shillings he was being paid, too. There were people everywhere, all the time, tripping under my feet, and I felt dizzy with it. Camera boys, a man who pushed a wagon along, eight riders, a girl to serve glasses of barley water and tea. In the circus, when you want to practise something, it's just you and the horse, and the sound of the dirt. In the pictures, even the rehearsals are a performance.

At one end of the shed, Dibbsey batoned with his megaphone. He was a fluster of nerves, too. All I wanted to do was ride, jump on Lordship and gallop the length of the shed and back, the way I'd done in *Starlight*. He kept calling at me, though, Dibbsey did: 'You need to be farewelling your father here, cry. Cry, for God's sake.'

And I couldn't cry: there was the feeling of sick in my stomach, and a terrible ache in my bosoms, anyway, which was distracting. I never was a crier, that's the thing. Couldn't much see the point.

No offence intended to those who do.

'Pretend. For God's sake, Jess, it's just pretend. Look sad, pretend to cry.'

I couldn't. I couldn't pretend to cry, for no reason that I could see. The girl – that was me – was just farewelling her father, who in this case was being acted out rather unconvincingly by one Mr Eugene Rider, a tubby Scotsman who kept trying to kiss my ear in an over-familiar manner. It wasn't just the kissing the ear, though. Or even the tubbiness of Mr Rider, or Dibbsey shouting from the ledge at the end of the shed.

Dibbsey shouted, 'And . . . rolling,' and I shook Mr Rider's off, leapt on to Lordship and galloped towards the camera at the far end of the shed. Got half way across the stage and Dibbsey leapt up, shouting something or other. Camera was still rolling, though, so I yanked at Lordship's reins, and speared him below the ribs, tugged on his bit until he bucked himself up. And then – what happened? – my hands slipped, and I couldn't hold on. I tumbled from his side, rolling almost beneath his hoofs. That horse, he'd been with me for a long, long time; he trotted back, still on his hind legs, and sideways, before he put his front hoofs down. Tell me horses aren't part of the family. Dibbsey ran across the stage; they were all of them suddenly around, swarmed, looking down. Dibbsey knelt, wiped at my face, bent my arm. Knelt there, silent, for a long minute, then said, 'Okay, let's take a break.' He looked up at the sky, beginning to darken. 'No, forget it, we'll call it quits for today. Start fresh in the morning. For God's sakes, Jess, what was that?'

'I thought it would look exciting. More exciting than bloody tears.'

It was all sorts of strange luxury, the moving-picture business. One slice of which was the notion of sleeping in a high bed, in a room, with a door, in a house. Like the acre-long studio shed, it belonged to Mr Dampier, and Dibbsey insisted that it was mine. I never even asked where he slept all that time. Curled like a snake, Billy slept on a chaise-longue at the foot of the bed. The living-room window was a fat square in the middle of the wall, letting in a neat wedge of light and a view of the brick schoolhouse next door. Tilly, Gladys and Heap slept in the high bed. Me, I couldn't bear it, the stillness of the house, so I shuffled outside each night to my caravan, mine and Ariel's caravan, slotted into the side yard of the little house.

I lay awake, listening to the wind touch the veranda of the house, rattle it, with nowhere to go. Thought once or twice about my daddy, the way he left with the empty hat-box there. Not even a goodbye. Ha. He'd be sorry, if he saw me. Couldn't think why I felt so tender and sick. God, Ariel. He was out there, I could feel it, and I wanted to shout at him, pull him to me; tell him to get me out of there, that stupid ruddy shed with too many people and too much noise.

Look at me — I'm beating round the bush like a bloody old goanna, here, trying not to tell the truth. So. Here it is.

I knew. Of course I knew. I'm no damned fool. I've watched two trick-cycle girls sicken and swell and disappear. Maggie never came back, but Gladys — another story, she was back with red eyes and a flattened voice. And there was Ariel. It will sound wrong — odd — but how else can I put it? Apart from the acrobatics, the hair-tugging, the whispered desperations after the rest of the crew rocked themselves off to sleep — and I want to make it clear here that it was me as much as him who whispered, 'I need you.' Apart from that, which, let's be frank, is a small part of it all, he was like my father. Not my actual father — God, I'd have run him off with his own gun — and I don't want any thinking there was any of that sort of rot with my father. Don't be ridiculous: that man was a greedy, useless piece of intestine but he wouldn't have come near me waving his — whatever you want to call it. And there are names, I know; but I'll come to that later. Meantime — Ariel filled me in on the gaps, the important ones, some of them accidental. One accidental one being the nature of humans, and the nature of fear. And, better, the nature of trust. That man — I'd have trusted him with my life. Did. Which isn't getting us closer to the truth. I knew, is the point. I knew before I said my great and fatal yes to Mr Alfred Yellow-moustached Dibbs; when I tumbled underneath Lordship's hoofs I knew, and in all my mad, brave additions to his patchwork moving picture I knew.

Do you see now? How to say it more plainly? I could not have thrown myself hard enough. Could not have rolled too close to those hoofs. I checked and checked for signs of blood and splittage and, believe me, I wept and howled like a chained-up dog when I saw that there was none. I wanted it, all of it, over. I wanted me to be over.

You're not the first to disappear, or to waver. There are thousands of us, millions, and we belong to each other.

Well, this one had other ideas, as they often do: I watched the patterns of the moon and thought about my daddy, and the way some babies just will insist on being made, and how this one was the last cinnamon taste of Ariel. It would be a half horse, half baby, if it was to follow the family way. It seemed pretty clear that no amount of gin was going to move it out and, God knows, I didn't have it in me to go to the places that Gladys or Maggie went to.

Ariel wasn't coming back, I'd settled on that, and the money from the circus was running down the river faster than I could leap off Lordship. I pushed the knitted blanket off me and pulled the tin box from under the broken saddle, inside the caravan. All night, I added up figures, then added them again, and none of the answers looked good. The knot across my belly grew tighter, while the moon beamed down on me, as if it was benevolent, as if there was someone out there, up there, who cared.

~

Head sharp against the speckled edge of the sink, something trickling. Tickling into her eyes, against her lip.

Powder was stuck to her lip and the last of the pills rested, leadlike, somewhere in the spoon of her chest. Rose could feel the weight of them; could feel, she was sure, the juices beginning to fizz at the edges, bubble away with the neat roundness of the pretty white pills, and the soothing powders.

The grain in her throat seemed to swell, to fill her chest, her head, too. Snow. Powder falling like snow. Children – two girls – lying on the snow, arms flapping up and down to make snowprints of snow angels. Snow angels, yes.

She could feel the sink sliding away from her, the coldness of it as her face slid down. Wall. Concrete. A thud, the bloody taste of rust. Each surface of her skin was grainy, but she was far, wonderfully far, away.

Everything tumbled, now, beautifully. Sammy – yes, that was him, her baby. Skin like silk, the smell of air. That was better. She could reach him, was sure she could.

It had all been—

It had all been—

What?

She hadn't always been here, she remembered that.

She was in a sparkling gown. Marquisette collar. That man was beside her. She couldn't think of his name. She kissed him some time, on a canal path. She was on a balcony, looking down at faces, blurred together, a bluish ocean. People were applauding, someone was shouting. No, no, it wasn't a balcony, it was a ship, a gangplank, and they weren't people, it was the sea. A dark-haired nurse handed her a baby.

The baby.

Oh, the baby.

She'd failed, that was all. She had failed.

There was a smooth slide, then. She was on it, sliding down, very far. She had red boots on, and mittens. He was at the bottom, that man. She could see him with his arms out, knew that she had blistered once with love for him, and that he had for her. She slid, slid down and past him, barely whistled, barely touched his cheek.

~

I can see you coming; we are joined, after all.

What is it that you want? More pictures? Something to pass the time? Trust me, there is a plan.

Lottie Lyell turned up in the last week of filming. Lottie – ah, what to say about her? Pure honey ran through her veins, I shouldn't wonder: heart of precious metal. Which brings me to another point, though: why would you want it, after all? A heart made of inedible, indelible gold. Lottie, in fact, had enough of the real stuff – gold – to keep her going, with or without a heart made of it.

We were filming a scene where Mary, trying to protect her father's land, and her own honour, shoots at a trap, knocks him dead – thus leading her on the terrible path to Outlawville. I swear Dibbs was making it up as he went along, in a ruddy blind panic.

Do you want to know what it's like to kill a man? I always did, I always wondered – do you think that makes me bad, or mad, or both? This is a story, isn't it? A flippit of entertainment, a diversion. Believe me, I know all about that, about diversions, flimsy stories, about something to while away the hours until the clock stops ticking and you realise that you wasted them, all those hours. Oh, come on, I'm no fool – *Captain Starlight*, *Mary the Outlaw*, *Girl from the Bush* – I know what they were, what they were for. I'm proud of them – I rode well, I held my head up, I made my eyes bright and my lips appealing; but they were mere stories.

What do you expect of me? Of course I wasn't Mrs Plum Posh – look at me, flicking around, half animal. I could outride any man, and outshoot most of them as well, though I'd never been called on to try. Never been called on to use a gun at all, if you want the whole truth nothing but the truth so help me God. Ha! Not the only time I've had to use that little phrase, you can bet your grandmother's nipples. I could be a crack-shot liar, too, if I had to be, as well as a straight crack-shot; I could bet my caravan on it, and Lordship as well. Well, I have to tell you that when I had that gun in my hand, it felt heavy and hard, but I knew something about myself, in that minute. Just this: that somehow I was going to head out to Nullo Mountain. That I'd do some looking, that's all. You just know these things about yourself, you know what you're capable of, even though all you've ever had to do is wave a gun around as if it's a fairy wand.

Same way I knew I couldn't cry, couldn't pretend, though Dibbsey was almost red with the frustration of me. What could I do? He didn't hire me to cry, he hired me because I was the best damned rider in Australia. The best.

They changed the scene, in the end: I waved the father off, and underneath, the titles were to say: 'She cannot know that she will not see him again.' If I'd been writing it, the title would have read: 'She knows that she will not see him again but is more concerned with getting some food. He wasn't much of a father, anyway, and she's got bigger and better fish to fry.' Dibbsey said if I didn't shut up, they'd write: 'She waves him off but cannot cry because she has no heart.'

As if he knew the half of it: me rocking myself to sleep at night, holding Ariel's cap to my face, just for the smell of him. Tears don't tell you if a person has a heart or not. If I had no heart, I'd be able to pretend. Lottie Lyell, with her metal heart, could cry when someone clicked their fingers at her, or offered her cash.

The day we finished filming, there was a party in the studio, and the sun sparkled through the glass roof, making even shadows look like diamonds. Dibbsey had managed to get a band in, and they were playing all that wild new ragtime. Heap insisted on joining in, standing in the clump with them, strumming along on his ukulele.

Dibbsey weaselled over, holding out the long camel coat he'd bought for me: a gift from the production fund, he said. 'Got a surprise for you, Jess.'

I could barely hear him, people were hooting and hollering around me so much. He put his mouth right next to my ear: 'Got someone who wants to say hello.'

We pushed our way to the end of the studio shed; the air cooled, somehow seemed thinner, away from the band, the shuffling that counted for dancing. Lottie Lyell was leaning back against the low proscenium. She leant forward to kiss me when I got close, twice on each cheek, then she pushed me in the direction of the grey-haired man standing next to her. 'Go on, Raymond, give the girl a peck.'

The man smiled, held a hand out.

Lottie slipped her hand underneath his elbow. Her nose wrinkled when she smiled. 'So, Jess, a new film actress has arrived.'

'Oh, Cripes, hardly an actress. One film is all, and all I can do is ride. Can't act, can't cry. Not like you.'

She tilted her head, laughed. 'I can do more than ride. I'm not— You're not frightening me, Jess. Who's getting me a drink, Raymond?'

Raymond loped off, towards the waiters who were lurking near the band. Every few steps he stopped, swung his hips, shuffled his feet and did a little turn. He was quite the pretty dancer.

Dibbsey watched him, then touched my arm, as though we were married. 'I'll go help.'

Lottie flexed her nails, catlike. 'Now, Jess. Dibbs tells me you're going to be a marvellous poster girl. What do you think about it all? Isn't it wonderful? Now, I know that Dibbs has the next one all planned – *Girl from the Bush*, something, anyway—'

'I've still got the circus, actually. I'm sure he'd rather have you—'

'Oh, good Lord, don't be ridiculous. I'm far too expensive for him, for one thing. Anyway, he says you start filming in a fortnight. Raymond and I are finishing a new picture now, and then – well, we need another woman, who can ride, for the next one. There isn't another woman who can ride like you.'

'There's you.'

'I'm already taken.' She touched her lips, wiped the corner. 'I know you might have some – difficulties—'

'Difficulties?'

'Oh, darling, only if you wanted to be silly about it. You'd be good in it, and it's important for the country. *Australia Calls*.'

'Oh, it's that one, is it? Then you know my answer. I can't think why you'd even ask.'

'It's not about – it's nothing personal. The Yellow Peril is a threat, we're all— It's not about men like him.'

'And your moving picture isn't about women like me.' I stood next to her, all stiff and awkward silence, until Dibbsey came back, holding up two glasses.

'Your lady outlaw is quite the determined one, Dibbs. You should take her under your wing, tame her.'

Like I said, heart of solid metal.

Dibbsey said, 'She's barely been a widow three months,' but he slipped his hand under my elbow and smirked down at me like I was a warm slice of loganberry pie and he wanted to be the cream on top.

Lottie glanced at my riding coat, buttoned up to the throat.

Earlier, when the party was just beginning, Billy had trailed me out to the back of the shed, where I was doubled over, vomit etching out of me like stormwater in Balmain. He put his hand on my shoulder, knelt down beside me and looked at my eyes. His teeth flashed, a yellowish moon in his black face: 'Reckon you got yourself something special in there, hey, Jess? Maybe Ariel hasn't left after all, hey?' The yellow moon disappeared then and a long shadow parked itself in his eyes. 'God, hey, Ariel—'

And I made him stop because sometimes – and you should remember this – there's nothing to be gained from knowing everything, feeling everything. Nothing to be gained from adding more tears to the world.

'Think about the film, Jess.'

I could feel the tightening of my skin, the quickening; Dibbsey's hand burning on my arm. Tinny saliva was swilling in my mouth. 'No. Thank you.'

Lottie tilted her glass to her lips. 'It's one thousand pounds.'

Oh, I could swear to you that I could feel a kicking in there, a beating on my ribcage, and my tongue was leaping out of my mouth, ready to say yes, one more foolish yes.

So I kept my tongue held back in my mouth, and I held my lips tight; knew that if I opened that mouth of mine, a yes would jump out. One thousand pounds – I could store some aside for this little mound growing inside me, get Billy and Heap and the girls paid off, keep the circus running while I was out of action. But I would not forget, not about Ariel dancing and rasping by the river, calling out to his dead daddy, his voice full of ache, a fatherless child, like mine would be.

'You can think about it. We'll be filming in four months. Jess.' She lifted her glass in a mild salute. 'It's just a story, you know that. A moving picture, that's all. Entertainment – it's what people want.'

I take it back. There's no such thing as just a story. I was wrong. Not the first time, or the last. I'll tell you when we get to the last; at least you'll get fair warning.

I can see you coming. You know you don't belong here.

~

Footsteps beside her. Shouting.

She could hear him, calling down to her. So far away; he was outside the parcel of green which embraced her. Was it green? Not deep and lush, not the night green of Cumnor Wood, this was flat green and pale. She was in it, and was blended with it: her body was unfolding, opening out. Each vein throbbed, was ready to explode. It was not unpleasant: the blood pulsed, then slowed. Everything slowed.

Except for the man, shouting, calling. Cool concrete ached beneath her skin, each particle of it pressing into her.

He was calling, 'Come back, Rose. Come back. Please, please, God. Oh, God, you can't let her go.'

She wondered why he shouted so, wetness falling from him, on to her body, on to the green. Hands against her skin, con-crete hard beneath her. Shaking. Slapping; something slapping at that bit of her. Face, that was it. Shaking her so that her tongue rattled, the powders swelling inside her sifted and resettled.

'Rose, we need you, we need you.' His sobbing sounded like a storm.

Briefly, she considered moving her mouth, asking why, and who: who was this 'we'? Perhaps she could do it, raise her tongue, resting so deeply; perhaps she could part her lips. It was so weighty, though, that tongue of hers, swollen in the cavern of her mouth. The storm of his voice began to lull, hushed by the choral whistle of the air breezing beneath her, holding her.

Smoke twisted in a column, pink and wispish, dancing; it was across a ravine, a bush-filled gully.

She stood on a rough-edged rock. Tilted back and forth. Did it require strength to get across? Because she had none. It was the air that would have to carry her, or let her fall.

Feet flexed. Push.

Rocks below her, sky above.

~

There was a big poster up outside the Parramatta town hall, all caged inside the glass case at the side of the pillared steps: *Mary the Outlaw*, starring Athene of the Antipodes. That was me. The picture showed a drawing of a horse, leaping across the page, and my face, all dreamy and made up to look like someone who wasn't me, tucked up in the corner. As if I was looking down on the horse. My lips in the picture were painted into a bee-stung kiss, and my hair was smoothed into a tight bob. Somehow, they blackened up my eyes, so that I looked more like Florence Turner than me. How could you ride through the bush, hold up a bank, and hide from the police, all while keeping kohl on your eyes? And in a dress? I stood across the path, watching the fringe-top surreys clicking past the sign, the horses lifting their knees high. Not a word or a nod from the drivers and it's funny, isn't it, how I wanted to call out and point, and stand myself next to grey-white sign and say, 'I'm her, sir, look at me'?

According to the red-veined newspapermen who wrote the columns, I was a fresh-faced girl star, who could ride like Lottie Lyell and smile like Florence Turner. Girl – ha! I was a widow, full of bitterness, was what I was. And I was fat as a sulky carriage myself – look at me, and how you could read the direction to Marrickville in the veins on my face. I was always more vain about my features than folk might have thought. Might have assumed given my other – tendencies.

The drooling newspapermen also wrote columns about the handsome rider Billy Awaba, ha! No idea that his 'his dark, wavy locks, his sunbeaten skin' were the marks of his people. Fools, the lot of them, if you ask me. Being a fresh-faced girl star did have advantages, main one among them being that I could afford to keep my caravan parked where the hell I liked. In the garden of the Metropole Hotel, for instance. That and— Well, money always comes from more than one place, doesn't it?

Ariel's Great Buckjumping Show to be exact. Now known as DeRabe's Travelling Circus. Or Drab's Circus. Something, anyway.

You can't say I wasn't trying to keep his memory, keep him alive, God knows – if there'd been a little bit more in the tin box; or if we weren't losing all our audience to moving pictures; or if Tilly and Heap hadn't decided to run off and get married. Or if he'd not been so ruddy determined to ignore the signs, so madcappedly willing to embrace fear, to soar with it, to see where it all led. Bloody Ariel: he was always willing to go along for the ride. Well – there are always thousands of reasons, for anything.

I managed to keep the posters, the big lump sticking out the front of me, and the caravan.

Mind you, it got harder and harder to waddle my way up and down the little wooden step, and every night during the winter, Mr Burns, the manager of the aforementioned esteemed establishment, came waltzing out, tapping on the window of the caravan and calling in, 'Would you like to come in to your room, Mrs Areel?' Once or twice I thought about it, too, especially given I was paying for the room. Only way I could park the caravan. And the more my belly swelled, the more uncomfortable that swag became. But it smelt of Ariel: the lemon of him, the starry minty-musk that strayed from his skin.

I managed to ride until I was more than seven months gone. Kept the buckjump shows on Fridays and Saturdays until the autumn started to keep the audiences down anyway. Tilly and Heap just ran off some time around then, maybe they got sniff of how tight it was.

Or – I don't know, Heap said once he couldn't bear the moving-picture people. Tilly left the note: *me and heap have ben in lov fr a lon tim now end we thort it wos tim to marri end hav a hape lif just us we ar sorry jessi for evrythen end we hop you will be hape end the sam for bil.* One trick-cycle girl, no music, and a lady rough-rider who was as round as a pig and couldn't keep hold of her breath. Before the nights started to drop down early, we knew we were finished.

If you look closely, in the last scenes of *Girl from the Bush* I looked more like a fat old judge on the back of Lordship than a sprightly young girl, and you can practically see me wheezing when I leap on for the ride off across the plains.

Most nights, in the winter, I had one other visitor tapping on the window of the caravan or, sometimes, the door.

Dibbsey knew what he wanted, and I'll give him this one thing, even now with everything that's gone between us: he told the truth about that. Never waltzed around outside, throwing roses up at me, calling, Oh, I want to be your dear friend, is all. No. He had his intentions, from the day that Ariel didn't come back. Before, that's the truth, isn't it? Watching me scissor my legs as I slid down off Prince Vic; his mouth watering while I rolled away from Lordship's hoofs, and swayed to Heap's ukulele. I wasn't without my charms. Men will waste a good deal of time and a good deal of money over a woman who can bend herself backwards while balancing on a horse. Such skills suggest certain – possibilities.

Some nights he didn't knock, but simply left delicate calling cards: a jar of macadamia jam; two caddies of black tea, one made from silver; half a ham, which I had no means of eating without his company. He was persistent, was what he was. Hung about waiting, like a town cat. Don't think I didn't know what he was up to; but when you've swollen to half the size of Hungary, and the last touch you had was the night before your husband – was the last time you saw your husband – you get clumsy, perhaps, in the whole matter of whom you let close.

And there was this, too, not a small thing: why would he bother? Just for the acrobatics? Which, frankly, he might reasonably expect to be spectacular, but – let's be brutal here – he could afford a little plaything. Plenty of them around, even then. Bob-haired girls who had seen the moving pictures in their local hall and wanted to be the girl on the poster; wanted to out-Nellie Nellie Stewart.

He didn't, is my point.

One night, when it felt like the baby was pressing up against my throat and setting all of my chest on fire, he rubbed camphor on my back, and dripped silver colloidus on my tongue and it felt fine, just fine, to be cared for. In the mornings, he collected me with a hired black carriage, placed a blanket on my knees as if I was a grandmother. During the filming, he had the Roy boys bring me endless cool glasses of barley water.

The day my baby boy arrived, Dibbsey was in a public house, celebrating. He'd made the final cuts to *Girl from the Bush*, had rolled the delicate, magical film into its canister and kissed it. The same day, *Mary the Outlaw* had two full columns: one in the *Bulletin*, one in the *Age*. And I stood on the corner of Collins Street, watching the line of men – and some women too – winding out of the town hall and round the corner, right down Chapel Road. Head down, and all on my ownsome, because even Billy took Dibbsey's offer of a free drink and buggered off to the drinking house.

And just then was when my little one decided it was time. And

I'm not going to pretend it was friendly or easy, or anything other than bloody terrifying.

I'm not a great mother.

I swear to do better, daily, weekly.

I could have done better.

He was a shell of a thing, my boy. Dark and cinnamony. God, you could have heard me scream when he came out – flat on my back with my legs up in metal stirrups. Stirrups – ha! Who rides upside-down with a dribbling doctor peering into your front passage? Sorry. Crudeness, I know. Ariel liked it, and that was the problem with me: I never remembered that others don't, that it was just him, Ariel, who loved me to swear and spit and talk like a man until I unwrapped the cloth from my chest and burst out all over him like a bud. But, oh, the pain of it, and the sheer indignity and – I have to say this – he was not what I expected. Hideously ugly, that was what. As for the force. Goodness me – see, I can be as coy as the next rough-rider – it wasn't what I would consider a fine afternoon's entertainment. Being shoved into a wagon, while a street full of men panic and bustle as if they're being some help at all. One gave the driver twopence and told him to rush me to the Parramatta hospital.

I will always think of that place with the smell of ammonia. The burn of it in my hair; it was a nurse who scrubbed at my scalp, her fingernails scraping, tugging until I screamed. It was the doctor – fat and red-lipped, if I recall, though you will appreciate my memory may not be reliable here – who administered the whisky douche and took no notice of my demands to have the bloody whisky douched straight down my throat.

He suggested I would not be a wonderful mother.

That there were families, couples – he could name them – who were keen to have a child, would pay substantial sums to take a child off my hands.

I have money, substantial sums of it, I said.

Or words to that effect.

After he'd been slapped and spruced and cleaned, my baby, my boy, he still looked like a red, lumpen fish. That was not when I first loved him. But when I did, I knew that I would not let go, even when it seemed I had.

~

The ambulance smelt of ammonia. The sharp metal tang of it stung Joe's eyes, wafted across Rose's nose. His head banged the metal roof with a sharp, loud clack each time the van swerved. Beside him, Rose was a creased sack, her lips an egg-blue. Saliva trickled on to her cheek, a meek sign of life. She seemed so wilted against the canvas of the stretcher, so – withered.

The driver lit a cigarette and held up the pack, an offering to Joe. He shook his head and shifted himself from the folding stool he was wobbling on; he doubled himself, knelt beside her, as though in prayer. He opened his mouth to pray, too, but found that the will was gone; or, at least, the sense of the right words, the correct form.

While the white van pushed its way out of the hostel gates, Joe tried again the words of prayer, but this was all he could get to: *Why did I follow you – why did I obey – I tried to obey you – where is she? Where is she?* And his words began as mutterings and then grew louder, took on the form of sermon, a Pentecostal fist-waving, foot-stomping shout. The driver sounded the horn, wound his window down and called to the crowd, who had swarmed round the vehicle, 'Will youse lot bugger off? Garn – mind your bloody business. We've got a sick – she's – if youse don't let me bloody through—' while he inched the van through the crowd of migrants and tried to block out the calling, shouting, wailing of the man in the back of the van. Rows of two and three deep, people pressed in all around the van, their faces flat against the windows. Worried faces, tempered with the hunger of curiosity, the appetite for a morsel to ease the stale boredom. Teenagers, lots of them, but adults too. A fluff-haired woman tried to help, pushing against the rear door, waving the teenagers aside. Tears ran quietly down her cheeks. Slowly the crowd began to part, a Red Sea making way.

Joe was sorry, he was sorry, he was, he was. The driver – Ray, late on the shift to earn some money for his wedding – knew that Joe was sorry. He knew it, because Joe called it out, wept it out, unknowing. Joe could not hear himself, it seemed, though the dead would hear him, surely.

The rain started as they pulled out on to the road, bucketed down, sluicing into the dirt. Spatters of thick mud coated the front windscreen.

He knelt beside her, rocking, calling out to God, until they reached the hospital. The ambulance workers ran to the back of the van and wrenched the doors open, leaving Joe exposed, huddled over the shell of his wife. He didn't hear the call, but there must have been one because suddenly there were four others, burly young men in white coats, pulling at the canvas stretcher, toppling him sideways, as though he were irrelevant.

Inside, he ran beside her, trying to keep his hand alongside hers, at least near her arm, her head, anything. She wouldn't know he was there, a nurse shouted, wouldn't care either, no doubt, but he couldn't let her go, like this, alone. Six people carried the canvas stretcher, though there seemed to be swarms of them; they appeared like bees, clustering round her, round the stretcher, as soon as the doors had been pushed open.

'The baby, Rose, the baby—' Joe tripped as he ran, lost his pace and the stretcher ran on without him. The swarm of doctors didn't break stride, pushed on, turned into a room. Joe tottered behind them. 'She's my wife,' he called, unnecessarily, to one of the grey-smocked doctors. To another, he shouted, 'I couldn't save her.'

An alarm clanged its way down the pale grey corridor. More

125

ammonia. He pushed at the heavy metal door of the room they'd pounded into, then pushed again.

'Sit.' Someone — a nurse? A woman, anyway — pushed him, physically pushed him, as though he were a child, into a hard-backed chair; the metal legs shone fiercely. 'Wait. Someone will come.'

Metal on linoleum, a scream of a sound. He rocked, back, forward, back. No one came.

The door beside him thumped mercilessly. Each swing outward released a puff of noise, the steam of controlled panic, filtering into the sweltering corridor. Someone was calling, 'Again, go again,' and there was a hammering, a high-pitched battering. A woman called, 'She's going.' The hammering noise again.

Two men ran, coats flying, past him, throwing their weight against the door. Shouts. He could hear them calling in there, even through the door: the metal kept nothing from him, kept him no more locked out than he had kept himself.

Then it was quiet.

He rubbed his hands against his trousers, trying to wipe off the sticky residue of sweat; he stood, walked three steps across the corridor, and three steps back; he picked off a leaf from the drooping pot plant at the end of the corridor; he stood in front of the faded print of a bowl of fruit, hanging lopsidedly on the wall, and breathed out so loudly that the plant's faded leaves fluttered; he sat down again, rocked forward and back. Still no one came.

He waited and kept waiting.

Footsteps beside him; polished black shoes, a soft squeak.

'Mr Dobell. I've just heard. I came to see how she is, and how you are.' It was him, from the asylum, Dr Dwyer. 'Would you rather sit?'

Joe stood, hands squeezed into fists.

'Your wife – I'm sorry. I believed that she would find her way. I suggested that I should perhaps speak with you, rather than one of the operating doctors. They're working very hard.' The doctor stepped towards Joe, and Joe backed away, as though from a burning bush. Dr Dwyer tried again. 'Would you like to sit? Or to walk?'

Joe stayed standing, made his back as tall as a piano. 'I don't want to hear from you, over there with your treatment that didn't work, that just made her unhappier, further away.'

'Yes, I understand.'

'With your machines and your tying her down and – making everything worse.'

Dr Dwyer kept his palms out, as though calming a dog, kept his eyes on Joe's. 'Mr Dobell. They may not be able to – they've said they may not be able to save her. They're working hard, and I believe she has a will, that she will fight. I do believe that.'

'I— Everything made it worse. She was – before— I didn't expect it, for her to disappear like that, after the baby. I haven't been a good husband, not really.'

'I'll sit with you, if you like. Or stand with you.'

Joe rubbed his face in his hands. 'No. Please. Just go. Go.'

The doctor lowered his head and padded softly down the corridor.

It was the thin doctor who creaked up later, much later. Grey hairs were slicked across the man's head, his hands were folded in front of his crotch, and he paused between steps. One foot, wait, next foot, wait. He creaked with careful sympathy. 'Mr Dobell.

We've tried hard. Very hard. We haven't — it appears we haven't been able to save her.'

Joe held on the chair, his fingers red against the plastic.

The doctor backed away.

There was no noise from behind the door, and Joe swayed up the corridor towards it, kept moving past it, stumbling from one wall to the other. He left no marks, but when he thrust his face into the air, outside, he lifted his fist. First one and then the other. He stood outside the hospital entrance, right in front of the red RECEPTION HERE sign, shaking his fists at the sky, calling out mad words, mad words.

There was a book of redheads on the ground, right at his feet. He picked them up, flicked at one and let it burn until there was black on his thumb. Not a flicker on his face. Burnt another until it blistered his palm, then pulled his money-holder from his pocket; his carefully folded teacher's certificate. No more words were falling from his mouth, but there was a high-pitched rattle, a hiccup, raw with grief. He balled the certificate into a pyramid, a pyre, then pulled at his cotton shirt, tearing at it, wrenching at the damned cufflinks. Two matches began to flame the shirt, red, then orange, a blue tip emerging near the collar. He wrapped the flaming shirt round the paper and kept it in his hand until the skin blistered.

~

It seemed sudden, unexpected, but surely it had always been true, that she could hear the dirt sing. Each grain, minute, delicate, was poised in an act of worship. The leaves, too. The scrubby sticks of grass, the spikes, the red paw of a flower bursting from a rock: a swelling, soaring, deafening chorus.

Then, quiet. She could hear the ants whispering a name for her.

There was the sky, the quiet; she was flying, that was the truth of it. Not with strength, because she knew she had none, but with the will of the air. Below her, though, the trees stopped singing, the ants stopped speaking. For a moment, darkness. Behind her, shouting, someone calling her, trying, calling with a different name. Heat fusing against her. Sound speeding past, whipping against her face, her ears. Water tumbling. A sudden propulsion, and the air popped. Everything changed: someone was running. There was light.

Wood smoothed behind her. Below, a window. Corner: she knew that word, could recall it. She was in a corner, high, quiet.

There was a woman. A bed. Around her, heads, peering down. One of the heads pushed itself close to the woman's. Breathed into her mouth.

They appeared to be anxious.

She could see that it was a room, with a rather unfortunate paint scheme. Grey was not good for walls or floors. People should realise that. White coats. She knew that this meant something, that she should perhaps understand it. The window in the room needed washing. It was irksome that no one noticed the worrymarks on the glass.

A man had a metal pad, booklike; he pushed it to the woman's chest, shouting over his shoulder. There was a thumping noise, the sound of someone being punched. He pushed the metal pad against her chest again. The woman on the bed jolted, then lay flat again.

Something happened in the room: they looked at each other, all of them, too quietly, too carefully.

Not the woman, she didn't look anywhere, at anyone.

She could see more, too. Outside the room, a street; four buses. A rag-and-bone cart. Six cars. And still, the ravine, the ants, the smoke, the singing. Amazing, the way she could count instantly, see everything, even him – Joe.

Joe. And the baby. And the baby.

She was tugged then, pulled from her centre. There was a cord there, and it pulled at her skin so sharply that shreds of flesh tore off. She could see them, the small filaments of skin and muscle, floating behind her as she whistled towards the smell of – flesh. Burning skin. The singing stopped, dragged to an ugly silence.

He was burning something – himself. Burning himself. Damned fool.

She remembered, then, remembered everything, all at once. Everything was laid out before her: the pink slipperiness of her own skin at birth, slapping against her mother; snow angels; the taste of dirty river water; throwing stones at a prep school boy; a white veil; Joe's first kiss, and his last; that long night, waiting for Joe to return home; the long grey face of her father, filling the church with his regret; and Joe, again, waiting for her with that smile slicing his face right in half.

And the ship, that was there, too. The infirmary: a blood-streaked cloth near her hand, the muck of birth surrounding her. She asks again for Joe, and finally the nurse says they've found him, passed out in a stairwell. There he is, later, red with shame, kneeling beside the bunk, pressing his head against hers.

And yet it all seemed to matter so little: the hula dance, the nameless woman in Hinksey, the cold, hard birth alone, the endless small disappointments. It was all there, laid out before her like a map, each territory marked out in green and blue. Troughs and peaks were marked with odd lines, shifts that meant more on the ground than from the air, and the lines were drawn in circles. Round and round they went, through blue territory, white territory, up, over and round, passing the same point again. The map spread out, covered her eyelids, her tongue, her underskin; and she could see it all, at once, drawn and marked, all the places she had been. But it didn't show her where she was, or how she would get home.

~

W hy are you here?

  I need you to see something, but that's not why you've come.

You see, there's nothing to be frightened of, nothing at all. Except, perhaps, of what you can do.

Oh, you'll see, you'll see.

Come here, now, and look at me like Lady Pig, all propped up with pillows – four, if you don't mind – and a tray beside me: chicken-pot pie, calf's foot jelly and my teapot. That milk jug was so fine that I could see my fingers through it; I thought it would break with my great bridle fingers. Do you see the bell? One tinkle, and a nurse would come running! Outside, on the lawn of the Metropole, my caravan stood as a lonely sentry; a coracle for all the minor mementos and Ariel's scent. It was on his child, though: if you could breathe him in, you'd know it. Yeast and cinnamon and – something else, something Ariel left behind: the scent of the eucalypt.

It was Dibbsey, of course, putting me up there, calling in every day with parcels of cocoa or jam, when what I really wanted was beer. Cabbage leaves steamed on my bosoms for the first weeks; what with the nurse dabbing cool water on my forehead I felt like a potted plant. That was Dibbsey's gift, too – the nurse, not the cabbage leaves. The Metropole kindly supplied them, from the kitchen, ma'am, at the nurse's request. It's funny that I have no memory of her name, now, when you consider how intimate she was with some of my body parts.

This little creature hung on to that one part of me as though his life depended on it. Which, come to think of it, it did. Felt nothing for him, then, not a thing but pain. Each crevice ached like the desert, and every time he raised that gummy mouth to howl for more of what was coming from my bosoms, I got struck by a flash of pure pain. More than the tearing of my posterior and interior, and more than the compounded milk. That scent on him, that nutmeg-coloured skin, the narrow black eyes: you'd think it would make me fall into him, fall into adoration, the way he seemed like a potted Ariel. More than just a *potted* Ariel. Truth was, it frightened me. He stared at me, little black holes squinting up, watching me, while milk trickled down from the side of his lips, guzzled into the folds of skin on his neck. It has to be said that, even for a baby, his manners were appalling. Light reflected back from his eyes, and sometimes I could see a smile there, could see the shadow of someone dancing. Folding and rasping and dancing. Staring up at me, he would be, demanding to know where the nurse had come from, the cocoa, the amethyst brooch pinned to the shawl. Even the shawl, for that matter, who had paid for it? I could see him in there adding it all up on his fat little fingers and red little toes, and waiting for Dibbsey to poke his head into the room. Not that he criticised, or was angry. Just – lonely.

I couldn't speak to Dibbsey. Not with him in there, listening. Couldn't bear the thought of hurting him, having him left out in the cold.

Lottie paid a visit: just one. She didn't like him watching her, either. She brought me a posy of asters and pink roses, tied with yellow string. There was a box of Anderson's Caramel Creams, as well.

Lottie barely looked at the baby when she came in, although the nurse was holding him when she opened the door. Though she may have been distracted by Nurse gasping, 'Oh, Miss Lyell,' and looking, terrifyingly, like she was going to faint all over the rose-covered rug.

'Jess, my God, you poor, poor girl.' Lottie handed the posy to the nurse, who seemed to think that they were for her, and buried her nose in them immediately. Lottie plonked the caramels on the tray and stuck her perky little *derrière* on my bed.

I waited for her to notice him.

She looked everywhere, but at him: at the dark tapestry on the wall, the brown picture rails, the willow-patterned washing jug on the edge of the marble dresser, the bed with its white canopy. Finally, me. '*Girl from the Bush* must have done well, by the look of all this. You must be pleased. He must have paid you well.'

I could see the nurse, patting him on the back. She looked at the clock wedged against the wall and gathered her carpet bag with one hand.

I nodded, but pressed a finger against my lips. I didn't want him to hear. Lottie raised her eyebrows and mouthed, 'The nurse?', so I shook my head, whispered, 'I don't want to hurt his feelings.'

'Oh, darling, I'm not sure he has any feelings. He does — I think he does rather like to have a medal or two, do you know what I mean? In the shape of a girl.'

The round chime of the clock rang out, three times, for the hour. The nurse hooked her bag over her arm and pushed the baby down into my arms. He leered up at me and immediately began rooting for my bosoms, the rascally pig. Cradle cap, milky yellow and crusty, was forming at the front of his head. I picked at the flaky skin with my nail and flicked the scabs on to the floor. Lottie looked away, pinching her little lips together. Nurse whooshed out the door without a word, which had become something of a habit.

Lottie took a caramel and held out the box to me: 'That Roger Wilts from The *Bulletin* was quite in love with you, I think, after *Mary*. Dibbs must be pleased, too. Well, both of you.'

I shook my head at her, hard as I could without him noticing.

'She's gone, dear,' Lottie whispered, a giggle mixed in.

'No. He's listening.'

Her giggle dribbled away. She stopped chewing her caramel.

'Ariel. I don't want him to feel as if – I don't want him to worry. To feel usurped.' I said it as quietly as I could, but he gave me a terribly fierce suck, and I jumped. Hit my head on the walnut headboard. 'See? He's very sensitive to it.'

Lottie left before the clock struck quarter past.

Let me make it plain here.

There was nothing of the acrobatic nature running between me and Dibbsey. Spare me: I was dribbling milk, my skin was patched red, and I smelt of cabbage. It was more – what would the word be? – the companionship. It was warming, to have cut flowers delivered on alternate days and notes slipped under the door: *You're wonderful! (PS We've made new reels of* Mary the Outlaw *– it's being distributed in England! And America!) (PPS Filming starts in nine days.)* Six weeks after he was born – I'm not having a lend, six weeks – we started filming *The Lady Is the Outlaw*, with me running back to him every hour to stick my breast in his mouth.

That was when I first loved him.

Milk squirted through my brown serge button-down, escaping through the bandages wrapped tightly against my bosoms, pressing them as flat as a boy's chest. His little thumbnail eyes curved into dark moons, and he lay tucked in a wooden drawer, at the side of the studio, watching everything.

There was nothing like him, never had been: his face smooth as a shoe, his black hair lying in one flat yell across his scalp. On the second day of filming, I heard his little caterwaul cry and Dibbsey stopped the camera. I ran over to him, plucked him from the drawer, saying, 'Okay, little hungry beast, milk time,' and his whole mouth curved open; his hand, bunched into a reddish-pink posy, stretched up towards my face. His mouth opened further, showing off his new pink gums: oh, he was pleased with them.

I couldn't bear to look away from him, after that. Couldn't tear myself from him. Kept touching his cheek, the roundness of it, I found any excuse to hold him close: a tickle, a snuffle. Oh, I immersed myself in him, as though he were air. Woke in the middle of the night, lit the lamp so that I could watch his upper lip flutter out with each breath. I needed a name for him; a name for victory. Victor: yes.

Somehow, for him, I could imagine overcoming everything, anything. I could imagine never giving up, never letting go. You can imagine it, too, if you'll let yourself.

I took Dibbsey up to Nelly's Glen, to show him what green was, what grey was, what space was: he stood in the middle of a stretch of flat rock and listened. I thought I could love him, or at least tolerate him, then. When you listen in the bush, to the calling back and forth, it's like a series of sobs, sad little stories being passed round. Anyway, when Dibbsey showed me he could stand all quiet and listen to it, well, I thought he would do. I had the baby strapped to me, all swaddled up in layers of muslin and grey blanket, the way Billy had shown me. Milky spurts were dribbling out all down the muslin, and Dibbsey came and stood right next to me. I loosened the muslin and held the baby, stood there rocking, listening to the sobs of the bush, and wondering if it would be all right, perhaps, to have some company, to think about it.

Dibbsey put his hand on my arm, and said, 'What do you think, Jess? What about it?'

The baby looked up at me then, and a gurgle, a shriek, tickled out. A laugh, his first laugh. I thought it was a sign; I thought he was letting me know. Yes. I thought yes was the right answer.

Later I realised that it might have been a hiccup, or a sob, or a shout, or — well, that's the difficulty with babies, isn't it? You can never quite tell what it is they're saying.

~

The tin on the roof was rusting, just a little, and just at the tip. Somehow that warmed me to it, made me feel like I could call it home. Four shillings a week. The docks of Balmain were at the bottom of the hill and the thrive of them, the noise of it all, thrilled me, made me feel as if I was on a journey, when I was just sitting at the little oak leaf-table. I'd never had a table before. I sat at it each morning, watching my baby catch the winter sun in his hands, squinting at me through his black moon eyes. Chairs, too: I bought them myself, from the man who left the cottage the day we arrived, dragging his furniture out on to an open cart. He charged me twopence for that miner's couch; he couldn't fit it on the trap. Ariel left, the day we moved my blue trunk in there. I didn't notice him go; when I picked the baby up that night, unwound him from his thick wall of clothes, he looked up at me, parting his lips, and he was just Baby. There was no one else there, and I laid him down on the yellow cowskin that Dibbs had thrown on the kitchen stones, and I put myself beside him and I looked right into his little black moons, trying to find Ariel again. He hadn't even said goodbye. The baby put his hand out, on to my face, his waddle-thick fingers kneading and poking, and I wished, just one more time, that it was Ariel, touching me.

Each morning, I paced from wall to wall, feeling the absence of earth, or rocking, beneath my feet. There was a kerosene stove to cook on; a fire in the middle of the sitting room. Sitting room! I could sit there, at the table, or on Dibb's green wing chair, and then put my feet down on the cool, still stone, and walk – eight steps – into the sleeping room. Yes, if you're wondering, there was one bed in there, one bed only. Perhaps that was why Ariel left. Dibbsey bought the lace quilt. Turkish, apparently, or Egyptian or somesuch thing. It was a gift, when *Girl from the Bush* opened, and it made a whole lot more sense on that big, solid bed than it did thrown across my crippled swag.

About the bed. Dibbs was— It wasn't what I was used to, with Ariel. No quiet whispered moments, no falling into each other. There were words, yes, of course there were. Things he liked to say, or liked to hear. The expectation – he was always keen on that. For all the flame that had lit up on Dibbsey's face when he saw me flip myself around on the back of Prince Vic and Lordship, when it came down to it, right there on top of the Turkish quilt, he lacked spark. Perhaps I did, too. Perhaps my spark had dimmed out there on Nullo Mountain.

Truth was, I was unsettled by the lack of movement. A caravan, even when it isn't hitched up to a workhorse, has a sway to it. When the wind blows, you can feel it, feel yourself to be part of it. Oh, I was as happy as a mudcrab when the rain was tipping down in diagonal lines and there was a fire in that white grate, and the baby was asleep in the middle of the high bed, with his arms spread out like a tree-branch, and everything, everything, smelt of warmth. Sometimes, though, I'd hear just the wind outside, and I'd get up and press my face against the window sash, and I'd feel terribly – locked out. As though the world was outside, and I couldn't get to it. I suppose that's the point; I suppose a house is meant to keep the world out. But I found myself missing the world sometimes, that's all.

Dibbsey stepped over the baby, usually, or around him. Sometimes, I tucked him up in my arms and offered him to Dibbs, hoping that for one instant he would notice, that he would know what to do with the fatness of my son. He tolerated him, don't misunderstand. There was no trouble, not in that way, and not then. Just – I longed for him, Dibbs, to see the glorious vanilla of that skin, to find himself unable to resist gathering the cottonsmooth flesh, gobbling the thick neck. I longed for him to know that the only thing to do with a baby is to fall in love with him.

I know, it's not always that simple.

Once, when the crawling was just beginning, the baby inched himself over to Dibbs, and pulled himself to standing. He puckered his lips and tried to blow Mr A. B. Dibbs a kiss.

'He looks like a Chink.' It was just a joke. Meant fondly. That's what he said. Anyway, what was I to do? I was in so deep, already.

There was rain the day he trod mud all over the cowskin, almost trod on the baby, and plonked himself in the wing chair, all sullen, silent. Sat and stared at the fire while I watched a bead of water tracing its way down the window, trickling in, across my palm and back out to the ledge. The baby watched, too, his gurgles mingling with the hiss of coal, and filling up the silence in the room. He gurgled like a billabong, then, gabbling versions of words, pointing, pushing himself up on his arms and legs and tumbling about the floor. So I let His Dibbs sit it out; waited for him to open his mouth and say what the mud, and the plonking, and the sitting there hissing like the coal was all about.

Finally: 'They're pulling out. Did you know it?'

I kept watching the waterbead: I had no idea who, or what, he was talking about. So how could I know it?

'Spencer's. They've got chicken spines, got the scares, somehow, and they don't want to be giving away any more precious pounds to moving-picture folk.'

I couldn't see it, couldn't see where he was leading me, so I collected the baby up, and snuffled him, snuffled his ear while he shrieked.

'Put him down, for God's sakes, for once. Just listen. It matters.'

I put him down.

'We made them a fortune, a ruddy fortune, selling into England, America, Canada. Now they're thanking us and – I don't know. I don't know what's put the scare up them. Something has. That bloody ban on showing Ned Kelly pictures in Vicbloodytoria hasn't helped. All frightened of the Irish frigging uprising, thinking we're gunna start one of our own.'

'I don't understand why – what it is that we need to be worried about.' Look, I wanted to say: a rug, a chair, a table made of oak. We have solid things here. Signs of life. Everything is here, except Ariel.

'We don't have—— All I want to do is make moving pictures. Bushranger films, no one makes them in England, in America – just us.' His moustache was turning the colour of pale rust, the effect of pipe-smoking, though you could hardly say he did it to excess. Blood traced the edges of his eyes, and it was harder to say what led to that. 'I can't do anything else. And the signs aren't good – I'm telling you, Jess.'

'Get another investor. Cozens?'

'He's put it all in an epic with that bloody Longford.'

'Then, the Hudson people?'

He was sliding down in the chair, peeling away from the air. Outside, the caravan creaked, rocking in the rain. The baby was beginning a high-pitched moan, a tenor underneath the swishing of the wind. I gathered him up and laid him down in the centre of the bed, right on the deep red cross in the middle of the quilt.

*

What I had found – and this bothered me greatly – was that I imagined Ariel. When Dibbs took me to that bed, when he patted his hands on the purple lace, and stroked me, I closed my eyes, and it was Ariel I felt beside me. His breath I swallowed, the eucalyptus of his scent. Sometimes it took real effort, removing the rough edge of Dibbs, imagining Ariel taking such lack of care, thinking of him in such hurried, rubbing form.

Once, Dibbsey whispered, 'Open your eyes and look at me,' and I did, I looked for a moment. But the sight of his yellow moustache, the pale sandy hairs drooping over his lip – oh, and his pale, freckled skin – well, it put me off my stride, if you will. Took the pleasure out of me with one breath.

Even early on, very early on, it was Ariel I saw, felt, touching me. From the first day, out there in Nelly's Glen, I made Dibbsey's fat, fusty fingers into Ariel's delicate, danceable ones. To be clear: it was Ariel from the early days I thought of, when we would both be all sweat-glistened from the sheer force of us. Not him later, when he so often wept, 'I am an old man, how can you love me?' and I would put my finger on the crease in his cheek and whisper, 'We are children together, and old bones together; and I am an old woman, you mad fool.' I have felt everything in me leap, sitting by that window, remembering the salty taste of Ariel's mouth, the cool pressure of him. Once, only once, I've thought of Dibbsey like that. In those mid-months of carrying the baby, when the sickness had stopped and I wasn't yet swollen. Oh, then, goodness, I couldn't ride on a pony trap without feeling flushed, red-cheeked. Ready to swoon sometimes, I'd be, after climbing off the bony back of Lordship. Well, then, I remember looking at Dibbsey's moustache

— the very one that now makes me hold my breath, holding in queasiness — and I thought of it tickling me, over the watery warmth of kisses, and I was more than a little warm myself, let me tell you.

The baby flung his arms out, and I watched his eyes droop.

From the sitting room, Dibbs cleared his throat and called, 'Are you coming out, Jess? I've got some thoughts.' A rattled note in there.

Victor's black lashes fluttered and he looked up at me, the lantern reflecting against his eyes. I knelt down beside him on the bed, patted his tummy, the way he liked.

'Jess? Let the baby be. He's had you all day, God knows. Leave him.'

I kissed the black hair of the baby and let the door squeak behind me. Stood by the wall, stretching my back out. 'What?' Already, I was running out of things to say to him, realising that he wasn't Ariel, not at all, and that maybe what I'd heard up there in Nelly's Glen was the sound of my own loneliness.

'There's no money.'

I put my hand against the wall and felt the solid marks in the pressed tin. 'There's money, of course there is: everything from *Girl from the Bush*. We sold it everywhere. And—'

'It's all gone into *Outlaw*. Everything. And now, with Dampier pulling out — it won't get made. Not without more money.' A puff of breath came out of him, making him thin, flattening him as though he were bellows.

A smudge of rain crept under the window; I could see it, trailing down the wall, towards the cowskin.

'It could be – I thought it would be our greatest. Really. We'll—
Well, I don't know, I don't know what there is, if this doesn't work.
We're mid-way.' He looked up at me, pale blue eyes thinning. 'You
could have taken the film with Lyell. One thousand pounds. One
thousand bloody pounds.'

'I couldn't, Dibbs. You said at the time, you said you understood
why – surely it's clear. Look at my son.'

'Rather not.'

I could see the line, then, of pale mould, tracing its way down the
wall, all the way to the floor. Looking at the flickerings of grey, I
felt a twist, a sickness, starting up in me again. The way it was when
I was carrying, but this time, I was full only of absence. I was sick
with something missing, something gone. Homesick, you might
call it, but with no idea of where home might be. You see, you're
not the first.

~

Joe stood beside the ashed remnant of his shirt. She could see him, she could see everything: the whole world, the inside of colours, the shape of silence. She could see the way he looked hollowed-out, his shirtless skin creasing limply round his waist.

He folded, slowly, a house of cards, tumbling. Arms first, then legs, buckling beneath him; back folding as sharp as a paperclip, as sudden as a punch.

That was where he was when they came out to him: the two nurses, both brown-haired, pink-lipsticked. Each had hair tied back identically, a neat French twist at the nape of the neck, beneath the winged cap. Angels, they looked like, or a child's idea of angels. Those hats, with their crisp peaks on either side of the head, folded, ready for flight. They stood slightly behind Joe, each with a hand on his shoulder – one left, one right – as though ready to lift him, pull him up. Perhaps they were, perhaps that was what they had in mind: they looked strong enough, in spite of the pink lipstick. One was thick-waisted, legs as solid as a man's. Even the smaller one, all delicate wrists and light freckles, had the mark of pure muscle beneath her green uniform. Joe looked up at them, his face red and raw, confused. An old drunk, that was what he seemed like, down there, his mouth gaping, his eyes flicking everywhere, trying to find some light.

The freckled nurse leant down, got down on her knees beside him, close, terribly close. She spoke: her mouth moved. The bigger nurse – the thick-waisted muscle-girl – stayed standing, a sentry. Joe looked from one to the other. Yes, he nodded, yes. He let himself be pulled to standing, then scrabbled on the ground, trying to pat away the ash of his shirt. Each of the nurses appeared kindly, patient; they held him up, folded the shirt neatly, as if it were something that still mattered. Supporting him by the elbows, they led him into the hospital ward.

Inside, life creaked into sound: his footsteps, knocking on the hard floor, a dirgish underbeat to the soft-soled shuffle of the nurses; the sucking sound of the metal doors; muffled scuffles of more soft-soled footsteps; *beep-beep-beep*; words humming; *beep-beep-beep*; a tin tray being dropped, echoing, further down the hall; the scrape of a metal chair leg as he sat down; howling, someone howling, owww, he was saying, like a dog, a wolf, oowwww. There was no needle in his paw, but there he was, doubled over, rocking back and up, his arms creased across his body. The doors opened, the thin doctor rushed out; mask round his neck, buttoned coat. He moved so quickly that it seemed like a glide.

'Mr Dobell. Good, good. Did you tell him?'

The freckled nurse, still standing beside Joe, nodded. Said, 'He didn't take much in, though. He was in a state. Weren't you, love?' Bending down to Joe, raising her voice, as though he were an old lady, or someone in a wheelchair.

Joe held out his hands to the doctor, palm up. Help me, the hands said. The doctor sat without asking and sighed with the creaking chair. 'Mr Dobell.' He sighed again. 'She's – it's a kind of – we don't know what will happen, you understand. It is good news, but – her heart stopped – well, longer than I've known to be possible. Somehow – she's breathing. Her heart is beating.'

Joe wept, then.

The freckled nurse stood watching, her wing-tips quivering with concern.

'You shouldn't—' The doctor was too young, had no idea how to do this, how to go into this territory.

'Oh, thank you, Lord. Thank you.'

'She isnae really back.' The solid nurse frowned at him, though her voice, with its Scottish sweetness, was barely a whisper. 'She may not come back, hen, not properly.'

Joe whispered, too: 'But she was dead and now – I want her to come back. That's all. And then to – she shouldn't have done this. It's a sinful, terrible thing that she's done. That she's tried to do.'

The nurse folded her arms so that her smooth uniform creased in harsh lines across her chest. 'It's not our job to be priests, right enough.'

'Well, that's neither there nor here, really, as it turns out. She— It's unlikely that she'll come back. You can see her. Sit with her. She might hear you.' The doctor creaked in the orange plastic chair.

The nurse spat out a huff of air. 'She won't hear. But you can talk.'

Joe stood up. 'I need a shirt. I don't want her to see me like this.'

She was spread out on the bed, all white, smeared across the sheets like Savlon on a bandage. Her dark hair curled round her face, and there were tubes, tubes everywhere. Fingers bunched like daffodils on top of the sheets. Pale yellow tubes snaked out of her nose and two wires travelled the long distance from her temples to a tall machine by the window. Joe tripped on the metal hanger lurking by the bed; a bag of liquid hung on it, the colour of saliva. He patted at the tube connected to the hanger, patted at the bed, at the chair.

The freckled nurse padded close to him and reached up to pull the cloth curtain round the bed. She stopped, right by the chair, and whispered to him, as though it were a secret, 'You can speak to her, love.'

He waited until she had pulled the curtains round. Hands flexed on his knees, arms straight. Sitting up in class, that was what he looked like, except for the ash marks on his neck and the scrubbed red edges of his eyes, and the hospital white gown, worn instead of a shirt.

A grey moth fluttered on the upper ledge of the window. Circles, like eyes, on its wings.

A dark, stray hair coiled on the sheet. Joe picked it up, ran his fingers along the silk of it and stopped at the grey tip. He pulled the hair to his lips and his eyes closed. He curled it, then, round his finger, tight enough to leave a white mark and to turn the tip of the finger violent pink. It snapped when he pulled it tight.

He sat, with the half-thread of hair dangling from his finger, until the dark began to creep into the ward and the nurse pulled the curtains back and told him to go home, that the buses would be stopping soon.

He laughed, then, and said that home would take too, too long to get to and how would he know it when he saw it?

The nurse – it was the Scottish one – touched his shoulder and said, 'You'll know it when your eyes close, hen, and they don't open again.'

He stretched his hands out. Opened his mouth, then looked up at the moth. Its wings trembled.

~

It wasn't entirely unexpected, you could say.

There was a whole consignment of traps sent down to Traytor's Studio, all of them waving their bright shiny New South Wales Police Force badges, some of them with guns, too. Good Lord, what were they expecting? Ned Kelly himself to leap out from behind the camera? The whole of rebel Ireland to be hiding under a trolley? We hadn't even heard then, no one had. We didn't think it would be possible.

We kept filming, anyway, waiting for them to come for us, trying to speed it through. What was the use, though? We wouldn't be able to show it, sell it, do any damned thing with it.

They did come for us, of course. Six traps, each on horseback, most of them looking like crumbling cake in the saddle. Ha! If that's the best the New South Wales Constabulary can offer, I'm amazed that the Kellys didn't cross the border and take over the state of New South Wales. Told them so, too, which you can imagine won me a whole cartload of trap hearts. Not that they were rude, or even forceful. No guns were drawn.

Dibbsey was behind the camera when they arrived: filming shadows of trees, if you please. No doubt it made some sense in his tobacco-stained skull.

A podgy trap sitting at the front of their little cluster, called, 'Is this the production ground for the moving picture *The Lady Is the Outlaw?*' and Dibbsey called out, yes, it was and what was it to them?

Constable Podgy took out a rolled paper from his saddle-bag and cleared his throat: 'I am obliged to inform you that for the good of the country's morals, any creation or distribution of motion pictures showing or promoting bushrangers and their doings will result in immediate prosecution.'

Three of the traps slid off their horses and started pacing the paddock. Poor mangy-looking beasts they were, too – the traps, not the horses, ha! – poking themselves where they weren't wanted. Victor was crawling around, concentrating hard on putting pebbles into his mouth, and one particularly scrawny trap, with white flecks of flaking skin on his lapel, said, 'Who owns the yellow baby, then?'

His mate slapped him on the arm and croaked out, 'You're the half-girl, half-horse girl, aren't ya?'

Podgy Trap still hadn't got off his horse, and Dibbsey called up to him, 'What is it that we're supposed to do? Can't you just let us finish?'

'Won't be anywhere to show it, cobber. Screening of all such films is outlawed. You'll not find a town hall between here and the black stump that'll show your flaming moving picture. Is that Jess A?'

And that was that, really. All six of them sat around on their blue serge arses while we gathered ourselves up. Dibbsey and the Roys dragged the cameras, the trolleys and the tall light stands over to the side of the paddock, huffing and puffing as much as they bloody well could. Not one of those traps offered to help lift or cart a ruddy thing, though both Sergeant Podge and Constable Scrawn did ask me to sign my name on a handbill of *Girl from the Bush*, each of them creeping up all secret, looking over their shoulders. Oh, you stupid ruddy fools, I wanted to say, it's a *story*. I'm not really a flipping outlaw – but I didn't, it's true, cowardice got the better of me.

Dibbsey was more courageous, sort of: he pointed his megaphone at the camera and said, 'See that? It's a flaming camera.

We make it up, you do know that, do you? Pretend. We're no more outlaws than you are— Strewth, you reckon we can turn the whole of New South Wales into bushrangers?' and Billy, sitting on an upturned billy-can, called, 'I bloody wish, boss. Then we might see some more cash.' Sergeant Podge said that if he heard any more lip out of us he'd see us arrested straight away, and the best thing we could do for ourselves was to pack up and move on.

When they left, all the puff went out of Dibbsey; you'd think they'd taken all his stuffing out and trotted off with it on the back of their well-bred horses. He was as thin as that cowskin on the stone floor in our little house. It was one of the Roys and Eugene Rider, the tubby Scotsman who played half of the bit parts, who went off to borrow two carts and four Clydesdales from Mr Hudson, and brought them back to the paddock. No one spoke while we loaded the carts. Everything went on: the blue costume trunk; canvas chairs; tenting; four metal tripods; the trolleys and stands; the lights. By the time we'd piled those carts up high, the sky was wrapping its red and pink scarf around the place, and still no one spoke. Stuffing indeed: we were like a bunch of scarecrows, plucked and scattered across the field.

Billy was the first one to open his mouth: 'I'm gunna go back.'

'Back?' I was stuck: where was there to go back to?

'The circus?' The smallest Roy shifted himself, started packing paper into a brown saddle-bag.

'Nah, mate. Back up my mob, Awabakal. *Kia-kia* land up there. Had enough of this sort of carry-on. No offence to you, Jess.'

Back. Going back. I thought about that, and what it meant.

*

We rode back to Balmain that night in the surrey with Lordship at the front; Dibbsey held tight on the reins and his bottom lip was pressed against his teeth so hard that it was white. Victor was all tucked up in a blue blanket bouncing on my knee, waggling his fat brown fist at the passing sulkies, and at the thin slice of moon creeping above the gum trees. I watched him, this little fat moon, holding my breath.

I sat at the oak leaf-table until the sun started to creep into the sky.

Dibbsey drank seven bottles of beer and the last two tumblers of whisky, then threw the cowskin out on to the cobbled path, calling, 'Help yourself, go on, come and take me for all I'm worth, frigging—' and kept going, muttering *frigging flaming traps* while I carried him inside and pushed him on to the bed. I lifted the baby off the bed, and he flopped over my shoulder, as soft as beaten leather; he slept on the cowskin that I dragged inside, skin on skin.

~

*D*ear Mrs Dibbs.

Thanking you Kindly for your letter dated Aug. 15 1912 which I received through the effisient offices of Parkes Postal Service. I take no Offence to your inquiry. De Rabe's Circus suffers no ill effects from the Success or otherwise of the Moving Picture field though I do Thank you for your concern in this inst. It was perhaps Poor Management which had unfortunant effects on the business of the travling horse show & I think that people are not so Intrested in horses.

Very kind of you to offer your riding skills but we are not very Keen on horses & like our ladies to be Ladies no disrespect intended mrs Dibbs however it has been my Experiense that people of new south wales prefer a circus with cyclists which are more Modern & we have been very happy with Gladys in this inst. she sends her Best regds & also we have resently Purchased three ceylon elephants. I was intrested to see reports of your Moving Picture resently people are not so intrested in the irish in this part of new south wales this is simply the word of Experiense.

Yours Sincerely & Truly

Mr & Mrs G De Rabe.

Prop. De Rabe's Circus.

Look at it; go on, just look. Flaming hide. Look at the quality of that paper. As thick as a tooth, and twice as smooth. Words scratched in so deep I could run my fingers along the edges, close my eyes and feel the letters. Waste, pure waste. He wouldn't know how to run a show if Ariel drove over him with the ruddy instructions dangling from the cartwheel. Ha. Gladys sends best regards inbloodydeed, does she? Dibbsey had ten such letters, too; oh, yes, they just kept coming, along with the requests for payment, final demands, threats. Twenty-three workers: riders; scene actors; musicians;

camera operators; film cutters. Suddenly it seemed that no one had been paid; news travels fast and a good deal of panic was being spread in that particular corner of that particular part of the colony. Did I mention the rent?

So:

He sold everything to Mr Hudson, of Hudson's Moving Pictures Company, formerly of Hudson and Devine Stage Company. 'I'm just doing you a favour for I don't even know what reasons – God knows, the arse, tits and everything in between has fallen out of moving pictures now. Old Longford is back to romances, but the likes of you and me are gunna have to find some new way around.' They were Hudson's precise words, or so Dibbs informed me, coming back to the little house with a bottle of green ginger wine under his arm and a sore and sorry tale under his tongue. Swindled, he was: made barely enough to drown his sorrows. Though after the visit to Hudson, Dibbs seemed to spend a lot of time down at the bottom of that particular ocean. The way Dibbs told it, Hudson had looked at the trap-load of cameras and costumes and said, 'Don't know what the hell I'll do with it all.'

What he did was ship the lot to America: he joined up with a young Mr Nestor in that new Hollywoodland, and made seventeen outlaw films. Ha! Could have been me, playing old dastardly custard. They forgot to ban those ruddy outlaw films over there, in America, where they were less worried about the flaming Irish.

Last anyone heard of Hudson, he was found in a swimming-pool full of pale sherry and naked young men. So, I suppose you could say he was drowning in success. In a manner of speaking.

*

My darling red caravan rocked in the square patch of garden, like an accusation.

Across the road and down a neat little side-path, there was a public house: the Gentleman's Arms. Dibbsey got keener and keener to take that path, to wander out looking for *contacts*. Oh, yes, if contacts is what you call the sucker who stands you for green wine and beer all night, then that was exactly what he was up to. Both of us ignoring the pile of notes slid under the door; big red marks cutting across them. Lordship was pastured on a strip of common green between our street and the Gentleman's Arms and me and Victor would take a little stroll each morning, with a bag of oats. Oh, my boy: I tried to breathe him in, watching him so hungrily. Listening to the sounds of him swallowing, the mad concentration on him when he ate. Each moment was a moment of loss with him: I tried to store it up, to keep him as he was, but as soon as I blinked, he'd changed, gone. Watching him trace a finger over the Turkish quilt, I held my breath, could forget – almost, or could convince myself that I had forgotten – the empty paddock, the lurking shadows of no work.

We were at the green when they came.

Dibbsey stumbled out of the drinking house, calling in some old voice, 'Jess Dibbs, you're my great big love.' Great lump of ginger, as though half-cocked words could win anything from me, as though I'd not had better words, and more of them, from a better man. He sludged his arm over me, so that his tobacco hand flapped in the baby's face and I stepped away, but politely. None of the hitting had started then, none of that, but any fool knows what too much of the green and the ale can do. He wanted to sing, and I tried to hum along: *Jess is a fine old dame*. Mid-chorus, and him in full voice, when we rounded the corner and saw them. Even the Turkish quilt had been dragged outside, draped over the leaf-table. Two men and a woman who looked like a worn whip were counting them all out. Dibbsey dropped his voice, and I patted the baby soft on the back, keeping him as quiet as a thirsty creek. I saw it then: the door of the caravan had been pulled from the rusted metal hinges, and the windows blocked with board. A bearded man with arms the size of redgum trunks was hitched in the middle of the wooden struts; he was grunting like a baby, tugging it away. I saw Ariel's face in the window: his mouth made the shape of dead, dry grass.

'Come on.' I tugged at Dibbsey's caterpillar-soft arm, yanked him back to the green. We unhitched Lordship and kept moving, just kept moving, until our feet were weeping and my face was dry.

~

Look at us, there in that lean-to, lined with potato sacks. Dust settled in my nose, not going anywhere, and the rough, salty smell of hessian sifted through everything. Each log was split from a whitegum, and I could slip my hand behind the hessian and run it along the silky grain of wood; each stroke like a kiss. Against one wall, a miner's couch, all littered with green-ginger wine bottles and scraps of chewing tobacco; oh, yes, make no mistake, we were living the high life, all right. Nothing like that bed all draped with a knotted quilt; we squeezed on to the couch, breathing in to make room, and Victor slept in a berry basket. Slept – ha! Wrong word: what he did was wriggle and slap his hands around, and climb out of the basket, and try to pull bottles from the narrow ledge; and then he cried, the high sound of a black cockatoo. Shriek, shriek. Once he started walking – waddling around on those thick, fat-rippled legs – he wouldn't touch any milk from my breast. I tried to stick my fingers in his mouth, to hush him, to shush him, but he spat them back, pulled another bottle from the ledge. He wasn't happy, that was clear. Poor mite. Cried and whimpered through the night, while Dibbsey beetled in my ear, 'Shut him up, can't you?'

Inside the house there were shadows flitting across the windows; they fluttered like moths. Nora and Reggie: Dibbsey once gave Reggie a job setting up the folding projection screen, with the Morka Brothers' Travelling Cinema, and Reggie made all sorts of promises about seeing Dibbsey proud, and if he was ever in trouble, oh, yes, he'd see him right, all right. The lion and the mouse, that sort of carry-on. But look how it turned out: poor old Nora didn't know what to make of herself, opening the door to a tobacco-stained man, a screeching child, and me. God, what to make of me?

Six months back, I had berry-sweet lips and a bob as smooth as that whitegum and I slept beneath a hand-quilted Ottoman rug. Now, look, who would recognise me? And up there in the mountains, it was so cold that my skin started to chafe, and the tip of my nose stayed red.

Reggie's sister was paying a visit the day we arrived: she'd come in a posh old trap, with a handsome young driver sitting out there all dozydoolally, and I thought I'd found my luck when I saw it. One of her eyes looked sideways while one looked forward, and her lips seemed barely to move when she spoke. She was in service she said, to Lord Someone-or-other. Dibbs and I stood politely, me with my bub all tucked up while she kissed Reggie on the cheek and shook Nora's hand. She peekabooed the baby, then climbed up to the handsome trap-driver, and waved herself off. Oh, I could be there again, riding around. It was a new town, Kandos, run by some rich old blokes who opened a factory making cement. Reggie walked down every morning and worked in the factory, came back covered with white dust. There was a big banner, as you came into the town: *The future is in cement.*

You couldn't say Nora wasn't kind. And that's the thing: you can always find them, people willing to hold a hand out, to turn a shining face to you. You will find that, if you listen.

On one of the early days, my little one was howling, all red-cheeked and furious, and Nora called from the house, 'Bring him in here to me, love.'

I pretended I hadn't heard: the thought of taking myself in there, into the house, reeking of shame, as a beggar – it took the breath out of me and left the sour taste of rotten beer behind.

She called again, though, and came outside. White sunstripes cut into her, so that she looked like a shadow, a luminous shadow, standing with the paperbark peeling behind her. 'Jess? It sounds like he's got teeth, that's all. Bring him to me, bring him over.'

I did take him to her, then, because I could see that the red mark on his cheek was spreading, a purple fruit bruising one side of his face. Nora had a piece of towelling cloth in her hand, all wet and wrapped tight; when Mr Howlbaby opened his mouth for another shriek, she slipped the cloth in and he clamped down on it, startled. 'Oh, Mister Boy.' She lifted him right up, and his mouth slitted into a line, with the towelling dangling out of it like a pipe, and he made me think of those old Chinese men in the markets, trying to sell magic powders. Nora's hand dived a kingfisher dive into the round pocket in her apron, then swooped up again. A stick of stale damper: the baby clawed at it, and whacked it in his mouth so fast that the cloth plopped out into the dirt. Nora touched her hand to his cheek, said, 'Oh, he's just lovely, just lovely,' and the baby waved his stick of damper as though it were a flag.

'My little one died. She was three. Talking, God, she could babble the crown off a daffodil. Scrumptious, she said once. Rice pudding. That's what she was eating. Yellow custard on top. Scrumptious. Can you imagine? Im-possible. That was another one.'

'He won't be talking for a while yet.' I didn't know what else to offer her.

'It was no one's fault.'

'No.'

We stood in the sun, watching the shadows ripple around my little boy, and her little girl's absence.

*

All afternoon, Dibbs poured gin down his throat.

How did I not notice this before, his tendency to throw himself into the bottom of a bottle?

Missing one thing can make you look awful hard for another thing, anything, to take its place.

At night, putting the baby down in the flat basket Nora had given me to use for a bed, I said, 'What about a job at the factory, Dibbs? With Reggie? It can't be all bad. Exciting, even, being part of the future like that.'

Dibbs snorted. 'They've threatened to lay Reggie right off, just for taking his ruddy hip-flask in with him. In this bloody cold – who wouldn't need it? A bit of warm comfort through the day?'

'Why not go and see Raymond? Or – someone. You can work running the camera, or making the lights—'

'Oh, for God's sakes – you stupid, stupid – I am worth ten of Raymond frigging Longford, right?'

'You are, you are, Dibbs.' Because I knew, in that second, that he was right, somehow, that I must have been stupid, a stupid flit of a girl, to be there, to be forgotten, to not understand how I got there.

'What I do is make moving pictures about bushrangers. Outlaws. That is what I do.'

'I know you do. That's what you do.'

'And you – for God's sake – do you think you could be an actress without a horse?'

'No – I'm not—'

'That's right you're not. Damned right you're not. You're just a horsegirl. There's no bloody – you can't make a moving picture with a horsegirl.'

The baby started swatting at the air, then, whimpering, scratching at his face, the way he did sometimes. His face was pale with the cold of the mountain air, fuzzing straight in through the logs.

Dibbs got louder: 'You just don't – you don't listen. If you listened—'

'I know,' I whispered, creeping round him, hushing my own fear. 'I know, it's true. Please, let's just – sssh – let's— Here, have some beer, Dibbs.'

He drank then, and for a moment it was quiet, and I thought I'd won. Then he reared up, all dingo-ish and rabid. 'If you had kept your bloody mouth shut—'

'I didn't say a word. I didn't make the banning happen.'

'Shut up. Shut yourself up.'

The baby started up, a scrawly call, the way he did when he was newborn. It stabbed at the lean-to and kept stabbing until I was shredded.

Dibbsey put his face so close to mine that I could see the dark spots inside his nose. 'Shut that child up, you hear me? Shut it up.'

And I tried; I tried to shut him up. When he finally whimpered off to sleep, I poured whisky down my own throat, as if that was going to help anyone.

Dibbs was drunk again. 'Bloody thing. Bloody Chinky kid.' He perked up at that little bit of rhythm. Repeated it as a beat while he danced around the yellowing miner's couch. 'Bloody Chinky kid-ha-ha; bloody-Chinky-kid.'

I stayed scrunckled back on the couch, the torn leather pinching at my bare legs. A burst of courage: 'Come to think of it, you're right. Don't go to Longford, or Spencer, or any of them. They wouldn't want you, not a drunk like you.' The whisky had gone to my head, too — who was to say I wasn't a bloody drunk myself? When was the last day without a soothing smooth from the green bottle? I reached for it again, tottling there on a milk crate beside me.

'Bugger off.' He stopped his dance and slapped my hand away. 'Call me a bloody drunk. Look at the face on you, God, yar like a friggen cow-dog. And I'll tell you this, cow-dog, I've got plans, plenty of friggen plans. I've got it organised. I'm gunna sail over there, and make outlaw moving pictures in that bloody America, and when I do, I tell you, it won't be with you.'

Curving his body upwards, he straightened himself: belly in, head straight on his shoulders.

'They'll get banned over there as well, you great lump. And you'll get spat right out.' Poison in my mouth and, damn me, I knew where it would lead. He started it, he did, started this goading, and I couldn't let it rest. Just couldn't. My tongue kept going, kept flapping about until Dibbsey started up his dance again.

'Your Chinky man is happy to be away from you, I'll bet. Lucky man.'

I lifted my hands from my lap and let them drop again. Reached for the bottle. His face was right in front of mine then, so close that I could see a small black blob balancing on the end of his nose. It was annoying, hanging there, swaying in front of me. He was talking, his mouth was moving, making the black blob swing right at me, and I couldn't help it, I really couldn't, it had to go, that was all. So I lifted my hand and wiped it away, flicking it on to the green rag-rug.

It came suddenly.

His hand a quick fist surfing through the air: a smooth curve before it hit my cheek, just below the eye. The wood of the couch-back cricked in protest as my head bounced back. There was no blood, and Dibbsey seemed puzzled about that: he looked at his fist, then back at my face.

I was paused, hand on my cheek. Just waiting for what happened next; it was the habit I'd got into. No, I haven't told you, but you might as well know it now. Usually, though, it was just a push, a shove, and only ever when he'd been drinking.

Anything could happen next: he could fall asleep right there, mid-swing, God knows, he'd done that before. Or — well, or something else: the push, the shove, or more.

'Don't hit me again.' It came out all quiet, all calm. As if I had the right, as if I was as tall as him. Just me, just sitting like that, and opening my mouth as if to talk about the weather, but it wasn't the weather that came out, it was that, that — command. That's what it was, a command.

It came in a shaft of light, like the moon, a sudden remembering: how I used to make a room full of men tremble, not just with wanting me, but with fear too, fear of how strong I was, how I could hurt them if I wanted to. Remembering the day I beat Bert Nooley at his own game, hanging on to a bronco's back for ten and a half minutes, one full minute over his lousy record. I could beat this one at his own game, too, if I could just remember where my fight had gone.

You can always get it back.

Before I had the chance to dig it up — my courage, my fight — he'd fallen into a heap on the floor, his mouth open and yellowish spit dribbling from his lips.

In the morning, he was red-eyed and swamp-breathed, whispering, 'Oh, God, Jess Dibbs. Forgive me.'

I watched him, didn't open my mouth. I'd said enough, I thought. Enough for a bloody lifetime.

'Everything I can do – that was it, in those rolls of film. What am I supposed to do, what?'

'You knew how to show moving pictures. We could travel around, showing them. Just – ones like *The Sentimental Bloke*.'

'And *Australia Calls*?'

He was right. There's nothing else. Not for me, anyhow.

'I hate it, Jess. I hate turning into – I mean, my God— It's the money, that's the thing. There's none at all, nothing.' He pulled me closer to his swampy mouth. 'Forgive me, Jess, forgive me.'

Words, I thought. Cheap as dry leaves.

Dibbs was gone by the time I got me and Bub up and dressed. A note dangled from a metal tack on the door: *V. good paying opportunity has come along. Back tonight with cash and kisses.*

Silt filled my mouth at the very thought.

All morning, Victor cried and bleated and pulled and pushed at everything in his path. He pulled at the spring of the miner's couch, tugging at it until it cut into the leather of the top cushion. Screamed when I took him away from it. I offered him everything: wet towels, a tinkling bit, Dibbs's bootlace. Even dry damper. He slapped at me until all around his face was blotched, pink and orange and brown, mottled like wallpaper. I banged on the house door, calling to Nora, but no one came out. Inside, I could see three pansies in a tin, plonked on the cool cupboard.

Thick black hairs covered the top of his head. He kept shrieking, kept going, and then – I can barely admit it even to myself, even to you, though, Lord knows, you need to hear it, you need to know the truth of it, the truth of me there shrieking into his tiny round nut-coloured face – I screeched right in his face, so close that my spit landed on his fat chin, so close that I could see every lash as he blinked. Could see, I imagined, his tonsils as he opened his mouth to howl before I put him down in the basket and stomped off into the rain, leaving him there to scream. It was better, much better, that the child cry like that than that he face the force of the whirl-wind of fury that whipped through me. He was just a baby – tiny, do you think I couldn't see that? All morning, though, all bloody morning, since long before sunrise, he'd been howling in my ear, and nothing would quieten him. Stubby hands pushing away the cool teething towel. I was thankful at least that I didn't have Dibbsey there, his voice beetling in my ear, 'Shut the child up, will you?'

Yes, and I could hear him all the way down the road, everyone on the street could, surely. If I stopped, though, if I went back – I imagined him bouncing against the wall, tumbling, his black hair streaking with fresh blood and I kept walking.

Nora was there when I got back, holding him in the sunlight. She said, 'Go and lie down, just sleep for a while.'

'I can't – I'm terrible, a terrible mother.'

Look at him, his dark face tucked into her shoulder, his back rising and falling with his hiccups; his hands kittening at his own nightdress. Come closer so that you can smell the yeastiness of him so that, like me, you can be swallowed by a great tide of adoration for him.

'If I could be a terrible mother – any sort of mother – I'd be – God, so grateful— Please, go inside, Jess. Let me, just let me.'

I took him from her and rubbed his back. His dark hair was like water, fresh, and clean. He was still hiccuping and he didn't look at me, not until I turned his face to me and whispered, 'Forgive me,' just like Dibbsey.

I held him right close to me, so that his sobs were muffled by my nightdress, and rubbed my face on his hair. Forgive me, I said, though I had no idea what the words really meant. Rather, I wanted to say: This didn't happen, that was not your mother. This is your mother, this one snuggling you, this one with the soft voice. Begin again, that's it.

The words were familiar enough, God knows. Dibbsey muttered them every time he woke up with his claggy breath, empty gin bottles by the side of the miner's couch shoved against the back wall of the lean-to. Every time he looked over at a bruise on my face he said it again, Oh, God, oh, God, forgive me, love, forgive me. And every time I looked into those red-mapped eyes and whispered, Yes, yes, I forgive you. But I wasn't going to turn into Dibbsey, I was clear enough on that, and it wouldn't be happening again, the shouting right in the baby's face.

Beginnings can happen any time. Believe me.

And you get a thousand chances, if you're wondering. You never run out.

It was afternoon when Dibbs and Reggie came back, both of them on Lordship. Looking like a pair of children, Reggie with his arms tucked round Dibbs, his face tilted sideways into Dibbs's back.

Useless in the saddle, Reg, and as excitable as a bird. 'We've got a plan, Jess.' He flopped sideways, collapsing like a cake, and stumbled back on to his arse when his feet hit the ground.

Dibbs stayed in the saddle, all regal for once, though it was only through the ruddy contrast. 'An opportunity, Jess Dibbs, my girl, that will turn everything back round.'

Turning everything back round: that was the sort of news I was after.

Of course, I forgot to ask what direction we'd be turning.

Barely morning, and Dibbs was outside saddling up Lordship; I could hear the effort grunting out of him as he pulled at each buckle. He stood at the end of the lean-to, blending in with the darkness, and whispered, 'I'll be back in less than a week, Jess, and you'll thank me. We'll have enough money to ride it out, this madness, until they let us film again. Or – we could buy up the circus from De Rabe, or another one. Whatever you want, girl. We'll do it.'

I watched him and held my mouth shut, kept my eyes looking all dozy. The little one was sleeping, tucked up on his stomach, a lumpish caterpillar, so I lifted my hand up in a salute as soft as skinned fish and waved him off into the morning dark.

Some time, my boy woke up and I pulled him next to me on the miner's couch, and he lay quietly, or slept, I couldn't tell which, and I dozed again. I wanted to dive under the cover of sleep and never come back. You know all about that, don't you?

Nora woke me. Standing beside me, a wooden tray in her hands, letting the cool shadow of her presence wake me. When I rolled over and opened my eyes, she was smiling, her eyes on the baby.

There was an enamel plate on the tray, piled high with porridge. Treacle dripped across it, the brown running into the crevices and swimming into the side of the white bowl.

'Here. Eat.' She stayed standing while I sat myself up and tried as best I could to brush myself down, smooth out the creases in my face. I spooned the sweet thick porridge into the baby's mouth, and then into mine while Nora stood, with her round eyes watching us.

She said, 'I used to smell her at night. Even after she was gone. I could smell her in my bed. Honey. She smelt like honey.'

Yes, I said, sometimes my little one smells of honey, too. He grinned up at Nora, his nose rippling like water. 'Or. Or.' When she lifted him, he waved his honeybrown hand at me, and his head tipped back with laughter.

When the night slunk in, Nora said, 'Come into the house tonight, why don't you? It's mad, you sleeping out here on your own with this little one.'

Inside, above the wood-stove, there was a narrow shelf, all lined with painted tins and a fine blue Ricketts teapot. Delicate roses traced the edge of it. Oh, the swell of longing in me – for a ruddy teapot, would you believe? I put my hand out, ran my fingers over an enamelled flower. Said, 'I had one like this. Had to leave it behind. Made the best cuppas in it.'

There was an alcove, on the side of their bedroom, barely bigger than a wardrobe. Pale green serge curtains hung on either side of the opening, tied with red cloth. She pushed them aside and smiled at me, hopeful as a nesting magpie: 'He can sleep here, if you like.'

There was a low cot beneath the window-slit. Yellow crocheted blankets, a corn doll, three round cushions.

'I couldn't – he's used to—'

'Yes. I just thought he—— The wee bed is there, not used. Seems a waste, is all.' A crease cut across the top of her forehead, hard and dark, like earth thrown on a grave.

Between us, my boy sat pouring dry rice on to the rag-rug. I watched the crease dig deeper down into her face, until it seemed that the earth would cover her, right down to her lips.

'Perhaps he could—— It might give him a proper sleep, and, well, and me too, and, God knows, I could do with one.'

'Yes,' she said, and her face was clear again.

Through the night I listened out for his cry, but there was only Nora, coughing and rasping as though she had a wall of violins caught in her chest. Above the couch in the main room, there was a high window cut into the roof. Harsh white moonlight shone through it, in one narrow stream, casting a square light on to the wall above me. It was as square and straight and bright as the stream of light that came from Dibbsey's travelling film-projector kit. If I raised my hands, I could make a shadow play: duck, dog, rabbit, cat. There was no baby beside me to watch, silent and open-eyed. Wind danced outside, and I waited for it to wake him, my body ready to leap up, run to the cot to comfort him. When I closed my eyes, I saw him clapping. Colours swam beneath my lids, my mouth opened, and everything thickened, the way it does before sleep.

There was a woman, dark hair, curled round a white face. A white bed. Too much white: coats, walls, faces. Something metal pushed on to her forehead; she was crying out, so loudly that only I could hear her.

My boy called out then, pulling me from that half-sleep. Before

I swung my body upright, Nora had shushed him. I could hear her, singing a soft song, and him making a shuffling sound, a slow clucking, then the deep breath of his snores.

My hands reached up to the moon-square; I made a rabbit dance with a snake; a dog yap at a cat. I twisted my fingers and made two birds bob on a branch; one flew away, dived down to catch a little worm. A kookaburra laughed, watching it all. I practised and practised, made each shape perfect and whispered the sounds. In the daylight, I would show him, as soon as the light crept down and the stars started blinking. He would sleep beside me in the lean-to and I'd hold his hand up, so that he could see his own shadow, make his own moving-picture show. Perhaps we'd make the shadows together, a *pas de deux*, a moving-picture show just for us, and we could call it 'Jess and Victor's Shadow Moving Picture'.

Yes, yes, that was how it would be. That was how it could have been.

~

He was outside, bleating away, before the sun came up. Sitting outside on the scrap of lawn that Nora had worked so hard to plant, pulling the heads off the bright nasturtiums, leaving the stalks tilted like drunks.

'Leave them bloody alone, Dibbs. They're Nora's flowers.'

'It's all right, Jess.' Nora coughed, her chest shaking. 'Lazy gardener's delight, they are – you can pick them and pluck them and they keep growing. Uproot them and toss them over your shoulder and they'll just put down roots and start again.'

I had Victor in my arms, and he shouted when he saw Dibbs, as though they were friends, as though Dibbs was someone who cared. Shouted and threw his arms up, face folding up so that even his cheeks were smiling. See? I wanted to say. See how little he requires from you; how much you promised, and how you give nothing. And even so, he can offer you this ruddy *gift* – because it is a gift, it is – of himself, this gift of being willing to embrace you. Dibbs did grin at my boy, I'll give him that, if you can call a lip-curl with teeth bared a grin. But I think – to be fair – I think it was a grin that Dibbs was intending.

'Didya sleep in there?' He nodded towards the house, towards Nora standing behind me.

'It was a damned fool idea, her sleeping in there on her own, with me in here and the cot there by my bed.' Nora was a wall of warning behind me, arms folded: *Just you start, Mister*.

But Dibbs wasn't up for a fight. He had his needing, pleading look on, a face full of crumbs. Reggie stood – *lurked* would be closer to it, to the truth of it – by the lean-to, feet scuffling in the muddish dirt.

'Why are youse back, anyhow? You said three days, did you not?

And what do you call this? One night, and I'll be betting on the grave of my daughter that you've been up to something useless, or you've buggered it up, whatever it was, the great plan youse had.'

'It isn't as simple as that, Nora.'

'Never bloody is. Leaving poor old Jess here—' She ended in a great splutter of wheezing.

'I'm all right. Happy to be here. Less of the "Poor Old". It's you who's a cause for worry.'

Dibbs grabbed my ankle so that I nearly tripped, baby and all, and tumbled down face-first. I could see that he hadn't come back with what he wanted, could see it in the droop of his moustache, and I could feel it in the sweatiness of his grip on my ankle, but I had no need to make it easy for him and, after all, he did promise. Untold bloody riches, circuses: *I'll treat you like a princess*, that was what he said, way back when. Don't think I forget such things. Like you, I forget only what I want to, or need to.

'So what'll we do, Dibbs? Will I write to Martini? You want to buy the circus, or – something else? You got another idea?'

Dibbsey's moustache drooped even lower, dipped right down into the well of his mouth, so that the tobacco-yellowed tips came out all spit-covered.

'What is it, Dibbsey? A problem?'

Nora called, then: 'Get yourself over here, Reginald, and you say what the blasted thing is what's going on.'

'We didn't—' Dibbs looked over at Reggie, still shuffling the dirt with his boot-toe. Reggie didn't look back, kept his shoulders hunched up near his ears. Dibbs started again. 'It's a great opportunity, Jess.'

'You said.'

'I did, I know.' The odd thing about Dibbsey was this: when he wasn't half-cut, strutting around like a butcher bird, ready to eat up all in his path, he was as weak-skinned as a geranium petal, and almost as pink. I could crumple him in one hand.

'Well, then?'

'We need to – the thing is, Jess, it is an opportunity, it is, and it's a good one, and it could fix us up, put us back in the square. Takes a lot of riding skill, but, and Reggie here – well, you've seen him, he's as weak as water in the saddle.'

'Like a sack of wheat,' Reggie agreed, lifting his head.

'We could make a lot – maybe fifty pounds – but we need a rider, someone fast.'

I bent down and put my boy on the grass.

'Jess?' Dibbs was trying to find some charm, but that had left him long ago, left him the first night he pushed me against the wall, if you want to know.

'Victor.' I blew my lips into his neck and rolled him on the grass, a bundle of laugh.

'Please, Jess. Fifty pounds.'

I looked right at him then, the stupid fool. Did he not think I wanted fifty pounds – even a share in fifty pounds – as much as the next person? It was clear, surely, that all I wanted was to get my circus back, and leap again from back to back. God knows, I didn't care about the lines of folk wanting to see me with my ruby lips – it wasn't that – I wanted to be riding, was all, and to know that this little one, this black-eyed pea, wasn't going to starve, to be sold off to the priests or to another circus, sold off somewhere that I wasn't. But – and I'm thinking here about you, too – they can be such fools, sometimes, can't they?

I held my boy up, a trophy, a shield. 'I can't leave him. He couldn't be on a horse even for a day.'

'I'll stay. You go with Reggie, and I'll be here.'

'Ha! You wouldn't know what to feed him, what to do with him. Anyhow, I don't even know what it is, this opporbloodytunity.'

'It ain't illegal, if that's what you're thinking.'

'It hadn't occurred to me, Reggie, till now—'

'Don't be stupid, Reg, you big-mouthed—' Dibbsey started twitching, itching for a drink, no doubt: I had started to recognise that old shake.

'Big mouth, and who's putting you up? One favour for all of us, one favour that would make a start for me and Nora, too, and youse two.'

'Right, then. Just tell me.'

Dibbsey swung his hands into a half-fist, he twisted his body right and left; he was like a hen, scratching around, unable to settle. 'Is there a beer?'

'When you've told me.'

'I'll get youse one, boys. And you, Jess?'

I shook my head and Nora – already shrinking – stepped into the shadow of the house.

'There are some cattle, a lot of them, that need moving, that's pretty much it. They have to be rounded up, and moved, the lot of them.'

'Moving where?'

'Across the border.'

'That's all – for fifty pounds?'

Reggie started rubbing Lordship down, keeping his back to me. Dibbs looked straight at me, clear-eyed as a possum at night.

'They're desperate to get them off the land. Desperate to sell them on so that they can switch to jumbucks.'

'Sheep? God, why would they? Who are they, anyway?'

'It's a property out near Goulburn. Friends of Reggie's. They want the cattle moved to Victoria; they reckon they've got a better price lined up there, a good buyer. Bill Lusty, the bloke's name is. And it'll barely take a week. Will it, Reg?'

Reg harrumphed a yes, without looking up.

But – it wasn't possible. I could hardly have my boy up there in the saddle with me.

Dibbs unfolded a pale grey map from his saddle-bag, ran his tobacco-yellow finger over it. 'Look – we head straight down to Goulburn, there, then cut in, here, and follow the Murrumbidgee for a bit, cut back into the valley there, and cross the border near Bombala. Easy.'

Fifty pounds. My mouth watered again, the way it had back in the stage paddock with all that talk of Nellie Stewart. Blind Freddie could see that I had no way of keeping my boy, my Victor, not the way we were travelling. Downwards, if you're wondering.

Nora eased out of the house, a brown bottle in each hand. She handed one to Dibbs and one to Reggie, and then she said, 'I'll look after him, Jess.'

'No, you couldn't. It's too long. He can do it himself or not at all.'

'We've got nothing left, Jess. Nothing.'

Reggie came in then, in a mournful voice that I had no doubt had been well ruddy practised. 'It's hard for Nora and me; it's just that we'll have to take *paying* lodgers in the lean-to. You know, soon.'

'Reggie . . .' Nora opened up her face, her eyebrows lifting, while the breath squeezed out of her like an old pipe organ.

'We will, Nora. There's bugger all in the kitty, and twenty-five pounds for each of us – well – it's just that, without it, I can't see how we'll get on. That's all I'm saying. That one way would be to get paying lodgers, you know. I'm just saying that.'

'Then go yourselves. I can't leave him, and I can hardly put him on a horse for a week.'

'Please, Jess. You've seen him with me. You know he'd be fine, you know it. He'd sleep in the cot and I'd watch him so careful. Wouldn't I, little Victor?'

My boy lifted his head and gurgled at her.

She stood close to me, so close that I could hear her whisper, 'I'd look after him so well, Jess. As if he was my own.' She looked at Victor, not at me. 'Please.'

Reggie gave me a pair of his trousers and braces, and when I threw myself up on the back of Lordship I felt like Ariel's girl again, all tucked into jodhpurs and caps; I looked more like a man than Reggie did, and Nora said she could quite fancy me. Victor, my beloved, darling boy, held my face in both hands and kissed my nose, my chin, my cheek.

I don't want to tell this, any more of this. I want to end it there, with the kiss, and my breath warming my boy's face, and Nora laughing as she waved us off, waving a handkerchief and calling that she was going to have such fun with my boy, such fun together. This is the way I'll remember it.

It didn't end there, though. It never does end where we want it to: and, in fact, I'd end it sooner, I'd end it before Ariel rode off to

Nullo, I'd end it before I ever met Alfred Dibbs. And then I wouldn't have him, would never have had my boy, so I couldn't finish it there at all.

Well. It still isn't finished, is it?

We rode out in the afternoon, the three of us, without speaking. Nora had tucked a chunk of damper in each of our saddle-bags, and a wedge of corned beef, and we ate as we rode. My whip was tucked into my jodhpurs, and every so often the leather tip of it weaselled against my leg.

Strips of red sunset were settling on the hills, but you could still see the shocking, sudden lash of green spread out like a rug. Pale sandstone cliffs loomed away into the sky, dotted with red banksias. There must have been three hundred head of cattle, all beginning to mope out their night noises and huddle closer to each other. Dibbs had the ropes in his saddle-bag. We huddled together, like the cows – though, admittedly, without the noise – and waited for the moon to get high.

'If we can get them out by midnight, we'll be near Bombala by dawn.' Dibbsey kept his voice to a whisper, though I couldn't imagine the cows would be bothered – they sounded like a whole orchestra of trumpets. 'They need to be moved at night,' he said, 'Bill reckons they get unsettled if you move them in daylight.'

The cattle trumpeted about, until Reggie said, 'You should lasso them, Jess.'

'Don't be a fool. What do you mean – all of them? I can't.'

'Course you can.'

'God, Reg. What's your plan?'

Reggie slouched on his lumpen bay mare. 'I don't rightly know, Jess. We thought – I thought, that is – well, no, I think it would be fair, you know, to say that we both thought – would you not say that would be fair, Alfie, to say that, that we both thought it? – that we both sort of assumed, Jess, that you'd know what to do, that's what.'

'I've never— Oh, ruddy hell, Dibbs! So you came back because you couldn't do it, you had no idea what to do and you've had this great idea – but it's down to me, is it?'

The cattle forming shadowy gangs around us grunted and groaned like lost ghosts. The dark was settling in, and Dibbsey had turned into a nodding shadow.

'Why don't we go to the homestead and ask your mate how he wants it done?'

'The homestead's eight bloody miles away, Jess, and Bill asked us to move them, sell them on and let him know when it was done. I said we'd be professional about it.'

Oh, God.

'Give me the rope, then. Go on, give it.'

Dibbsey fumbled in the moonlight, and pulled out two lengths. 'I thought you could just lasso them or— When we filmed, you could lasso anything.'

'This isn't a moving picture. I can't lasso twenty cows, you flaming idiot. No one can.'

Reggie's limp voice niggled into the darkness. 'I thought you'd know how.'

'Fine. Get your whip, Reg.'

'I haven't got a whip.'

Dibbsey gave a little groan beside me. What in Hades he was groaning about – when it was him who organised it, him who should have checked it – well, I didn't bother asking, for fear I'd take my whip and wrap it round Lord Dibbs's flaming neck. Instead, I held my hand out for the rope. 'This is what we're going to do. Listen.'

Reggie started up, ready to add something or other, so I lifted up the whip, flicked my wrist back, and let the tip come flying past, so close to Reggie that it almost brushed his cheek and made his bay mare rear up. Reggie's arms flung round the mare, and he didn't fall off; but he did shut up. When he settled, I handed him my whip. 'Take it. This is what's going to happen – are you listening? I'm going to use the rope as a whip, and you're bloody useless, Reg, not having one. Give us your knife, Dibbs. Now. Get out of my way while I try. Go on, both of you.'

They clicked their heels and edged their horses back – Dibbsey was as smooth as a spotted gum, but ruddy Reg flipped and flopped so much that even the cattle were startled into silence. I slipped a knot into the end of the rope and unravelled the other end, hacking at it with the knife as best I could.

The trick with a whip is not in the wrist. No. It's in the fingers. All in the tips of the fingers. That's where you feel the rhythm of the whip, it's where you put your strength and your softness. What you do is you spread your fingers out, as if you're cradling a butterfly. Or sometimes, the fingers become the butterfly, each fluttering point. You let the whip get comfortable beneath your touch, let it sit all warm and ready. You keep your fingers like that, remember, open and buttery-warm, just till you feel the weight of the whip. Then you close up, a gentle pinch; lift up and circle. You need the wrist right at the end, that's all. Only a woman can crack a stockwhip properly. Only a woman can make it dance. That's what I believe, and experience has never proved me wrong. Not once, not even now. And even that rope, cobbled together as a poor-man's whip, even that I made dance, and made cry out the way only a whip can: a squeal of surprise, and echoing bolt, that made the huddles of cattle call out and hobble clumsily towards the rocks.

We spread out, me at the back, Reggie and Dibbs on either side, so that we made the points of a triangle. Or, another way of seeing it, a better way: half a star. I cracked my rope-whip, it made a paltry sound, but still the cows looked wild-eyed and rattled sloppily away, towards Dibbsey, on Blaze. He kept the whip low when he cracked it, and the cows backed away, all as one body, as if they actually were lassoed together. Reggie flapped his whip and a half-whistle came out and the cows stood, watching him, not sure what to do next.

He tried again, and a group of them – maybe six – backstepped, watched him, and then bolted clean past him.

Reggie lifted his whip, waved it uselessly, and then turned right round, watching them go, and calling, 'Hey, bloody cows.'

While he shouted after them, like a good fishwife, ten, twenty, thirty of them pushed past his bay mare and clambered off towards the rocks. The rest were grouped near me, and Dibbs started to follow, to make a run, so I lifted up my rope and swung it, whipped it out so that it cut across the valley and the sandstone. The cows stepped back towards Dibbs; he lifted his whip and they ran towards Reggie. His hand went up, the whip circled, flipped back – in the *fingers*, Reg – and a bolt of lightning sound shot across the field. The cows – maybe there were two hundred and fifty left – stayed where we needed them after that. So we cracked one after the other, until we had them moving, the ones we hadn't lost, and after a while, it started to feel that we were one body, too, the three of us, and the cattle, that we were all moving together: the cows, stumbling across the rocks, away from the pasture and towards the border, and us, whip-cracking cattle-drovers, heading towards fifty ruddy pounds.

When we got out past the edge of Goulburn, I couldn't help myself; I lifted up my head and let out a battle cry.

~

We rode all through the night, and the next, taking turns to kip, and cracking the whips back and forth; I was as alert as a black cat, I tell you. We'd lost hours on Reggie's sheer uselessness – there's not another word for it – and we'd lost another forty cows or so somewhere around Queanbeyan when ruddy Dibbsey had insisted on dismounting to relieve himself and Reggie had taken the chance to set up a dawn picnic. Truly. Everything had been lit like a ruddy moving-picture set, too, the moon, and the pink of early light. Dibbs and Reggie were full-sized shadow puppets running against the great circle of the sun, sliding up into the still-grey sky. We let the cattle graze, and Reggie managed to light a fire. Dibbs tugged a billy from his saddle-bag, but I stayed mounted, there was something about it all I couldn't trust.

When Reggie was pouring the tea, I heard something cracking and crackling in the bush. I whispered to Dibbs, 'Listen. Someone's there.'

'Nah,' he sucked at his mug like a great monkey, 'it'll just be possums.'

'Ruddy heavy possums.'

'They are, around here.'

The moon had sunk, well and truly disappeared, when we creaked into a low valley. Ahead of us, the sun was so bright that I had to keep my head down. When we neared Bombala it was almost above us; I could see my shadow caterpillering next to Lordship's hoofs. Beside us, there was a wall of bush, high and dense eucalypts crowding over us, spreading a line of shade.

Dibbsey flicked his whip back, snapped it down to the ground and called, 'Smell that Victorian air. Nearly there.'

Behind me, Reggie shouted, 'Smell that sweet money.'

Oh, and I could, I could almost ruffle it with the end of my whip.

I thought it was a whipcrack I heard, then, so lifted my rope-whip and twirled and tried to crack it in return. Sharp, flat: the crack came again, and it wasn't a whip. I knew it then, that it was a revolver shot. Lordship pig-rooted, his hind legs flicking up in the air, his ears flat against his head, the barrel of his body heaving. Flat against him, I tickled his ears, whispered the sounds of the sea: ssshush-hush-shssh.

Three shots called out then, one after the other, and voices with them, firing down from the cliffs: 'Halt there. Show your brand.'

Both of them – Reggie and Dibbs – were way at the back of me. Dibbsey had trotted behind at half-speed, and Reggie was trailing at the back, complaining every so often of a sore arse. When the noise came, Reggie called, 'Bolt, it's the traps,' and yanked on his reins so hard that the bay mare nearly toppled back on herself. Dibbsey said something like *frigging frig* and I heard the scuffle of Blaze's hoofs on dirt. Behind me, a revolver clicked; I pulled at Lordship's reins, tugging him round in time to see Dibbsey lift up his revolver and fire up to the traps. The cattle were thronging right and left and lifting their heads to the red morning sun and lowing almost loud enough to drown the shots. A group of them galloped away into the green mound of hill, as fast as young brumbies.

I called back to Dibbs, 'Have you got the brand, Dibbs? Just let them know – what are you doing?'

He flicked his revolver up, firing towards the cliff. Lordship was skittishing about, sidestepping, and I leant down to him, huddled my hands on either side of his face, making them into blinkers. By the time I'd calmed him, rubbing his ears, stroking his back, Dibbs was gone and I knew what a bloody fool I was.

Above me, there was another shot, one of the traps calling, 'Get them, they're off.' I twisted Lordship round, ready to bolt off myself, but the traps had galloped down behind the cliff, each one with a bright, shining revolver.

Dibbsey, damned Dibbsey – they were gone, just buggered off, both of them. If I could have, I would have taken the revolvers from the traps and shot the pair of them myself.

There were two traps. The younger one – face as flat as a dead koala, shoulders stretching beyond Timbuktu you could say – said, 'Leave 'em, Jack. We've got this one, and he was heading up front, so I'm guessing it's his doing – that right, laddie? Howdya let yer mates gettaway? Great mates, hey? Why doncha tell us who they are?'

His mate sidled alongside me. 'Or do you want to show us the brand?'

I shook my head, trying to think how to lower my voice. What I knew was that my voice would show me for who I was, a mother wanting to get back to her child, that was what. And what was I to say? That I'd not realised? Taken his word for it? Sure and certain, it wouldn't have been the first time they'd heard the claim of innocence; and did I need the world to know what a flaming fool I'd discovered myself to be, after all – after all my hard-learnt toughness?

Koala-trap said, 'Can you talk?' and I made myself husky and rough, said, 'Yep,' because I knew I couldn't play at being a mute, not me with my love of talking back.

'Got a brand?'

I shook my head, and he tied my hands behind my back so tight I could feel the blood talking.

Riding there, with Lordship hitched to the trap's horse, and me with my hands tied – well, I got an idea, then, of how it might have felt for Billy's mob, being hitched up, chained and led along like dogs. Except they didn't get to ride. And they hadn't pinched anything, most times, neither.

They rode me along like a dog all day, though the wide one fed me a piece of oat biscuit he had in his saddle-bag, holding it to my mouth so that I had to nibble like a tamed and broken animal. They pitched camp along the Murrumbidgee, before we got to Goulburn, and set themselves up a nice bush prison.

But me – ha! I'm Jess, half girl, half horse – who could keep me locked away? How would they?

Later – I've heard the rumours, legend even, you might call it, like I said, you'd be surprised what we hear – they used to say that I dug myself out of the back of a brick dunny using a teaspoon, but the truth is more ordinary and more obvious than that. They were men, weren't they, those traps? See that wide one, with the grey eyes? He hadn't been with a woman for a year, not since his wife died. I always had limits, but I had plans, too.

When I scampered off into the bush, I wasn't sure where I was going, what my plan was – *Victor, Victor, Victor*, that was all that rattled through my head. You'll know how it is, when your brain is full of feeling not thought and – that tug, that pull at every bit of you. Policemen can be fools, too, like any man – but that one had his own baby at home. Drake, his name was – the trap, not the baby. When they nabbed me, of course they thought I was a bloke – who wouldn't, when I was rigged up to look like one? Though now I think of it, I might have had a better chance if I'd dressed as a woman and played the delicate lady out for a ride. Mind you, it'd be a fair point to wonder what a lady was doing out for a mid-morning ride with two hundred-odd head of cattle, miles from the nearest station.

Unlike the legends, there was no brick dunny. I never was a miracle-worker. Handcuffs – click-click, and then roped on to a low branch of the redgum weeping alongside the camp. My cap came skew-whiff with the effort of trying to sit comfortably under the gum; my hair started to sieve its way out. Somehow, too, with my hands pulled back, one of the front buttons of Reggie's shirt had popped right off. The young grey-eyed cop looked at the lump beneath my buttons, and at the strands of hair falling down on to my shoulders, then looked away, said nothing. In the middle of the night, with the other trap snoring like a goanna on a rock, I called the young one over, whispered that I needed to pee.

'Please, please,' I said.

He looked at my chest again; even in the half-moon I could see him.

'I've got a baby at home,' I said, and when the words came out, I saw him, as sharply as if he was there, placed in front of me. My little one with his muttonfat arms – God, I'd been trying not to think of him, not to see him – and there he was, curled on his belly like a fat frog, and how would Nora know to give him sago if he was miserable, sago with sugar, that's what he loved; and when I didn't come back – how long would they keep me, these traps? How long would my boy wait for me? And right then, I tell you, I was ready to bite through the handcuffs and run all the way to Kandos, but before I needed to start gnawing, the young trap said, 'I've got a kid at home. Little one. Me mum's taking care of him,' and he looked down at my handcuffs, all sad and sorry-looking.

'I need to pee,' I said, 'please.' Tears were streaming all over me, down on to my neck, my shirt, because I knew I had to get back to him.

The trap nodded and said all right, and I added, 'I can't do it with the cuffs on.'

He looked at me, still and quiet, and I turned round and stood with my hands held out behind me, waiting, hoping for him to open the cuffs. Tears were all over my face and I was sniffing and trying to remember that I could do this, I could do anything – *half girl, half horse!* – but the tears were all over my face and finally he slipped his hand into his pocket and said, 'All right, *young man*, you win,' and he opened the lock to the cuffs.

'I need to be alone to pee,' I said, and he looked away, shrugged his shoulders and muttered that he'd wait by the bottle tree.

Lordship, bless him, was tied up with the coppers' horses, and how hard do you think it was to slip the rope through and whistle softly for him to follow me?

When I first walked off with Lordship, I just walked, whispered through the bush; kept my head down and my arse up, as they say. That young copper kept his back to me and was fast asleep by the time I crossed the dry creek, or at least had the decency to pretend he was. Maybe that's where the story of the spoon sprang from – good on him, if it helped keep him in the bacon.

All I wanted was to get to my boy.

I'm still skirting, aren't I?
Loving him doesn't make me good at it.
I had to leave him, didn't I?
I should never have left. I know, I know.

~

Nights were quiet, just the shuffling of the night nurses, their feet moving like breath along the wards. Someone moaning, perhaps. Once or twice, the smashing of a glass at the end of a corridor. Muffled voices, a wheelchair squeaking past. Soothing whispers: 'Mr Dobell, would you like something?'

'My wife, that's what I'd like.'

'Yes. Of course.'

'I'd like her to speak to me. Rose! Speak!'

As if he could command the spirits, as if he could raise the dead, cast out demons, all with a flourish.

As if he was Jesus. Or Billy Graham himself.

Nurses came back, flicked curtains aside: 'We need to check her fluids. Any movement? None that you've seen? No. It's – unusual. To recover at all, you know. I've never seen it before. She's a miracle girl, so far, that's all, so we can only hope.'

'Pray. We can pray.'

'Of course we can. It's only that the buses will be stopping soon. You might want to go off and get some sleep. You might like to—'

'I'll stay. Doze here in the chair.'

'Work?'

'Yes. A factory. I'll go straight in. Splash some water on. Easier from here, really, than from the hostel. Want to watch. Keep watch.'

'Yes. Would you like anything?'

'My *wife*. I'd like my wife back.' Later: 'I'd like to turn the clock back. I'd like the chance to – to undo things.'

Bored nurses hummed a tune outside the room, by the ward desk. Laughter, spurting like fireworks, an unexpected brief burst.

They laughed again, shoes slapping: 'It goes like this, two-three, *swing* your hips, *twist*, *twist*.'

'Oh, shoosh, you.'

And off again, hushing down the corridor.

'Rose?' He tried it as a question rather than a command. 'Please?' Then: 'I have prayed. I have used the words of the Lord. I don't know. Nothing comes to me now. Without you. We'll go back. If you want to. Please.'

He whispered, put his head on her bed, right next to hers: 'I was wrong, I was wrong.'

Silence for a moment, then: 'I didn't feel anything, before. I don't think I did.'

He snored when he dozed, guttural, suffocated sounds. Agonising death rattles, then startled grunts, pulling himself awake. His sleep was never silent. Doctors' rounds in the morning; the rattle of trolleys tottering with medicines, up and down the wards. The curtains clicked as they were pulled back, Joe still snoring, stuttering gently into the dim light of sleep.

'Mr Dobell? Here, have some water. I think you've missed the bus, were you not getting the dawn bus?'

Joe's words were slurred from sleep, still thick with saliva. 'Whatimesit?'

'Oh, after eight.'

'Missed it. I'll stay and watch.'

'Yes. Well. About that – ah, here's Dr Anstey – do you need me, Doctor?'

'Not now, Nurse. Ah, Mr Dobell. Sad business, your wife.'

'Yes. She is. My wife.'

'Sad business, all round.'

'I wrote home, a letter. Asked them to pray. Everyone. It won't have arrived yet, the letter, of course, so they won't be praying. Not yet. But – she's much better, isn't she? Definitely, wouldn't you say? I'd say so.'

'Mr Dobell—'

'Only that I know I'll be needing to find a house, to take her to, the hostel won't do, I can see that, only it's hard to see the way out.'

'Yes. I'll need you to sign some forms for us.'

'Forms?'

'We need to know – I'm sorry, it's very difficult to talk about these things, I know. It's simply that we need to have your consent, you see, to move the body.'

'What body? There isn't a body.'

'No. It's simply that – simply this – that if something were to happen, if the signs drop again, as they did earlier today – if they drop to dangerous levels and you're not here – I'm sorry. You need to understand, Mr Dobell, that we are doing our best. We really are. But it's unlikely – I say, *unlikely* – that we'll be able to save her. Highly possible that we won't be able to, that's what I'm saying. We need your consent to, ah—'

'No. That won't happen, you see. It won't happen. I won't – no.'

'We're doing our best, Mr Dobell. We truly are. For your wife.'

'She – you're all here, all the bloody time – what are you doing then, if you're not fixing her? I see you here, all the time, all of you; listen to that, that's breathing, that is. Breath. That's what you can hear. And she blinked today, when I told her – when I said we could go back.'

'Perhaps I'll come back later. Have you had some tea?'

'I don't want tea. I want my wife. I want my wife.'

'Yes.'

'She's a mother, she's — we've — got a baby. A baby.'

'Yes.'

He whispered, through a mask of his hands, 'I know that she wants to come home.'

~

Stupid girl I was. Stupid as a girl. Stupid as that damned nutcase of a girl who rode out all tall and hopeful on— What was that one's name, that palomino gelding, his tail combed? No matter, I could at least remember the rough touch of his stubbled neck, the bristle of his trimmed mane. And hadn't they plaited his tail? Oh, yes, that was me, all right: the first show as Athene, in my spangly skirt, hands waving, goatskin over my shoulder.

Sir Edmund Barton himself was there, the time I won the rough-riding plaque. God's truth. He stood up and applauded when I rode in the winner's parade. I stood up on the horse's back, with my hands raised in the air, and I believed everything was ahead of me, everything was possible. Delicate as a flower, you'd have thought, to look at me. Breasts barely yeasting. Who'd have thought I could out-bronco the toughest boys?

Oh, it's odd, the things that come to you, the things you recall.

That girl, where was she? All hopeful, not expecting to be wandering in circles with a scrap of sweaty cotton tied round her leg. I stopped, bent double, tucked loosely in two like a dangling bridle. Breathe. God, just breathe. My feet padded, encoding the worm-black earth. Each crunch of soil sweeping beneath me, sweep, scrunch, crunch; my mouth ached with dryness. Ahead of me was the deep dark of the bush, as thick as silt.

Among it somewhere, if I could hear him, find him, Lordship trotted riderless.

I hadn't counted on the dark of the bush, or on me not knowing where it was I was pointed. When I leapt on to Lordship and spurred him in the rump, there was a slice of moon above me, just thin enough to shine between the clouds. I rode for hours before I found the denseness of the bush, and wove my way into it, pushing

Lordship on to be faster, faster. I wanted my boy; as for Dibbsey –
no more of him, that was over. I'd find a way, some way, to take my
boy away and manage. Something. I'd manage something. Maybe
domestic work. I'd find a lady, someone nice, kind, someone like
Nora, to care for him. Or – well, it was true that I had never
cleaned a whole house, never polished silver – I could break horses,
dress as a man, no one would know. Something, I'd find something.
No more, no more of this. And there I was, full of those thoughts;
it was so black that I couldn't be sure if my eyes were opened or
closed. Just the noise of Lordship's hoofs smashing at the ground,
and my thinking loud in my head, almost as loud as the thudding of
panic that beat through me.

With the moon gone, and the traps behind me, I was pushing
Lordship on, as hard as I could; pushing him to get home to my son.
Lordship leapt up, across a log, and I rose up – and something, I
suppose it was a low branch, swung me hard in the face, with the
force of a hammer, an anvil. I felt myself knocked back, felt the air
as I toppled to the ground. I think Lordship's legs kicked at me, at
my leg, as I fell. Hard ground, a log or – something – twisted
beneath me, scraping into my back, a swirl of sound as I hit the dirt.
Strange, how unexpected it was, how quickly the fall came, and
how I could hear music. Blood, the sweet salt of it, trickled behind
my teeth.

All of one leg was scraped, wet; when I stood, it was as solid as
a chopped tree beneath me. Useless. Fumbling at the buttons of my
shirt in the dark, I unbound my breasts; I took the strip of cotton
and bolted it round my leg, tight as I could, until I couldn't feel the
bloody trickle. Hobble one, two: pain slashed up my leg. One hand
pushed against wood, I waited, tried to breathe. Remembered this:

the pain of my boy tearing through into the world. I whistled out for Lordship, but heard nothing. Two steps, hold a tree branch, wait and breathe. Like an awkward, darkened dance, stumbling through the darkness and then the gradual dawn. I could have gone in circles, or backwards, just following my nose and whistling out. Some time, a wet morning light filtered through the leaves, and I grabbed at a branch lying on the ground, a solid walking-stick. Something crunched ahead, the heavy heave of hoofs. Weight on the branch, I pushed towards the sound, whistling, calling. Light fell through there, too. I could see a stream of light, as though the bush drifted out, maybe on to a ledge, or a cliff.

The light pushed through, a dull brightness, enough to see that branches were buffed, lower ones trampled – the marks of Lordship pushing through the bush. Whinnying; I could hear the snort of a horse, but – not right, the wrong sound, or—

I stopped dead-still, as still as I stood when Ariel drew his pistol and shot my dress off in the Amazing Outlaw Show, the bullet whispering past my hair and me standing there like a statue made of water, made of life. Nothing could touch me when I stood still like that; you could blink and swear I wasn't even there. There were two horses there, I could swear, I would swear. I stood.

Three red ants danced across the black toe of my boots. One pearl of sweat dawdled round my ear. Still I waited, and the horses kept breathing; no voices, though. A copperhead slithered across my boot and still I didn't move.

I heard a stamp of hoofs, a whinny that I knew was Lordship, and I crunched forward.

There was a stampeding of noise.

Six traps, they'd sent. Six. They pounded into the bush, shouting for me. Oh, they knew I was there: they had Lordship tied up, and a telegram from Bombala Police. He'd given me time to get away, that young one, given me a chance, no doubt about that, but a chance wasn't enough, and there they were, lined up and waiting and full of fire.

They hauled me off in a wagon to the Cootamundra clink, with Lordship trailing, his ears flat and his head low. They kept me in their rattling tin shed of a lock-up, and no amount of me saying I was just a woman out for a ride was going to shift them. Even pleading that I needed to get home, home to my baby boy, didn't raise a flicker, an eyebrow of concern. 'Haven't you been a boy?' I shouted. 'Imagine if your mother didn't make it home.'

One of them, a copper with a face so fat that the skin ran over, on to his shirtfront, said, 'My mother would never have left me to go off riding in the bush on her own, *wearing trousers.*'

For almost ten days, I rattled on the bars like an organ monkey, and it took all that flaming time for the young trap from Bathurst to get there. When he did he stood in front of the cell – and I must have looked a pretty frightening sight – and nothing moved on his face. Even his lips barely flinched when he said, 'Didn't the telegram say "man"? Can't you blokes read? I've never seen this woman in me life, and you should make sure you give her a good feed before you send her home.'

Thanks anyway, boys, but I'd rather stuff your tucker in my pocket and get home to my boy, who will never forgive me for being away so long; my boy who will be wailing for me right now, howling, inconsolable; or worse, happily snuggling into Nora and forgetting anything I have to offer him, or knowing the truth about me, as the fat trap knew, that I wasn't good enough, that I didn't deserve him and I would surely, surely be punished.

Oh, and I was, I was.

I pushed Lordship at a hard gallop from Cootamundra to Kandos, only stopping for water somewhere around Trunkey Creek, then carried on as best we could. I hadn't slept for days and I was as wild and half-cut as any old circus drunk.

But now look, there I am, back, squinting through the thick green-glass slats, and I could see the pile of split logs, spread out, drying in front of the wood-stove, and Reggie's revolver shining silver on a three-legged stool.

'Where is he?' I threw open the door to Nora's kitchen-nook, ready to grab him, snuffle him into me, swallow him up. 'And as for those two bastards— '

'Jess? Is it you?' Nora was like a blind woman, huddled deep in her bed, eyes thick with paste.

'Is he sleeping?' My arms were out and I pushed my way over her, past her, to the empty cot. 'Where is he?'

Nora had her face pulled down again, earth on earth, and she chewed at the air, a choking, hacking cough. 'Jess — you came back. They thought you'd never manage, that you'd—' She coughed again and a speckle of blood landed on her hand.

'Where's my baby? Where is he?' I turned to each corner, then, sniffing, pushing, and trying to step aside from that creaking anvil being dropped inside me. Nora wiped at the red on her hands and her lips. 'I'm sorry, Jess, I got sicker and sicker and – God, it was only a few days ago – you'd been gone so long and—'

'I left him with you; he was with *you*.' The strength was in my arms again and I was ready to tear down that shanty house and its little lean-to, ready to throw the lot of them single-handedly down into the valley if it would tell me where my boy was, blood-speckled hands or ruddy not.

'He – Dibbs – and Reg, it was both of them. They came more than a week ago—'

'Has Dibbs got him? Ruddy useless lying—'

'They said you'd been pinched – I didn't know, Jess, I swear, had my doubts, but I didn't know that it was a duffing job – they said you'd ridden off alone when you saw some traps and left them to talk their way out of it. Victor was here, happy, we had a lovely time, a lovely time, and he called out that night. All night he was calling, Mum, Mum. It was the first time he'd stayed up like that. Kept us up—'

'*Where is he?*' I didn't want her stories, her night-worries and Dibbsey's lies. I just wanted my boy.

'Oh, God, oh, God.' Tears had started to streak her face. 'What's he done? Oh, God, Jess, I got sicker and sicker—'

'*Tell me.*'

'Reggie's sister came – her family were having a weekend party, with friends, in their – they have a summer house—'

'Just tell me where he is, and get him, get him now.'

'I'm sorry, oh, Jess – I'msosorryoh.' Her words became a long moan, and I had to shake her, hard. The truth, if you want to know, is that I wanted to kill her. 'His sister came, just for a visit, and she talked to Dibbs for hours just outside, and I could barely move, I've been spitting that much blood and there's not a chance that we could afford a flaming doctor, prices they charge. Dibbs came in, said it looked like you were stuck for good in the clink and fat lot of good I was, lying here – and, God, Jess, if it's TB, you know, I couldn't bear it, if he got it, if Victor got it.'

'God, no.'

'And Dibbs said the family Reggie's sister was with had been – had been unable to have a little one – and, oh, Jess, God – it seemed that – we was trying to do the best thing, the best thing for him.'

'Where is he? What have you done, Nora?'

'I don't *know*. She – she rode off in the trap to see about it all, and came back the next day, no, maybe it was even the day after that one; and – she – God, Jess – she took him, he was all wrapped up and he had a bag of rusks, and Reggie sat up front with the driver, it was the carriage she came in that time, when she came back, not the trap, and Victor was smiling like all get out—'

'What's the name? Of the family? Where has she gone?'

'I don't know, I just— It was a wealthy family, someone important, that's all – a summer house in the mountains.'

And I was shrieking then, and pushing at Nora, when it was Dibbsey I needed to get my hands on, that chasm of a man, that lumpen liar, right there outside in the lean-to.

There he was: half crumpled on the quarter-sprung miner's couch; one boot on, the other toppled sideways on the rag-rug. Before I was inside the lean-to, I could see the ball of green spit dangling, settling on his chin. I kicked at him, shouted, 'What have you done with him? What have you done?'

Dibbsey barely shifted, but I could feel it again, that strength in my arms, in my legs: he would tell me, and he would take me there, to that house. I put my hand inside his boot and swung it up high, then pounded it on to his stomach, three times. Dibbs bent upright on the third hit, hands up in salute: 'What?'

'Where is he? What have you done with him?'

'Jess – I thought they'd – I thought you were done for, that you'd not be back – we was worried – both of us, me and Reg. Didn't know what to do. Thought you were done for, really done for.' He leapt into affability, as though he had invited me round for a tea-party.

'What? That I was stuck in the clink for you? Is that what you thought? Stuck for years in a hell-hole because of your lies?'

He blinked up at me. 'I just—'

'Where is my baby, Dibbs? Where's Victor?' I kicked at him. 'Get up and take me there right now. Nora told me.'

'Jess, darling—'

'No, you ruddy well don't – I'm not your darling, not your frigging darling at all. Get me there now.'

'Jess – think, just think. You weren't here. Nora got so sick and – we thought you'd not be back, it's true, and I couldn't care for him, God knows. Even you – go on, tell the truth, you're useless at it.'

'You liar, you bastard liar.' I hurled the boot then, threw it behind his head. 'I bloody am back. Get a trap from somewhere, and you take me to him, Dibbs, you take me there right now.'

'I can't take you to them, I don't know where it is. The family have left the house by now, and I don't even know it. I don't know where they belong.'

'Where is it? Where are they? You tell me. Reggie knows – he must know, he must have told you.'

'He doesn't know. His sister has taken him to Mudgee, he's got some business there—'

'What business? What bloody business? My son – is that the business?'

'Jess, think on it. He'll be happier. Better off.'

I thought my face was burning, that the blood in me was falling down, bursting out. 'Not without me, he won't.'

A crack-urn grin creaked unsteadily on his face. 'They left some cash. For compensation, and for trouble taken. Costs incurred.'

'Compensfriggensation? Take me to him, Dibbsey, please, just— I'll find some way of getting you money, more money, just, please, let me have him.'

'I don't know where he is. They've gone. An English couple, that's all I know. Rich, he'll be well cared for. They – I don't know – a house, it's in the mountains, that's all I know, no, not the mountains; it's two hours maybe from here. I don't know where, don't know the name. And the deal was that Reg wouldn't know. Not even his sister would have all the names. They want to care for him, Jess, as their own boy. But look, Jess.' Dibbs knelt down, and lifted a tobacco box. It was full of crumpled pound notes. 'We can get back on our feet. You can be free, you know, back to your old ways.'

'I don't want to be free, not of my son, you fool.'

'You'll come round. It's a shock, I can see that, but we had to do something, and that was – it seemed the best. We did the best thing, I think we did, Jess.'

There was a bottle, empty of green wine, on the ledge behind him. I was a whirl, a wind, and I picked it up and hurled it.

Dibbsey was like one of the big old circus cats, swaying on his feet, not sure what happened next: glass had shattered, smashed against his head, and the green glass flicked down on to his shoulders. There was a shard right on his cheek. He put his hand up to it and looked at the blood on his finger, then at me. He stepped forward, arms out, his mouth stretched open so far that it seemed for a moment that he was going to try to swallow me. His hands came to either side of my neck, and he was roaring, roaring and squeezing. His face rushed up, so close to mine that I could see the pits on his cheeks, the grey hairs in his moustache. His thumbs pressed at the base of my neck, he pushed harder, his thumbs digging to the centre of my throat so that I couldn't cough, could barely choke out whispers of air. I mouthed Stop at him, and tried to make it louder than a gasp, but he heard only his own frenzy. The thumbs pressed harder, spit dripped from his mouth on to my face.

Behind me, the metal chair leant against the wall, knocked back by my toppling. I reached behind me, grabbed at one leg and lifted it high. With Dibbsey's blood and spit slipping down on me, I lifted it; I lifted the chair as high as I could and swung it down with all the strength of my arms, on to the crown of his head. Couldn't have been a better aim if I'd lined it up like a rifle. He tottered, his face a swelling mess of shock, and fell sideways, hitting the floor with the sound of a half-cracked whip.

~

Reggie's trousers bagged round my waist, and his revolver felt odd, digging into my thigh. Nora – I'd backed out of that house with the revolver in my hands, a dead man in the lean-to, and without my baby boy. Ariel's boy. She gave me the revolver, though I would have taken it anyway. She'd gathered a saddle-bag full of clothes by the time I ran into the house, shards of glass on my shirt-top, blood on my face. Tears were still bubbling in her; she washed my face, hacked at my hair, and tied Reggie's trousers on – but she couldn't tell me where he was. Mudgee, maybe. Anyway, that was where Reggie had gone. Or Orange. Or – she couldn't say, she just couldn't say. Reggie wouldn't know, no, surely not, and she'd pushed me out then, saying, 'Go, hurry. Mudgee. Try Mudgee, but wait until it settles down, Jess; I don't want you swinging from a rope.'

Lordship was soft-footed, and I kept my head bowed; I followed the river. Mudgee. It was something. Somewhere to start. If I could just be close – I knew the traps would be out, soon enough, after me, or someone like me. And they'd hunt for a few days and then settle down, back to their rustlers.

I thought of Dibbsey's hands: the blue veins straddling his fingers, rivering to his wrist, the wrist that flicked, quickety-split, just like that, neat as a pin, as a whipcrack, as a brumby flying over a creek. His wrist which – God, how many times had I seen it, crick-cracking up and down with his daks round his knees while he called out to me to roll, to ride, to beg, to— Enough. I would not let him jump around like that, prancing dakless through my already torn head. How could I? Who had room for dakless Dibbsey when there was my boy to think about, the finding of an English family, a someone-or-other with a cinnamon-coloured son?

A fat wallaby plopped itself out from behind a scribbly bark, ears up, watching. The hollowed-out space of my belly felt cold, aching with emptiness. My hand fluted round the revolver at my hip. Startled by the twitch of my hand, the wallaby looked up. It didn't stand a chance. Like Dibbsey, really. Except that if you looked at it properly, with your eyes open and without the pounding of blood echoing in your ears, it was pretty obvious, pretty damned obvious even to blind Freddy that, really, it was me, Jess A, who didn't stand a chance. Not one chance in bloody Hades. All that pretending, waving revolvers around in three moving pictures, and I couldn't hit a wallaby standing right at my feet.

I scrabbled in the saddle-bag for my money-purse and felt something hard, round. Wrapped in a white shirt – Nora's Ricketts teapot. I wanted to hurl it, though, smash it against the rocks: Nora, careful enough, thoughtful enough, to remember that I loved this pot, and wrap it, to protect it. But not careful enough to protect my boy. Damn her, damn all of them, all people, everyone.

Damn Dibbs and his poor bloodied body.

Anyway, there was less sympathy leaning against my back when I thought of Dibbsey and his tall red— I never found a word for it, never something I felt right with, though he loved me to say 'cock' – he'd ask me to call it again. 'Ask for it,' he'd say, 'ask for my cock to come out.' Oh, yes, there are things I haven't told you. He was never acrobatic, but he liked his words, liked to – well, to get ready. He liked the preparation more than the event, is how I would put it. Mouth clinking on the words as though they were a cold bit, I would call out, just the way he wanted. Well, anyway, that was that. Dibbsey and his cock. There: look at that. The word had no problem, jiggled up and down in my brain in a little dance, to the tune of that ragtime song. Forgetting Dibbacy and his blue wrists and his fat fists, I let the word out, a soft whisper. My voice barely dented the air, and I tried again, tried to speak it louder, loud enough to make the gang-gangs fly up from the branches in righteous shock. But my voice had packed its bags too, gone up and left me there in the grey spread of bush, only capable of a whisper and a creak.

I cracked my wrists, thought: I have run a circus, I have been a moving-picture star, I beat every man in the 1908 Rough-riding Championship, and this is nothing. Finding food, finding shelter, finding my son, finding, well, everything, all over again — this is nothing for me, because I am the Amazing Jess, Girl Trickster, that is who I am. I will not lie down and curl up in that mass of leaves, and bury myself and not come back, though I have hope pulled out of me and nothing but cold fury left in its place. I will not lie down. Do you hear me?

I'm telling you this because you have to remember how you've got fight in you; to remember who you are, what's possible. That's what stories are for, after all. Everything is possible, that's what. Even now, where I am, I'd say that, would keep saying that, keep believing that.

Along the edge of the creekbed, kangaroo paw burst out, great red tears marking the way. I slid off Lordship and walked alongside him, stepping over the thick mounds of scrub, trying to keep close to the creek, trying to keep my heart still. Lordship stumbled down to the water's edge and drank, while I stood, watching, hand at my hip.

When the creek started to gather into a fine point, becoming a drizzle of mud, I pulled at Lordship's bridle and we started to push through the bush, away from the creek. Branches and leaves scraped at my face, but we pushed and ducked, and I walked towards the eye of the sun. I could hear the crunch of cartwheels on road, and I was going to find Mudgee, and find my boy.

With one pound in my money-purse, I pushed out on to a flat road, the pale dirt of it scattering into the edges of the bush. Eucalypt branches dangled from the saddle on Lordship's back, and mud was caked on the bottom of my trousers. I spat and scraped with the hoof-pick until I resembled someone clean. Then I clambered up on to Lordship's back and tried not to look like a woman who had killed a man that very morning.

Mudgee – and it was Mudgee, or so the painted sign outside the big hotel said – was two wide streets, three hotels, a stone church and a small store. There appeared to be a guest-house behind one of the drinking houses, and a gentlemen's tailor. I tethered Lordship at the trough, in front of the cream-painted hotel and he lowered his head as though in prayer. Two wagons drove past, and I watched to see if there was a child in either one, but each was driven by a solitary man.

Inside the store I gathered up a bag of flour and one of sugar, a packet of tea, two candles, a box of redheads, oats for Lordship.

'All right, love?' A woman with mud-coloured hair sat on a stool behind a low counter, stitching at a petticoat.

I looked at the floor, trying to keep the shadow of my cap over my eyes. Dirt was caked into my nails, and lined my hands thickly.

'Working on one of the farms?'

I shook my head and slid the shilling coin on to the counter.

'No?' She was determined to talk, to extract something more than money from me. 'Down at the hotel?'

I scraped my bags up into my arms, in a fierce embrace, and walked back to the street. Behind me, I heard her call, 'Change, love?'

Next to Lordship, there was a high chestnut mare tethered; they were nuzzling at each other like lovers. Watch yourself, I thought, it will come to no good, believe me.

'Looks like they've chummed up.'

Clown-like, I looked around me, trying to find the voice.

'I think it was my girl what started it.' He was on the veranda of the hotel, sitting back on a wrought-metal chair, an echo of the Paddington lace fencing the upper veranda. I looked over my shoulder: a wide hat, beardless face, as smooth as a stone.

A brown carriage, three horses, drove past; I watched but saw no one resembling Reggie, or the crooked-eyed sister.

'Come up and have a beer. Let those two get to know each other.'

I poured a handful of oats into Lordship's nosebag and slipped it over his bridle, then stepped up on to the cool veranda. Through the windows, I could hear someone singing 'Alexander's Ragtime Band', or perhaps it was a gramophone. For a moment, a fist squeezed at me, at my chest, my waist. I sat down, trying to breathe, next to him. Skin like pebbles.

Closer, I could see yellow hair sprouting half-heartedly around his ears. He held out a thick hand: 'Magic Jack.'

I slipped my hand into his and squeezed as hard as I could. Coughed, and pulled my voice back into my throat. 'Frank — Frank Heap.'

'Orright, Frank? Let me.' Magic Jack pushed himself up from the table, hands spread like a great dog. 'Keep an eye, wouldya?'

When he came back, with a brown bottle in either hand, we sat together on the veranda, watching the two horses nuzzle and guzzle.

'That's Lottie.' Magic Jack pointed his bottle at the mare. 'For Lottie Lyell. Aw, you gotta love Lottie. That little round face, you gotta love it.' He seemed to be challenging me not to love that little round face; Lottie Lyell kissed me, I almost said, but sucked the words back in time. Lottie Lyell didn't kiss me, not me, Frank Heap. Jack waved his bottle again, towards the narrow hall squeezed between the church and the store. 'The moving pictures get shown there. You like the pictures? Yep, me too. You gotta like moving pictures.' He took a slug of his beer, silenced for the length of a gulp. 'The best one, aw, nah, that would be *The Sentimental Bloke*, hey? Hard to go past it. But that flaming *Captain Starlight*, that was a doozy, weren't it? Aw, yes.'

A carriage – perhaps it was the same one – rattled down the cross street; I leant forward, peering, trying to see into it, holding on to a flimsy thread of hope.

Magic Jack nodded in the direction of the carriage. 'Lord and Lady Muck.'

'Hey? Lord and Lady who?' I hit my lip on the edge of the bottle, I leant forward so hard. I coughed again, tried to bring that voice of mine down to my chest, or lower.

'Just a name, mate. Settle. No bloody lords round here. Just trumped-up ones who think they are.'

How to ask? Any with new babies? Any sudden babies with slate eyes and black hair?

But Magic Jack was somewhere else. 'Yep. That ruddy Lottie Lyell, hey. Wouldn't mind giving her a poke.' A sour burst of laughter puffed out of his mouth, as unexpected and awkward as a fart. 'Yep. Yep. That Starlight fellow, he was up here, had his hideout here.'

It's just a story, I wanted to say, he's just a ruddy story. But my mouth would give me away and keeping my head down with the shade on my eyes was the best I could do for myself. Anyway, who's to say the story hadn't taken a life of its own, grown legs and walked these parts, hushing fear into the publicans and storekeepers and ladies in their carriages? Who's to say that the story didn't keep them up at night?

'Yep. Aw, yep. Up there, old Starlight's cave.' He waved his hand in the air, as though Starlight's cave was floating above us, right now, between my head and the tin floor of the upstairs veranda. 'That Thunderbolt bloke was there, too. Aw, they all hid out there. Could hide out there for months, they reckon. Years, prob'ly. My dad was storekeeper then, back then. Bloody lucky he never got shot, never even got held up. Starlight, Thunderbolt, the lot of them wandered round here.'

'Where's the cave?' I tried to speak into the bottle, to look down at my feet, disinterested, just – making conversation. The only way I could find my boy was by being hidden, I wasn't so much of a fool as not to know that.

Magic Jack lifted his bottle, tapping the end, draining it. He plonked it down on the table with a gust of breath. He looked at the empty bottle, then at me.

'Ah, I'll get us another one.'

The bar was cool and dark, and the singing had moved on. It came from another room: banjo music, an unfamiliar tune. The publican had a yellow moustache, drooping into his mouth, and I felt a swill of puke, the way it was when I was full of Victor and still trying to twirl myself upside-down on horses, or leap from back to back. 'Orright, mate? What are you having?'

I pointed to a row of brown bottles, and held up two fingers, as though I were mute.

'Twopence, mate.' The publican pounded the bottles on to the walnut counter and wiped his hands with the white cloth flopping over his shoulder. I watched his hands – blue veins, long, snaking fingers. 'Mate.'

His moustache quivered. 'Twopence, mate.' He leant over the counter, and I could smell the tobacco.

'Sorry. Forgot meself.'

'Bloody right.' And he took the twopence, snapping the white cloth as he turned his back.

Magic Jack had moved on from Starlight's cave. He was on to the glories of the Automobile. There was one in Bathurst, apparently. Bright red. Owned by – aw, someone or other. He suckled on the bottle, then stood up and wiped his hands on his trousers. 'Right, Frank. Must be on.'

'Yep. Course.' I walked on to the path with him, and unhitched Lordship's nosebag.

Just as Magic Jack swung himself up on to his mare, I said, 'If a bloke wanted to have a poke at that cave, how would he find it?'

Magic Jack squinted down at me. 'Oh, you'd be lucky, mate, real lucky. Not easy, not easy at all. But it's ruddy up there, I'll tell you.'

'Up where?'

'Up Nullo Mountain, that's where you've got to go.'

The street seemed, for a moment, to float above itself. I was floating, too; I could see my boots, far below me. Nullo Mountain: there was a whole army of fear between me and that place, and I'd never been brave enough to go and see. But he was calling me, I knew that, the way that I called you.

~

Crows battled with eagles, their cat-sounds, baby cries, echoing over the valley. Everything was washed out, the colour strained from it: diluted green, soapy blue, faded yellow. Even the ground was neither red nor brown, not dirt or rock. Washed out, half-hearted: a tired, worn place. Ancient, but with no wisdom to it, just – tiredness. Even the eucalypts were spread out, grey-leafed, unwilling. A creek ran through, though, and the water was fast and clear. Magic Jack had drawn me a mud-map, sketched on to the back of a match-book: 'Somewhere around there, mate. Best of luck to you.' And there was an arrow where it was. Or might be.

All there was, though, was a face of unyielding rock, and crows.

I unflipped the match-book, and tried to make sense of where I was, of where the knotwork of caves leading to Starlight's Cave might be. No signpost hanging out the front, and whoever bloody Captain Starlight was, he wasn't the most hospitable of hosts. Black cockatoos shrieked above me, swooping to a row of lilipillis, clawing at the red fruit, then spitting it down to the gully. Lordship was scrumping on scrubs of tall grasses; I shoved my way through greyish bush: a wall of banksias, red and gold, danced in front of me, a sudden burst of colour. In front of them, a slow drop, a blue sea of eucalypts. The rock below my feet was solid, and on either side of me the ground slid away. Two cockatoos swooped, dived straight for me, and dipped at the last minute. *Below me*. Ha! Of course, of course. I scrabbled down the curve on to a lower ledge, full of thick, green bushferns and yellow rock daisies. Hand pressing against the rockface, I edged along until – there. A great mouth, a gaping hole, yes, indeed; I had to squat like a bilby to get myself in there, but once in, oh, yes. Groping on all fours – you'd have thought I was a ruddy dingo – I wriggled in, then knelt back and lit a stub of candle. Further in, the cave roof was raised; I could stand and walk straight through, dance if I wanted to. Candle in front of me, I squizzed around: rock ledge jutted out on one of the walls and – something: a shadow at the far end of the cave, a darker shape against the wall.

High up, above the ledge, it was a painting: a horse, a long-necked beauty. Beside the horse, the dark shape of a man. Maybe a man – trousers, legs, jacket, gun – they give away as much as I do. They were painted in delicate colours: the horse, ochre, brown, and a mane in gold. The man was shadow, but – like a dandy – he had red trim on his pocket. There was a five-pointed star etched above them, like a guide, a sign. A kind of welcome mat.

When I scrabbled my way back outside, up the rock path and round to Lordship, I was blinking and spluttering from the light; a worm living in darkness, and I'd been in there minutes, only minutes.

I dragged the saddle-bags back round into the cave; trees had dropped everywhere – branches, twigs – and I gathered it all, giving thanks. Took the billycan down to the creek and gathered up water, first for damper, then for tea, and when I rolled the damper in the ashes of the fire at the mouth of the cave, and poured water into my Ricketts pot, I could, almost, forget why I was running. But not what I was looking for, God, no, not for a minute.

So, that was how I lived then: damper and billy tea, and bush tucker – lemon myrtle, lillipillis, bunya nut – and I slept by the fire, huddling under the pile of Reggie's old clothes. I waited for days and nights to pass before I moved, because I thought they'd be out there looking for me, combing the bush for the mad-chair-wielding-murderer. I didn't mark off days, but I knew that they were passing, and – I'm no fool and never have been – I knew with every sunset that it was one more day of my boy forgetting me, one more day of him calling someone else – Mrs Lord English Someone Muck or Other – Mum. Ha. Mama, probably, would be her preferred term. I sent kisses to him on the night-winds, sent smoke signals across the hills.

Nights were cold, and the ground was hard, ruddy hard.

Four times I tried to shoot – three kangaroos, and once, a wallaby. Each one got away. Lucky I didn't try to shoot Dibbsey. The fifth time: a wallaby, sleeping on the grass. Ha! Useless, laughable shot that I was – that was the only way I could get the poor bugger. I used my knife to skin it, blood slipping everywhere, great hacks of flesh coming off with the skin: but roasted in the ashes of the fire, my God, what a hole it filled.

Each night, I edged closer and closer to the fire, trying to catch the warmth of the embers and keep them in my body. I laid leaves on the ground for a bed, and they crackled and crunched all night.

I went down into the town. Walked Lordship to the edge of the bush, then tethered him and walked along the wide road, looking in at all the carriages, poking my head at all the wagons and surreys, but there were no cinnamon babies, no ladies with unexpected gifts. One shilling I had left, and no ruddy idea how I was going to live beyond that. I weaselled my way along the road, counting in my head, *flour, oats, better hope for another wallaby*, and I walked past the church and outside there were two traps, in their blue uniforms and their shiny riding boots. I kept my head down, all right, kept walking towards the store, but not looking in either direction, and on the corner what's up but there was another one, his back to me, talking to a big-hatted bloke.

'Frank! Oy, Frank!' Magic Jack, standing there with a blue-suited trap, blabbing away to him, waved his hands at me, both of them, like he was a flaming windmill. I lifted my hand up, nodded at the copper, and turned straight round. Headed back to the cold of the cave with not a scrap of flour, and the last match of my book. Ate lillipillis and lemon myrtle for dinner and dug up some of the round nubby yams that Billy used to cook up – *kokobai*. Bloody delicious when Billy roasted them. Raw, they tasted like toenails.

In the night, smoke rose up from the embers, twisting, a dance. An ember caught on me, snaffled on a thread of Reggie's trousers, draped over me, dangling in the black coals. The burn snapped me awake, properly awake. I thought I was: I sat up – that would mean I was awake, wouldn't it?

There was a man, standing on the other side of the dancing smoke. Red traced the edge of his pockets; there was a whip – a neat half-stockwhip – in one hand, a revolver in the other. He didn't frighten me; I didn't even reach for the gun. Strangely, his horse was right by him: a dark-haired creature with a dappled mane. I felt – stronger, braver, somehow, that he was there. He didn't talk, didn't raise his gun, just watched me, and smiled. I let him stay.

Daylight dragged its way even into the hard ground of the cave. I knew I had to make some things happen.

There was still one shilling in my pocket, which wasn't going to get me much more than a bag of meal for Lordship, and maybe a package of black tea. Here is what I thought, when I woke up with a burn-hole in Reggie's old trousers and the smell of smoke caught round me: *I can do this. I will*.

Because there isn't another way, that's what I thought, and there isn't anyone else now, only me.

All of those outlaws: Ned Kelly, Thunderbolt, and bloody Starlight himself, they didn't start off as bushrangers, did they? None of them had a son to find, a reason to keep going, to keep looking. You already know this: you never have to give up, not until you're gone. Maybe not even then.

Lordship was sweaty and calm under me, as we rode away from Mudgee, back along the creek, until we came to a track that led up towards Gulgong. There was a house on the side of the track: low veranda nosing down the shade. I slid off Lordship and whistled outside. No one came out. I went round the back, stood behind the low paling fence and whistled again; no one came. So I went to the door, and I tapped on the door and there was no answer – but it opened when I pushed it.

I only took what I needed: flour, a square of butter, a cake of sugar, two tins of corned beef. There was a purse left on the dresser, two shillings inside. I took one, and left a note: *Please forgive. A passing hungry traveller*. I didn't want anyone thinking it was the blacks. There was a basket of pale red apples by the door, and the sight of them made my mouth as wet as a baby's bathtub; I put one in each pocket and one in each hand.

Riding back to the cave, I kept my head down, my stomach sick with the thought of what I had to do. In the cool dark of the cave I had a feast under Starlight's horse, and I put my Ricketts teapot up on the ledge as though I were a real lady, and I kept thinking, Glory, glory, now my son has a mother who's a murderer and a thief.

Glory halleluyah. And I wondered if he had a mother after all, a new one, the new one, who would be better than the dud he'd been born with.

So that was how it was, and how it was going to be. I rode over to Orange and stood on the main street, counting the carriages and the wagons and the surreys, and none of them had a lady and a man and boy who was growing out of being a baby. I bought a map from the lady with the mud-coloured hair, and I drew a circle round Kandos, all the places, all the other towns that he might be. Marked them, one, two, three. Bathurst, Richmond, Cessnock. I rode to other houses: from one I took two blankets, and from another a china cup and saucer. In Millthorpe, a tin house tucked into a slice of bush provided me with a tall water jug. On the edge of Mudgee town, there was a homestead with a kitchen garden: early in the morning, I took pumpkin, carrots, squash. At night I baked them in my fire, pulled the seeds out and dried them in the sun. From a house in the fields near Millthorpe, I took a small spade, and rode back up the mountain with it dangling over my shoulders. Above the cave I dug up the hard dirt, scraped at it with the spade, and spread Lordship's shit across it, a fine topping. I scrabbled all around that bit of bush, down near the creek, into the valley, gathering billycans full of dark soil. I thought about those bright-headed nasturtiums of Nora's finding roots wherever they were thrown. And I sprinkled the seeds, and I hoped that something would grow.

I was, truth be told, a poor copy of a bushranger. But I wasn't swinging from a rope, and I wasn't starving, and I sure as hell wasn't giving up; I would keep strong and keep searching until I was ruddy swinging.

Autumn drifted to an end: the dark came faster and more fiercely, and the ground beneath me was like ice. I tried to sleep on the ledge, tried putting the blankets beneath me, tried waking at night and sleeping during the day, but my body felt stuck, coated with ice. I rode out near the Capertee valley, to a big guest-house. Kept my cap down over my eyes – they left the house on Sundays, and on the table: ham, pies. Before the autumn, I'd walked into the back kitchen and walked out again, with a pork pie and a boiled cake under my arm. Cake! Oh, I felt for a moment that I'd been forgiven, when I squeezed the rich dough into my mouth.

Sunday, and the guest-house was empty, as far as I could see – but at the front there was an unhitched wagon and on the wagon, the metal frame of a bed. What was I to do? It was a gift, surely? I hitched Lordship up, clambered up to the front, and flicked the reins. Poor old Lordship didn't quite know what to make of it all: his ears flicked round, and he tried to sidestep out of the wagon, but I talked to him low and quiet and he started to settle. We cantered back along the road, as fast as I could get him going without drawing attention, me with my head down. We got to the edge of the town before they started after us: two men on foot, one with a gun. He fired straight up at me, and it startled Lordship so much that he reared up and galloped on like it was the old days and he was leaping, with all the lights on him. The bloke fired again, and I remembered my revolver, pulled it out and fired back at them; I could see the dirt flying up near their feet, could hear them shouting, 'You bloody thief. We'll have the police on you,' and I pushed Lordship on, whipping those reins.

I drove the wagon half-way up the hill, and dragged the bed off, scraping my arms on the metal hinges, then drove it down to where the creek narrowed. Crossed the creek, then unhitched Lordship behind a great boulder. I'll tell you now that I didn't like it, whipping at him like that, unhitching him half-way up the hill and seeing him covered with sweat, his rump shaking. I walked alongside him back up the hill, and I dragged that bed with my own strength, one corner at a time, wriggling it through the scrub and up the dirt hill. Dragging it behind me to the front of the cave was ruddy hard work, and I was so bloody buggered when I got it in there that I lay on the bare metal springs and I slept with no fire and no food in my belly.

I went through a spring and a summer, marking out the age that Victor would be, taking only what I needed to eat, and to live. Enough to keep me strong, to keep me searching. Above the cave, the seeds sprouted. Every week, I rode out to a place in my map circle and stood and looked, and sometimes bought a beer for someone who seemed like they might talk. But no one knew anything, ever, about that boy.

He would be walking, talking. Calling her Mama.

My throat dried at the thought, the knots in my stomach swelling so that there was barely room for air.

In Cullen Bullen, there was a schoolhouse. Garden at the back, bicycle at the front, one of the new ones. I whistled, waited, and clambered in through a side window. Gathered ham, oats, tea: that was all. I never took too much from one place; it wasn't that I wanted other people to starve, only that I didn't want to, either. A greatcoat was hanging on a peg, and a pair of garden trousers, so I gathered them up, lumped them into my arms. The front door was solid, oak, with beams crossed against it. It squeaked as it opened, and I dropped the trousers, hand to my waist. The man who had his hand on the door, pushing it open, was thick-limbed, but barely higher than me, and with skin that crinkled over his bones. He looked up the hall at me in the kitchen, coat at my feet, saddle-bag full of food in one hand. 'You bloody scavenger, get, go on, get.'

I started to back away, keeping my eyes on him, though he had nothing like a gun anywhere, but he crackled at me: 'And leave the goods, Mister.'

'No, can't do that, sir. I'll be needing them, and you'll see I've not taken much.' I came out sing-song, half bloody Irish, half liar-bird.

'You drop them, young laddie.'

Ha! To think he'd call me a young laddie, even now, with the wind hollowing out my face and my hands caked like the back of sandstone.

'Drop them and get.'

The revolver was cool in my hand; I held it high, straight at his chest, and you would never have seen the shake in my hand, never.

His hands went up into the air then. 'Don't shoot me. Why are you here? Why would you come here, of all places? Go to the public-house, there's money there. You'll find nothing here.' His skin crinkled, like dry leaves. 'Please.'

I kept the gun aimed at him, and picked up the saddle-bag. 'I'm taking only what I need. I don't want to hurt you, Mister—'

He stepped towards me then, so I clicked the trigger back and said, 'But I will, I will if I have to. Now get back, go on, get down there and lie on the floor – don't make me shoot. I've killed men before, don't think I'm frightened to.'

He backed into the narrow, dark room alongside the hall, and creaked down on to his knees. When he lowered his head, I could see the shake, all across his neck, such a strong tremor that his hands could barely hold him up. I unlatched the door, and said, 'Don't come after me. But – please – I won't be back, I promise you. And I've taken no money.' He nodded, or perhaps it was the shake in his neck. A tear dropped on to the floor near his hands.

I ate the ham alone, without damper, and it stuck like dust, like dirt, in my throat, and my stomach ached on that metal bed all night.

~

Heat danced above the ground, bending the shapes of the trees, the rocks. Whip-birds called back and forth across the hill, soprano bellbirds sang. Everything was still grey-green, the way it had been when I first walked up that hill, and with a half-washed colour. The ease of it, though, now — the grey, the limpid rocks — calmed me, let me breathe. Among that pale colour, there was room for me. By the creek there were white wax flowers and orange black-eyed susans sprawled like slatterns; in summer, there was no shame by that creekbed, everything was loose and undone. The ground at my feet burst open, a great line of plump mud coiling up from the creekbed, and yellow grass sprang up from it.

When I unpeeled the cotton cloth from my bosoms, I coiled up like the mud. Stretched my arms up, shook myself out — I was like a wet dog, ah, the relief of it. They ached, just sometimes, from the effort of being held in. Like I did, like you do. Down at that thin creek, I could unravel and soap myself down, scrub my chest and belly; I could pour the water down myself, and sing. I bent down, poured the water on my hair and scrubbed at it with flakes of lemon soap; I left my top off and let the suds slither down my back, into the stream. White bubbles, round as flowers, bobbed against the rocks, swung down to the deeper creek.

Lordship heard it first: he lifted his head and snorted into the dry air. One hoof patted at the ground, ears back. Water pitted into my ears, I heard nothing but petals of soap. Only when Lordship whinnied, flicked his neck in a welcome dance, only then I looked up. Water dripped down my skin and it took me a minute to clear my head, to focus on the shape in front of me. I blinked away the water, wiped at my eyes. A horse. A man.

It was Magic Jack. Sitting high on his mare, spreading his arm in a great welcome sweep, as though I'd invited him, as though he were my ruddy brother. His mare stepped her legs high, and Magic Jack was as back-straight as a whitegum. Hand high, mid-wave, words drying out in his throat before he'd got them out to the air.

My feet were sunk in pebbles and mud; the cool of the creek swirled round my ankles. Water spattered, dripped down my bosoms, down to the shirt tied round my waist. Magic Jack slowly dropped his hand down to the saddle, swallowing so loud I could almost hear the spit travel down his throat.

It had been a long time since a man's eyes had cut into me like that, since I'd watched a man's chest heave, seen the bobbing of his throat.

When he spoke, he had the weak voice of a fig-bird: 'Frank?'

I could feel the white of him, watching me.

I knelt down into the water, head bowed, back bare, face red-hot.

Magic Jack clambered down, his feet kicking dust into the low, rough scrub. 'Frank?'

My hands crossed over the front of me.

'God.' Magic Jack backed away, scuffling through the low scrub. 'I'm sorry, Frank — I mean — it's not Frank, is it? I just thought— Aw, shit.'

'Let me put my shirt on, Jack. Please.'

'Of course, yep, just do that, you do that. Put your shirt on, mate. Love. Aw, shit.'

'Jack, turn round. Would you?'

We walked back up the hill in silence. I boiled the billy, poured black tea into the teapot. Gave Magic Jack the china cup and kept the thick enamel mug for me. He slurped at it and bowed his head down, peered inside at the ledge. I gave him a candle and let him look, and I was grateful that he didn't see the painting on the wall.

Lizard-like, we sat on the flat rock above the cave, warmed by the sun. Magic Jack kept his eyes away from me; he looked down at his boots, at the sky, over at Lordship or his Lottie. If he had to look at me, he spoke to my feet. Amazing, the power of bosoms.

He looked up at the red banksias. 'I've tried, God, fifty, twenty times to come up here. Kept wondering if you'd made it, if you'd ever come up, if it really was here, and each time I see you in town you're head down, arse up, and I kept wanting to ask if you'd ever seen the cave and where are you dossing – here? Are you dossing here?'

He wrapped his thick hands around the teacup, then looked down at my feet. 'I thought your name was Frank.'

And who was to know whether I could trust him or not? But – what now? He'd found me, hadn't he?

And to tell you the truth, I was starting to wonder, starting to doubt. I had begun to believe that I would never see Victor again, and more than that: I believed, when I dug away at myself, I believed he was better off. Without me.

So I told Magic Jack – not everything. In the story I told him, Dibbsey was left sitting at a kitchen table in Marrickville. Details are sometimes better changed. And there was no talk of Captain Starlight or moving pictures or cattle-rustling. It was a button business that went wrong, a visit to a dying aunt, and when I came back – you know the rest. The details were changed but the heart remained the same. All the time, Magic Jack listened and looked at the trees, or his hands, or my feet, but when I got to the bit about

Victor, my nutbrown boy, he leant forward and looked up at my face. 'I saw a brown boy with an English woman, and he called her Mama, and I thought it was – unusual. I was in Windsor, trying to buy a horse, which was a ruddy disaster. Knock-kneed. And I noticed this boy, who looked – a bit – I thought he didn't completely look like her, that's what I noticed.'

Before Magic Jack rode off back down to Mudgee town, he called, 'Frank? What's your name?'

I didn't hesitate. 'Jess A. The A is for Ariel, if you want the whole story.'

Windsor was an overnight ride, I had no doubt of that. I had no supplies left, and no money from the small amounts I'd pilfered. Fifty pounds – surely if I had fifty pounds, they'd let me have him back, my son? I could compensate them, the way they'd tried – the flipping hide of it – to compensate me. Blood-money, that was what it was. That night, I lit a fire beneath the painted man, I watched the smoke curl round him and I waited for him to appear with his half-whip, and words to make me courageous. There was only paint, and flames, but I tried to wish on the smoke, just the same.

I took a piece of brown cloth, to cover my face, black trousers to change into, and a dark brown shirt.

I rode across the back tracks, and across the river, and when I got to Portland I stopped, camped by the river, sleeping under the weight of a greatcoat. When the first light came, I washed my face in the river and waited. When the sun began to pierce the water, I rode into town, to the Portland Bank of New South Wales. Remembering how I could be as still as air, as still as metal, and all across the field, and down the dirt of the town's road, I thought: *I am as strong as a star. I am his only mother.*

There was one teller behind the counter: dark hair flopping down almost to his ears, a narrow face, pointed at the bottom – the man resembled a writing pencil. I tied the cloth round my mouth before I walked in – he knew what I wanted as soon as I swung open the door.

'Hands on your head.' I kept myself steady, rock-hard, strong as starlight. Revolver pointed at his eyes. 'Open the drawer.'

He fluttered, his lips pulled back, sucked in. 'Don't – please.' Trembly voice, hands shaking on his head.

I kept the revolver there, aimed at his eyes. 'Open the drawer. Take out one hundred pounds, put it in a bag and – there – put it there.'

Something sour in the air. Piss, stickysweet. The poor, trembling kid – someone's son. Hard as rock, that's what I had to be. He put the money in the bag and the bag on the counter, and I kept the revolver up, lifted the bag and backed out of the door. Lordship was right there, not even tethered: I leapt on to his back – ha! I could still do it, too, could have ridden standing, if I hadn't needed to hold my gun up, ready to shoot any trap who ran out across my path. I would have, too.

I cut across the back field, away from the town. After we'd crossed the river, I changed my shirt and trousers, and left my cap off. Hands shaking, I took the bag out, counted out the notes. Eight pounds and three useless shillings.

~

'I have no faith now, my faith is gone.' Joe's voice was as torn as paper.

The nurse was there, clinking a medicine tray, offering Joe drinks. The soft-voiced nurse, milk of kindness. Joe stayed beside her, talking, talking – to Rose, to the nurses. Asking how they kept it up, all through the night sometimes, offering words of comfort, drops of consolation. He said it again, 'No faith, what's the use of it? The bloody use.'

She padded closer to Joe, said, 'You keep your faith, honey. You keep it right there, because she needs you, she needs you to believe and to keep your hope.' She rustled as she bobbed down to Joe's level, bedside: 'No matter what those doctors say. I've seen it before. Miracles. Do you understand? You keep believing in her.'

Joe stumbled over the words: 'It's not her, it's not her I've lost faith in. I've not believed in her, not enough. Not – I've believed in the Almighty, the invisible Almighty, and – oh, God forgive me – I forgot about flesh, about here, where my feet are and my life is. Even when he – when our boy, our baby – was born on the boat. I wasn't there. What sort of a man? Drinking enough for three men. You forget where you are. Which is no reason – and all this time, she's been slipping away, going further away, and I didn't know – how was I supposed to know? What to do? I thought, a job, a house, those things. And now – look. A letter, too bloody late. Another posting, a house. Look at it – everything. *Sir, In response to your visit* – and I never even paid them a visit. It's all too bloody late.' He stopped. 'I'm sorry, you don't need to hear this, all these private—'

'Oh, love, we hear everything. We're counsellors and playmates and arse-wipers, you name it. Faith-givers, priests, too. Sometimes that.' She tinkled something down on to the tray, added, 'Well, you keep believing in her. She's not gone yet, much as she wanted to be. It's never too late, love.' The trolley creaked out, into the echoing ward.

'God is not in these words.' Joe dropped the weight of the book on to the hard, polished floor. 'Words – they're useless, bloody useless. But I'm waiting, Rose, I'm not going, not unless you do. Sammy needs you, Rose. I want you. Here. Not there, wherever you are, in that – underworld.'

The trolley squeaked again outside the room. The pad of the nurse's footsteps, coming back in. 'Look,' she said, 'there's only this.'

'Yes?' You could hear hope in Joe, dangling its feet on the edges.

'How old do you think I am?'

'Forty?' Cautiously, a hint of hesitation.

'Oh, you're sweet, love. Close enough. When I was a tiny tacker, my dad used to go out drinking in pubs. I've got three brothers, and we were all at home with my mum, and Dad was off drinking, and it was impossible for her, impossible.'

'Of course.'

'The point is, not to tell you how sad my life was, nothing like that. Because it was a long time ago. This is the thing – Mum got more and more . . . How would I put it? She couldn't really cope, being left alone all the time, and us – well, you can imagine, kids like to have a laugh, like to muck up. One night she asked a neighbour to come and sit with us, and she marched all over town until she found him in a pub, and she stood in the middle of a pub full of boozy men, and she told them all to shut their gobs while she talked to her husband. Get home, she said to him. If you don't stop this nonsense now, stop this drinking, and come home to your family, we're going. You've got one hour and no second chances. And then she walked home. She was shaking like the billy-oh when she got back, I can still remember it. I sat up, waiting. The four of us kids didn't know what she'd said, not right then, but, my God, you could feel the sparks coming off her in the hallway.'

'And?' Joe was polite, unsure.

'And Dad came home, and smartened up. And now he's got four kids who adore him, seven grandkids who think he's perfect. St Grandpa, no joke. He got another chance, and he took it. That's all, that's my point. And at the end of a marriage, or a life, these great enormous things – they're just tiny ridges in the map, that's all. Little bumps that add texture.'

'Or chances,' he said.

'Yes. Or chances.'

She squeaked off again, down the corridor. A door pushed open, swallowed the sound.

Nothing then, but the sound of Joe's breath. The sound of Joe not leaving.

Meals were carried along the wards, visitors gathered up their parcels and bags and shuffled off into the wind. Joe stayed. He had not left for days, had washed his face in the sink at the end of the ward, had not shaved but had managed to clean his teeth in the gents' washroom. Regularly, several times a day, workers and visitors to the ward told him to go, to get some rest, visiting times were over, and he replied that he couldn't, he couldn't go while she was tipped into the bed like that, how could he?

*

'Rose?'

Nothing. Of course nothing. They had said, they had all said: She's in a coma. You'll be very lucky. She'll be very lucky. Highly improbable, one said, sounding like a book, the wrong sort of book.

He called an aide in, 'Are there buses? Still running?'

'Do they run on weekends?' Doubt lacing her words.

'I'll have to walk, then. I have to get him. I have to get my son.'

'I'll find out, will I? About the buses? Is it the hostel that he's at? That migrant hostel?'

'No – a lady, an aunt of someone in the hostel. She's got him; wanted a boy to foster, no kids of her own. I needed to – I thought it was best, I couldn't – how could I care for him, climbing the wire at dawn to get to the factory, coming back and there he was still not fed; Rose gone, or as good as – I—– what could I do?'

The aide made a sound, which could have been There-there, or may have been Tut-tut.

'And then when she was gone – having that – the treatment – I caught the bus out once to see him, only once, and I couldn't bear it, that I'd given him away, failed so badly. So I didn't go back. She wants to keep him, the woman, I know that.' Joe was crying then, the cawing, crowlike cries of someone who has forgotten that they are in public, or ceased to care. The smell of his longing filled the room. He added, 'I didn't go back. My own son.'

The aide said, 'Where is he?'

'Parramatta. Do you think I could – surely I could get him back? He's my son. I want him here, with me. And her. I want to—– We'll find a solution, we will.'

'I get off in half an hour. I'll drive you. Okay?'

There was a long pause.

'Thank you,' he said. 'Oh, God, thank you.'

~

At the back of the town there was a track that led to another town, not much bigger than Portland. Wallerawang. We played there: Portland. Oberon, Lithgow: we played everywhere. All those years hiking around in Ariel's caravan, soothing the bickerings of Tilly and Gladys, and the others who came through and didn't stay – who'd have thought that I could store it up, this knowing the shape of the hills, the rocks? I didn't know: it was like talking – I opened my mouth and I could do it. Each bit of this corner of the country was imprinted; I carried a map in my belly. Not with the shapes and contours and land mass: I could never have explained it that way. It was just – I knew. I knew where I was and how to get to wherever was next and all I can think is that it came from that, those years. Or it was Ariel, guiding me. And I wouldn't put it past him, I tell you – I know it sounds unlikely, but that man was as determined as a wombat stuck in a log: and he loved me, more than anything.

I could get to Wallerawang by back country. Some of it was a scramble through bush, down rock hills, stopping for Lordship to drink, and slipping hay into his nosebag, which was the best I could offer him. Eight pounds would not get my son back. And my hand had been steady: rock-hard I had been, though I wanted to stroke the cheek of the poor clerk, pissing himself with fear. And who was to say that they'd be in Windsor, the English pair with my boy? Or where in Windsor, for that matter? We took the show once to Windsor; had to turn people away. Back then, way back. A man with one eye proposed to me in Windsor.

Closer to the town, the track widened, got broad enough for a sulky, if I'd had one, and we cantered down it, me and Lordship, as if it were an avenue and we were out for a Sunday trot, off, perhaps, to a ladies' luncheon. There's a thing: I never was invited to a ladies' luncheon, not once in all my life. It was busy in the town, busier than I'd expected, and I tethered Lordship outside the square bricks of the Bank of New South Wales, squatting there on the corner, and I walked lengths down the main street. Three times I walked down it, and three times back up, and there was a trap standing at the crossroads, and on the third time up, he called out, 'Can I help you, laddie? Are you lost?' I said I wasn't, but it wouldn't have been a lie to say that I was. On the third time I pushed open the door to the bank: this time my hand was nothing like starlight, or rock, or anything except river water, flowing and swirling round the rocks. Pictures of that clerk kept coming to me, the gulping noise he made, trying not to cry; the smell of piss seeping through the bank. Be lucky if he was fifteen, that was what I was thinking. Could be my boy one day, imagine that.

There was a queue of people in the bank, orderly, lined up near the counter. Two tellers, and I couldn't see their faces or even hear their voices, there were so many folk chattering in the line. Chattering about something or other, all of them seemed to have something important to say, but I couldn't listen, couldn't get distracted. I'd missed my moment, though, forgotten to cover my face, so I joined the queue, and when I got to the end of it, I smiled at the teller, and at the gentleman behind me, and I pushed open the door and walked back out. So that was ruddy Wallerawang.

I dossed under an overhang in the bush outside Wallerawang, and on the way to Mudgee the next day, I stopped three times, pressing my fingers to my eyes and crying with sounds that could have been the baby-bird shuddering of that clerk in Portland.

In Mudgee, I pulled my hat right down, and put the cloth over my face and walked into the corner shop with the oats. I was crying when I held the revolver up at the mud-haired woman. I said, 'Just give me five pounds. That's all.'

She opened the cash box and put it on the counter, lifted up the lid.

I said, 'No, you take it out. One pound, all right. Or two.'

I didn't care, it didn't matter. She slapped two pounds on the counter, as though they were slabs of butter; I took one and backed towards the door. I pushed out on to the street, and someone behind me was saying, 'Mr Lloyd George has declared war on Germany, England is at war,' and the woman inside the store started yelling, 'Police, police.'

I could hear Magic Jack, across at the drinking house, calling, 'Jess – I mean, Frank, Frank.' He'd be waving his windmill arms, I knew, but I clambered up on to Lordship, and nudged him, looking ahead, only ahead. Lordship's great rump barely moved he was so plain buggered out. I shoved him hard with my foot until he moved – a canter at first, but when I kept kicking he picked up a gallop. Two traps were behind me; one fired at Lordship's hoofs. He lifted them up like a dressage king. Another shot, and Lordship leapt: no jump could have held him. I held the revolver down and fired back at them, and galloped back towards the hill, and you'd have thought I was Captain Bloody Starlight himself.

By the time I got to the hill, there seemed to be a team of traps behind me, all shooting and shouting: they sounded like barking dogs, that's what. We galloped up through the hills, with them firing shots just to let me know they were still there. When we headed up across the lower stream, Lordship slipped, skidded in the water, and two of the traps bore up on us. I pushed Lordship back towards the cliff, fired a shot, and skidded down to an overhang. Lordship's barrel of a body was heaving, and mine was too. They were above us, calling, 'We can see you, so you'd better give yourself up.'

I knew that they couldn't see me, and I knew that there was only one person who had led me there, to a dark overhang, cowering in the cold shadow, with my belly heaving in and out like great, broken bellows. It was Ariel. Or if it wasn't Ariel – here's the truth – it was me.

They kept talking, calling that they could see me, that they were going to get me, and I tried to keep my breathing as soft and steady as a spider. The horses' footsteps crunched away after a while, and the voices murmured away into silence, until I could only hear the sounds of the whipbirds, their high whistle cracking through the trees. I slid off Lordship, and eased back under the overhang. Tried to pat him down, quietly; poor old horse, he'd been pushed harder than he ought.

Beneath the overhang, back against the rock wall, dry blue-green lichen crept down, making a soft cushion for my back. I hadn't slept for days, was half demented with the lack of it: eyes like sandpaper, skin crawling, that deep dryness in the head. Lordship was tucked under the rock, his head hanging, and I patted him down, had his legs curl under him. He still had it, one squeeze to his ear and down he went, legs folding. Crows harked out, black angels, circling. Behind me, the lichen felt as downy as those pillows plumped up behind me in the Metropole Hotel. One thousand years ago, was it? Sunspots flickered in front of me, hopscotching on the ground in front of the overhang. The sand behind my eyes rubbed, and grated, and the only way to ease it was to close them, and let the sunspots keep dancing.

I slept. Dreamt of you, dear one, just as you have dreamt of me. Dreamt that we found each other, that we tore a curtain down the centre. It was thick, heavy with tapestries: pictures of men on horseback, leaping across fields, ships tumbling on blue oceans, deep woods, ploughed fields, a priest in a white robe, women bent over cradles. Stories, just stories, sketched and stitched in a curtain so high it covered the very deep. We reached our hands up, both of us, and tore it from top to bottom; it split with the sound of buildings falling. Our hands touched. Children applauded.

Who knows, who can tell if Lordship wandered because he heard something, another horse, some words that sounded familiar, or because he was tired, too tired and old to keep leaping and hiding and being fed on poor oats and scrabbles of grass? When I opened my eyes – later, much later – he was gone. I jerked up like a bucket from the deep well of my dreaming. Footsteps coming closer, traps' voices bellowing. Crunch, crunch. Feet pounding, right above me. One of them shouted, 'Here, look, you can climb down here, bet he's gone down here,' and his footsteps pounded down the rock, closer. I scrambled out from the overhang and looked behind me. Two of them, grinning like hunters. A bullet exploded into the dirt, and I ran then, my feet scrabbling against the pebbles and the traps scrabbling behind me. Another shot. I could have fired back, I knew that, but it wasn't what I wanted.

Above me there was a ledge, a leap above, the kind of leap Jess Girl Trickster might have been able to do with barely a breath. They pounded behind me – more of them, all of them – and I stepped out, flexed and leapt. My hands caught the rock, it was nail-hard. Tried to pull with my arms, to lift. Another shot echoed past; it hit a scribbly bark by my foot. I swung my leg up, tried to heave; I could see them, flitting closer, blue birds, flecking in and out, dappling through the trees. As I swung my leg, another shot – a young one, a trap with a face like a yellow pear – right there, near my hand, and what was I to do but let go, and feel myself tumbling, toppling back with the glorious grace of a dancer, of a trick-cyclist, of a rider like me.

I am here, now. Crooked, at the bottom of this mouth-like ravine. Oh, yes, the green fringes like teeth.

Today is the day I die. I can feel it in my flesh, in my fingers. Where I have always known things, in the tips of my fingers.

Will my boy know who he is?

Here are the things I am sure of: how to make the whip circle before it snaps; how to gentle a horse using nothing but breath; how to beat a room full of men, every one of them, at their own game; how to hold on to love. And this, too: today is the day, the very moment, that I will die.

The ground is opening up, a blue flower, budding. I can see through it, deep into it.

When Billy came back to me, shaking like rain, with scratches clambering up his arm, he brought a red flower, a kangaroo paw. Ariel had tucked it beneath his saddle, for me. The red fingers of it settled against my hand, and I kept it beneath my swag until it was dust.

*

There were five of them, Billy said.

They waited until Ariel and Billy were close, up here in Nullo Mountain, till they were near the gaping mouth of the ravine. Two of them tied Billy to a high whitegum, like that one up there, perhaps, bending. The others held Ariel, shouting, Chink, Chink, and Kill the Yellow Peril.

They let the horse free, listened to him snorting in the trees.

Billy said they swung him twice, holding him at each end, as though he were a sheet, or a dead dog. They swung him out, counting down from five. Ariel didn't cry out. That was what Billy told me. He looked up at the sky, opened himself to it: he was part of it, he always was.

They let go on one.

He made the shape of a star when he flew, high up, arms and feet pointed and not a sound coming from him. Only a hum when he hit the ground. Billy waited until the crows circled.

He knew I'd find him.

I waited here, with this crooked body, the grey and yellow stone around me; the earth beneath my skin. Rocks below me, sky above. Waited with the sound of my breath weakening, the ocean sound of my blood. Ants calling someone's name, the dirt singing. And you came here, down here to the deep.

How could we be sure whether you dreamt me, or whether I called to you? Like blood and dirt and bone, in the end, we're part of each other.

Rise up: the mountains and the trees, and the son you grew, all know your name. You can be as fast as water, as strong as starlight.

There's one thing, only one thing for me to tell you, the one thing you have asked of me. And in return, one thing for me to ask of you.

~

Find my son.'

The rasp-voiced nurse was heavy on the polished floor; she nearly slipped on the tiles. The tray she was carrying was bell-loud when she slammed it down and ran from the room. In the corridor, the matron, all crisp vowels and clicking fingers, called, 'What's this about, Nurse? We're not in school.'

'No, Matron. She's flickering.'

'*Flickering?*'

'Stirring. Mrs Dobell.'

'I don't think so, Nurse.'

'Her head lifted from the bed, Matron. And she spoke.'

'Ring the bell, then, Nurse. There's no excuse for dance-hall frolicking. Not in my ward. Move. *Quickly.*'

She was in water. Rocks poked at her skin, tore at her arms; she was pulled by the rapids. Head above water, gulping air. Above her, grey-green leaves, leaning over a ravine edge. The water pulled her further, down. The rapids churned over her. She pressed back against the rock, beneath the cool parade of water, shushing down, pillowing out at the crown of her head like a blessing, and curving out from her face. Behind the torpedoing waterfall, she was as still as a coin. The water made a clear cathedral, and she was the bishop, the queen, the cut-glass. Ahead, there was the smooth bed of the river, tonguing through the rock-bed. Behind the glasswater, she saw it suspended in sky. An upside-down surrender. Everything would be here, offered, opened up. Her eyes would close, at last, at last.

A hand, pushing in, wet. Flesh on flesh, the shock of it.

And on her shoulders, pulling her, tugging her. Chest, then face,

' pulled through the water, smashing the cathedral. She gulped air, her face pressing up, into the dry.

Someone said: Be strong. Fight. Do what I asked. Will you? What do you choose?

She could choose. Could fight, could imagine not giving up. Swimming up, up. Remembering who she was.

Rose could see herself, flat on the bed, a cut-out doll, hands arranged over the sheets, mouth a neat, straight line. A nurse slammed a tray down, ran from the room, her feet skidding on the floor.

Beside the bed, Joe jumped up, scraping his chair back. Sammy was in his arms, holding a purple plastic cup. Joe was shouting, shouting, and Sammy lifted up his cup, banging it on Joe's head, taking part in the celebration.

She could shed her skin, a snake, a watersnake.

She could feel that the skin had already been peeled away, pulled from her, a thin mask, which was left somewhere far below.

She could see herself, a dance of smoke, could see she was coming back, coming to somewhere that might be home: herself, but changed. New skin.

Darkness, then. Hands pressing on her skin. Prodding at her eyes. Get off, she wanted to call: I've had enough of that carry-on. Poke at your own self.

A strange thought echoing in her head: *I am you. That's why you came: to find me.*

When her eyes opened, inside her skin, it was Sammy she saw first. She watched him through narrow slits, her eyes barely letting in light. Hungry for signs of change, she lay, barely letting out breath. Fragments, broken snippets, markers of growth hung off Sammy, they were everywhere: the baby was gone, she had missed it. She knew that, even now, barely blinking, only beginning to remember the shape of words, of breath. He had – so quickly – become a small rabbit-eyed boy. Hair that flopped over one eye so that just the long shadow of his lashes could be seen, and his skin had darkened, ripened into gold.

She couldn't tell, couldn't guess when all this had happened: she had, after all, been gone for so long.

She reached out her hand, touched the boy's cheek.

Joe's hand – his wide knuckles on narrow fingers – stretched down to hers. 'Rose, Rose. Are you back, are you really back?'

'Yes,' she said.

'They can't believe it. You're a miracle girl, that's what they're saying. You asked for him – you said to find him, "Find my son", and he's here, look, waiting. Things will be different, so different.'

Her eyes opened then: a marble of green against the white of her face. She rasped out, 'Bet your ruddy arse they will. Bloody better be, or else. I'm – whatever I need to do. I'll fight, now, not give up. I want myself back, Joe.'

Joe waved the letter from the Department, then lifted a paper cup of water to her lips. 'You did fight, Rose. And you won.'

~

The hospital garden is damp; the morning has been full of rain, spitting intermittently. Sammy is in blue wellingtons – gum boots – shining with the scattered water from the grass. He toddles through the flower banks, arms outstretched, weaving precariously from side to side. Joe lays a cloth on the wooden bench, and waits for Rose to sit. Every day they have been here, leaning over each other, whispering, talking, while Sammy picks leaves and petals from the flowers that line up along the edge. They sit on the bench beneath the statue of Sir Edmund Barton; sometimes Joe rests his elbow on the statue's knee, as though they are old mates.

During the first days, when Rose hobbled out there, leaning on Joe, both of them paper-fragile with each other, she stopped first at the frangipani tree. She would pause to gather strength, and to kneel down to Sammy, to show him the white petals. Each day, each week, the walk round the garden became longer.

In the mornings, now, while Joe is at the new school, she walks here with Dr Dwyer, talking, talking. She stops, touches the trees and learns their differences, their names: grey box; green wattle; spotted gum.

On the bench beside her, Joe sits as close as breath, says, 'Are you ready, Rose? It's not much, the house. A square of land. Three trees. We'll do what we can, begin where we are.'

She nods. Pulling Sammy on to her lap, she says, 'Look how high the sky is here. How spread out. Later, you know, perhaps next year, I'd like to learn to ride. Horses, I mean. I have a feeling I could do it.'

Across the garden, Dr Dwyer waves his arm, making a long shadow across the hospital wall. He hurries over to them, his coat flapping behind him. Closer, he stretches out his hand to Rose. 'I wanted to make sure I saw you before you left, Rose. I'll be seeing you each Tuesday, in the clinic, but – I wanted to wish you luck and, well, joy, I suppose.' He nods towards Joe. 'And to you, Joe. I was hoping to be here later but – a family engagement has called me. Well. Anything you need to ask me, Rose, before you leave, anything that can't wait until next week?'

Rose smiles up at him, at the sun filtering through the whitegum behind him. 'There is one thing. I've been thinking about it, and – your first name, Victor. Did your mother give it to you?'

He looks at Joe, a little uncertain. 'Well, yes. I suppose – I mean, yes. That's what normally happens.' He laughs. 'That wasn't quite what I had in mind—'

'Your mother would be so proud of you, so pleased.'

He clasps his hands together, as though holding flowers. 'Well. Yes. Thank you. I'm sure—'

'She loved you, very much. And she didn't give up. Not ever.'

He holds the bunched hands to his chest, and is silent for a moment. Then, 'Yes. I've always chosen to believe so. And – nor did you, Rose, after all.' He lowers his head – a polite gesture of farewell – then walks towards the red-walled building. Inside the glass door, a pale-haired woman is waving at him. Two tall boys, dark like their father, lean their faces against the glass, hands up in jubilant greeting.

Half-way across the damp grass, he stops, pointing to the far corner. 'Look, rosellas. In the nasturtiums.'

A patch of sun is tangled among the nasturtiums in the corner, and a flock of red and blue parrots parade busily among the flowers. Rose puts her hand on the back of Joe's neck. 'Nasturtiums. We'll have some of those, in our garden. Perfect. You can uproot them and toss them over your shoulder and they'll just put down roots and start again. They always find a home. Amazing, really.'

Joe turns his head to look at her. 'How do you know that? You've never even had a garden.'

'I don't know. I really – I just do.' A smile flutters across her face. 'Trust me.'

A thread of sunlight weaves, flickering, across the dew, touching each corner of the garden: the quartet now embracing behind the glass doors; the birds hiding under the flat green leaves, the brown bench that holds her and Sammy, and Joe. Rose slips her hand into Joe's and watches the sunthread drawing a circle, knitting a pattern with them all. From here, the whole garden looks like a jewel-lit, perfectly woven tapestry.

Acknowledgements

Jess A is a fictional character inspired by the life of Elizabeth Hunt, known by various aliases including Elizabeth Martin, Mrs McIntyre and Jessie Hickman. A circus performer, it is believed that she won the Australian Rough-riding Championship in 1905, was arrested for cattle duffing (rustling) and petty theft, and lived for a time in the cave in Nullo Mountain known as 'Starlight's Cave'. Beyond those details, the characters and circumstances in this novel are the work of imagination.

Local historian Pat Studdy-Clift has written about Hunt in *The Lady Bushranger* (Hesperian Press, 1996).

The production and distribution of bushranger films was banned by the New South Wales government in 1912. Although Lottie Lyell and Raymond Longford created a number of Australian films – among them, *Australia Calls* – and were major figures in the early, thriving cinema, neither person had, in reality, any encounter with any of the other characters imagined in this work.

Jim Hammerton and Alistair Thomson generously let me read early proofs of their marvellous book *Ten Pound Poms: Australia's Invisible Migrants* (Manchester University Press, 2005) and I am deeply appreciative. I am grateful, too, to Dr Bill Routt, who provided some useful tidbits on the early Australian cinema – any misconstruing is, of course, entirely mine – and to Caleb Williams, who let me while away rainy hours in the archive room of the Justice & Police Museum in Sydney.

I made use of David Roberts' *English to Awabakal Dictionary* (University of Newcastle, 2002). In using Awabakal words, I acknowledge the Awabakal people as custodians of the language.

For the various spaces – Marra Marra, Hardy's Bay, the Stroud Hermitage – in which this work was created and redrafted, and the opportunity to spend time in retreat, I am thankful to Sue Woolfe and Gordon Graham; Tom and Diana Macken; Marian Macken; Bruce Shaw and Alfred Leong; Bethan Birch; Rosemary and Markus Michalowski.

I am endlessly thankful for Richard Griffiths – who enabled the writing of this book in countless ways – not least for his ability to translate Greek texts on demand, and his wise and incisive notes. For other sustaining gifts of conversation and insightful readings, my thanks go to Judith Murray; Charlotte Mendelson; John Dale; Debra Adelaide; Paul Ashton; Abi Parsons; Steph Leach; Sarah Leach; and Jill Dawson.

I am particularly thankful to my mother for being brave enough to tell me of her visions.